P9-AQE-451

FORTUNE'S FAVORITES

The sweet, liquid notes of the larks' distinctive song lulled her into humming along with them as she reached down to pick some of the white heather springing up beneath her feet. She had been surprised to find the rare plant on the moor, growing here and there among its more common purple and lilac cousins. She reached over and put a sprig in a buttonhole of Jack's greatcoat. "White heather for luck," she smiled at him, and he turned toward her and smiled his heart-stopping smile. Her heart lurched in her breast as she gazed at her handsome tormentor; she dropped her eyes and tried to catch her breath.

"You think we need it then?" His low-timbred voice affected her strongly.

"Oh assuredly, sir, if we're to reach civilization without further mishap." Jillian turned aside to hide her blush and hoped that the sudden strange feeling in the pit of her stomach was caused by hunger. "We've had enough *bad* luck in the last three days to last a lifetime."

"What! You would call meeting each other bad luck? I would rather call it the best turn fortune has ever done me . . ."

THE ROMANCES OF LORDS AND LADIES
IN JANIS LADEN'S REGENCIES

BEWITCHING MINX   (2532, $3.95)

From her first encounter with the Marquis of Penderleigh when he had mistaken her for a common trollop,
Penelope had been incensed with the darkly handsome
lord. Miss Penelope Larchmont was undoubtedly the most
outspoken young lady Penderleigh had ever known, and
the most tempting.

A NOBLE MISTRESS   (2169, $3.95)

Moriah Landon had always been a singularly practical
young lady. So when her father lost the family estate over a
game of picquet, she paid the winner, the notorious Vis-
count Roane, a visit. And when he suggested the means of
payment—that she become Roane's mistress—she agreed
without a blink of her eyes.

SAPPHIRE TEMPTATION   (3054, $3.95)

Lady Serena was commonly held to be an unusual young
girl—outspoken when she should have been reticent, lively
when she should have been demure. But there was one tra-
dition she had not been allowed to break: a Wexley must
marry a Gower. Richard Gower intended to teach his wife
her duties—in every way.

SCOTTISH ROSE   (2750, $3.95)

The Duke of Milburne returned to Milburne Hall trust-
ing that the new governess, Miss Rose Beacham, had in-
stilled the fear of God into his harum-scarum brood of
siblings. But she romped with the children, refused to be
cowed by his stern admonitions, and was so pretty that he
had the devil of a time keeping his hands off her.

An Alluring Lady
Meg-Lynn Roberts

ZEBRA BOOKS
KENSINGTON PUBLISHING CORP.

The giant elm, known as the Dancing Tree, across from the Almshouses at the corner of Cross Street in Moretonhampstead, Devon, was damaged in a snowstorm and succumbed in 1903.

ZEBRA BOOKS

are published by

Kensington Publishing Corp.
475 Park Avenue South
New York, NY 10016

First printing: May, 1992

Printed in the United States of America

Chapter 1

It was a wild night—wet and windy. Well, what could one expect, Jillian thought resignedly. It was, after all, typical English spring weather.

A delicate shiver coursed through her small frame as she sat in the creaky old stagecoach that stood in the muddy yard of the Masked Hangman Inn in the little south Devonshire town of Yelverton. She and her fellow occupants of the coach waited for two more passengers who were expected to climb aboard before the stagecoach undertook the dangerously winding climb across the bleak high moorland and stony crags of Dartmoor on its long trek to Exeter.

Jillian St. Erney sighed as she sat in the musty old vehicle and listened to the distant thunderclaps. She pulled her heavy cloak more tightly about her slim shoulders as an occasional gust of wind buffeted the old coach and set it to rocking on its ancient springs. It was decidedly cold waiting in the damp coach. She wished the driver would hurry.

Jillian gazed disparagingly at her dingy surroundings. Even in its dim and distant past, she mused, one would have been hard put to describe the coach as an elegant equipage. The clientele had not much to recommend them either, she thought humorously, as she surveyed her fellow passengers then looked down at her own unfashionable cloak of gray worsted. At least the garment was thick and warm, she reflected ruefully.

She must make the best of her circumstances— and the other passengers—she supposed, for they would all be cooped up together for quite some time. The stagecoach would not stop again on the high, wind-swept moors until they reached Moretonhampstead, some thirty miles to the northeast. She had been informed that the journey would take them some six hours. The slow, lumbering coach and the treacherous weather would undoubtedly decrease their speed.

The coach door opened, taking Jillian's breath away for a moment as a strong gust of wind blew cold droplets of rain directly on her face while a passenger mounted into the vehicle.

"Ohhh!" she uttered in surprise as a sharp pain shot through her foot.

"Excuse me, ma'am."

Jillian was surprised to hear the well-modulated tones of a gentleman as he trod on her toe. And a very well-dressed gentleman he was, too, she could see at a glance. She peered up at the chiseled features of the man whose attire seemed oddly suited to a tedious journey in the rather dusty, decrepit old vehicle. The man wore a finely tailored, large-collared black greatcoat over a lighter-colored suit, and he carried an important-looking leather valise cradled tightly against his body. Why would someone who obviously could afford better choose this inexpensive and exceedingly uncomfortable means of travel? Jillian wondered curiously.

"'Tis a trifle cramped in here, is it not?" she smiled slightly as she looked up at the new passenger and quickly tucked her feet out of harm's way. The man turned at her remark and lifted his well-shaped blond brow haughtily. He bowed, somewhat ironically, in her direction but seemed disinclined to pursue any conversation.

Well at any rate, Jillian thought, it was a relief to see a respectable person board the coach. She had been sitting betwixt a stout woman who muttered constantly to herself and an elderly farmer who had slept since Plymouth. The latter smelled of onions. Two rather unkempt and slightly shifty-eyed young men—local farm boys, she supposed—who had been on the stage before she boarded in Plymouth had disembarked in Yelverton. She had let out a sigh of relief when the two yokels got down, for they had directed several unmistakably leering glances her way.

The taller of the two had poked the smaller in the ribs with his elbow exclaiming, "Lawks, Jem. What a corker!" They had tried various gambits to engage her in conversation, but Jillian had not answered their questions nor responded to their remarks. She snubbed them as best she could and directed her eyes out the smudged windows, trying to make out any landmarks or scenery that could be distinguished through the gloom and the intermittent rain.

Reg, fault-finding husband that he had been, had told her many times that she had no charms to attract a man; she had no reason to disbelieve him. She just assumed these two local lads were unused to seeing a young woman traveling alone and had

7

thus mistaken her for a woman of loose virtue. Although she had taken care to wear her oldest dark blue woolen gown, covered by her serviceable, if somewhat worn, gray cloak and had tucked all her hair up under an unattractive straw poke bonnet, her manifold attractions, despite what she believed, were all too evident anyway.

What had attracted the boys to her, dressed so dowdily as she was, Jillian knew not. She was a small woman with large sherry-colored eyes, a well-curved mouth that she tried—unsuccessfully—to hold in a prim line. She had a lovely, soft complexion and long, golden brown hair that caught and held the light easily. It was her one claim to true beauty. She always took care to bind her hair up in long braids and pin them tightly to her head—the gleaming tresses were well-hidden now under the ugly bonnet. Remembering how often she had been abused by Reg for her lack of looks, she thrust her pointed little chin in the air and thinned her mouth.

Jillian thought to change her seat since the bench opposite now had only one occupant. The handsome-looking gentleman, however, rested his heavy valise on the seat beside him, not leaving a great deal of room for one of even her rather small, compact size. She made a move to get up but then reconsidered. Would she appear rather presumptuous if she deliberately placed herself next to the gentleman? She feared so.

Her eyes strayed to the man again. He seemed a fine gentleman, but then fine gentlemen did not need to sink to the necessity of riding in a common stagecoach.

"Are you bound for Exeter, sir?" Jillian asked tentatively, knowing even as she did so that she was violating her gentle mother's strictures on conduct befitting a well-bred young lady. But she asked nonetheless, hoping to engage the gentleman in some civilized small talk. As a widow of two years, she considered herself no longer young, and was confident that her status gave her the right to ignore precepts set down for girls.

The gentleman seemed startled at being addressed and looked at her suspiciously. "Only as far as Moretonhampstead," he replied abruptly. Jillian flushed at the sharp response, regretting her attempt to initiate conversation. All her distrust of men returned in a flash as she turned away.

But then, to her surprise, the man seemed to recollect himself, and he made an effort to answer more politely. "I take it you are for Exeter, ma'am?" he inquired in light, even tones.

She bowed her head briefly in acknowledgement, somewhat mollified.

"What a disagreeable night for travel, is it not, ma'am? Do you think the roads will hold across the moor with all this rain?"

"I do hope so, sir. I must catch the Mail in Exeter by nine tomorrow morning. However, I have never been across Dartmoor before. It is a dangerous journey, then?" Jillian questioned, to prolong the exchange.

"Why, 'tis a very bleak and lonely wilderness. 'Tis not my business, ma'am, but if you could postpone your journey until daylight or until the weather clears, you would be well-advised to do so." This was said with an urgency that Jillian was at a loss to understand.

"'Tis impossible, I'm afraid. Thank you for your concern, sir." After he turned his attention

9

away from her, Jillian stared at the man curiously until the farmer to her left shifted his position and poked her in the side with a sharp elbow. The old woman continued to mutter in a sort of chanting rhythm, perhaps praying for a safe journey, Jillian thought irreverently as she was squeezed between the two old folks.

The fine gentleman was definitely nervous, Jillian concluded, as his eyes darted frequently to his fellow passengers. Whether from worry about the journey in the bad weather or from some other cause, she could not determine. Even in the dim light of the coach she could see that his knuckles were white where they gripped his bag.

"What can be keeping our coachman?" she wondered aloud.

"He is undoubtedly fortifying himself with warm flannel in the inn," the gentleman remarked sardonically.

"Oh, dear! I do hope not. Surely he will need a steady hand—and head—if the road is as slippery and steep as you say, sir."

The man lifted his pale, shapely eyebrow in skepticism and was silent, effectively putting an end to their conversation as he turned to gaze out the window into the damp darkness. Jillian noted that he was a rather tall, lean man of about thirty— quite handsome, too, with his light blond hair and fine blue eyes and dressed in such well-tailored clothes. She began to speculate on his possible occupation. He looked a true gentleman, but since he had stooped to traveling on the common stage-coach, perhaps he was only someone's land agent or man of business, or even a solicitor. She entertained herself in this fashion so as not to think of what lay behind her—or what lay ahead.

Jillian had had no other choice that afternoon but to board the old coach at Plymouth for the long, arduous journey to London. The first phase of her trek would take her across the sparcely inhabited, harsh moorland of Dartmoor to the cathedral city of Exeter where she expected to change to the faster Mail Coach for the journey to the metropolis.

It was all her own fault that afternoon, as usual. She could not keep her tongue between her teeth and had finally told Mrs. Jenkins that the two schoolgirls she was governess to were a pair of spiteful, lazy baggages who were no more willing to learn the lessons she was endeavoring to give them in music, art, French, needlework, and poetry than they were to comport themselves with the propriety and well-bred manners to be expected of properly brought-up young ladies. The two Misses Jenkins lacked application, discipline and manners, Jillian had stated flatly to her employer, the girls' mother. She had not lost the quickness of tongue she had sharpened in her girlhood to protect herself against her two rather rackety and bullying older brothers. Instead it had been made razor sharp in her bitter battles with her dissolute scoundrel of a husband during her brief marriage.

"A pair of rag-mannered peagooses, not fit to be received in genteel society." Jillian smiled slightly as she recalled her exact words to their mother. Intemperate they may have been, ill-judged possibly, but they were certainly honest—frank to a fault she had often been called. 'Twas just that she had become too much in the habit of speaking her mind since her unfortunate marriage six years previously.

Mrs. Jenkins, the girls' doting mother, naturally

11

dismissed her on the spot and ordered her out of the house before nightfall. Thank goodness quarter-day had just passed, so she had received her modest wages. Jillian was thankful, too, that the woman was not so lost to all propriety as to make her walk the five miles to Plymouth. She had grudgingly offered the gig, and Jillian had gritted her teeth and accepted with humble thanks before running upstairs to pack her few belongings.

When Jillian arrived at the posting inn, she discovered that there was a stage due in at seven that evening which was expected to reach Exeter sometime before eight the next morning. She thought luck was on her side, especially when the booking agent told her that a faster Mail Coach would leave from the Golden Lion in Exeter at nine and make good time to London. Her wages would just cover the double journey with enough left over to buy a bit of food on the way but not enough for any extra overnight accommodations. She had some qualms about descending upon the St. Erney household unannounced but no doubts that Reginald's father would receive her. She was confident that he would not be such a nipfarthing as to begrudge his son's widow bed and board when she reached London—but only until she found employment more suitable to her temperament would she impose on her miserly former father-in-law, however.

She sighed again as she gazed out into the rain-soaked inn yard. It was on just such a black and wild night that word of her husband's demise had been brought to Jillian Ford St. Erney a little more than two years previously. She thought back to that night, as she sat in the creaking, shabby stagecoach.

*   *   *

Jillian had been shocked at first, but not surprised on later reflection, when she received an express from her father-in-law informing her that Reg had been killed—broken his neck in a fall from his horse. Only later had she learned that Reg had tried to jump a five-barred gate for one of his stupid wagers. He had been dead drunk, of course. And then he had been just plain dead. The horse had been killed, too.

She had tried to feel sorrow at the death of a fellow being, but the only sensation she had experienced had been numbness. Her marriage had been too wretched for any of her tenderer emotions to be touched by her husband's death, and she was not sorry to be released from such an ill-fated relationship. Reg had left no provision for her, of course. He had gambled away the small settlement his own father had made on her at their marriage.

She still harbored a great bitterness toward her wayward brothers for the financial arrangement they had made with Lord St. Erney that had made her Reg's wife in the first place. These two older brothers, at home on leave from their army units and ready to kick up a lark at a moment's notice, had assured her jovially they had won a great boon for her—she was to marry the son of their wealthy, titled landowner neighbor.

In one carousing night's round of dicing with their equally wild childhood pal, Reginald St. Erney, her brothers had made her the object of a bet. Reg had lost the staggering sum of twenty thousand pounds to them in drunken play but had agreed to pay them only two thousand pounds and

13

to marry their sister, if the next throw of the dice went his way. He had won with a pair of sixes. Her brothers proudly showed Jillian Reg's promissory note next morning, written in an unsteady hand on brandy-stained paper.

When the brothers confronted Lord St. Erney with the note, the wily old man bargained with them further, deceitfully telling them the note would not stand up in a court of law—and as he was the local presiding magistrate, the Fords believed him. In the end, her brothers had been forced to agree to accept a settlement of one hundred pounds each, while Reg, partly as punishment, had been forced to wed her. His father hoped that if Reg married little Jillian Ford, his spendthrift, gambling-mad son would settle down and be less of a drain on his own pocketbook. How wrong he had been!

And Jillian knew now that her brothers had hoped to profit further when Reg's father died, for they hoped to entice Reg to gamble with them again. But alas for their plans, the son had predeceased the father.

It was true that her own parents lived in comparative poverty and had no way to make a provision for their young daughter's future other than teaching her what few skills they had acquired in their own youths. From her father Jillian learned about plants and flowers, poetry, and sketching, and from her mother, French, music, and needlework. She had made use of these gifts to acquire her position as governess in the Jenkins' household, but they had been wasted on her charges.

Her dear impecunious, scholarly father was forever ensconced in his study pouring over his botany books and making sketches of specimens he had found while out wandering in the lanes and fields. Her gentle, well-bred, but wholly impractical, mother had never learned how to hold house in more than twenty years of marriage.

Neither of her parents had a head for household management—not that there was anything to manage, anyway. They lived on the charity of Mr. Ford's elder, clergyman brother in a house on the edge of the St. Erney estate. Mr. Ford had been the studious second son of a minor landowner and Mrs. Ford, small, dainty, and beautiful with thick, honey-colored hair, the daughter of the Oxford don who had been Mr. Ford's tutor when Jillian's father attended university on a scholarship. Mr. Ford's father had objected to his son's proposed academic career, so the newlyweds had settled to a life of genteel poverty with their three children, accepting the charity of various relatives to make ends meet. But their funds had dried up as the various elderly relations had died, leaving what money they had to nearer and dearer kinfolk.

Jillian's two brothers in their youth had brought endless trouble to their parents. The parents had no control over the outrageous starts of their two sons, and Mr. and Mrs. Ford had been quite thankful when both boys had enlisted as infantrymen in the army when they were but eighteen and nineteen, respectively. That left only their dear little Jillian at home. Jillian recalled that both parents had frequently said what a comfort to them she was. When old Lord St. Erney had called and proposed the marriage of Jillian to his youngest son, Mr. and Mrs. Ford had been astounded, but had agreed, quite happily at the time, as no other option seemed open to Jillian.

15

They had hoped to secure their daughter's future comfort by wedding her to Reginald St. Erney.

And Jillian, for her part, had agreed, partially because she wanted to take the financial burden of her support off her parents' shoulders and partly because she felt a romantic thrill to be marrying the neighborhood's most eligible young man. She had heard the older girls at church sighing over Reginald St. Erney, calling him "impossibly handsome," "a romantic figure," and saying, "Wouldn't he make a heavenly husband?"—and she was proud to be his bride, despite the irregularity of their betrothal. Of course at that tender age and with her complete lack of experience, she had no idea that such "romantic" characters could be complete scoundrels. It was only now that she realized what a young innocent she had been.

Living with Reg had been far from "heavenly," she thought ironically, remembering him constantly berating her for her lack of beauty and her failure to excite him. He often laughed at her and called her prudish and unwomanly, telling her that she was uninformed about what it took to please a man. Well, what could he have expected from a gently bred, untutored eighteen-year-old, she thought resentfully. A fleeting smile crossed her face as she remembered shouting at him once that she wasn't one of his overlaced bits of mutton, coarse and lacking in taste.

Reg was usually foxed when he was with her, which thankfully wasn't often. She preferred her husband's neglect, when he was off with his cavalry unit or his other women, to his "attentions." His gambling fever had never abated. He was forever spending all their money on drink, cards, dice, horses, and his numerous mistresses. Eventually Jillian had had enough—she brangled with him like a fishwife every time he came home. It had seemed to her the only way to give him some of his own back. Her already pointed tongue was made rapier sharp in an effort to protect herself from Reg's cutting remarks and wreckless behavior.

Bah! She had had quite enough of marriage. And when those two rascals, her brothers, had urged her to "bag" another husband as soon as her year of mourning for Reg was up, protesting that *they* didn't have the funds to take care of her, she had turned a blistering scold on them, letting them know in no uncertain terms what lowdown worms she thought men were, especially in their dealings with women.

Never again would she allow herself to be taken such advantage of, she vowed, slamming her fist into the palm of her gloved hand as the old coach again rocked and swayed in the strong wind, causing the lantern hanging on a hook by the door to flicker as it swung to and fro.

She thought again of her father-in-law. Lord St. Erney, a tight-fisted old clunch, had agreed to the marriage because he had had enough of his youngest son's running about stirring up trouble, creating scandal after scandal, gambling and losing wager after mad wager. His heir had married well, his second son was climbing the ladder of promotion in the church, and Lord St. Erney did not much care what happened to Reg as long as it wasn't a drain on his purse. He hoped to settle him down in marriage, even going so far as to give the newlyweds a dowry of five hundred swampy acres that he didn't want, hoping Reg would first drain and then farm them. Futile hope

17

that had been!

Reg didn't let matrimony stop his wild starts, however. Indeed, after the wedding he was wilder, if anything, than before. As soon as she and Reg were wed and the papers for the land signed, he mortgaged the farm and used the money to join a cavalry regiment with whom he spent his time in various camps all over England. He never was posted abroad, Jillian thought ironically. And then he got himself killed for that stupid bet, riding an untamed horse over a five-barred gate in the middle of the night! In his typical neck-or-nothing style, Reg had ridden the animal straight at the gate—his neck and that of the unfortunate animal were forfeit in the futile exercise. Horse and rider had both expired instantly.

Her parents had both died during the four years of her marriage and Jillian, with no funds of her own, had nowhere to turn after the funeral. Certainly not to her spendthrift brothers—neither one ever had a feather to fly with. Her father-in-law had generously—by his close-fisted standards—come to the rescue and offered her an annuity of fifty pounds a year. She had accepted, penning a terse note of thanks, but with nowhere to live she had then proceeded to supplement this negligible amount by hiring herself out as a companion to an elderly lady of genteel circumstances in Plymouth.

Dear old Mrs. Bakewell, Jillian sighed in remembrance. She had been relatively happy in her employment with the old lady. And Mrs. Bakewell had enjoyed Jillian's spirit and had encouraged her to speak her mind. The more outspoken Jillian had been, the more the old woman had laughed.

"You remind me of myself in my younger days,

you know, Jillian, my dear," Mrs. Bakewell had remarked on more than one occasion with a nostalgic gleam in her rheumy old eyes. "Except that your tartness is all on the surface. You have a sweet nature underneath your thorny exterior, however much you try to hide it. . . . I was prickly to the core and still am. Pickled in vinegar—that's why I've lasted so long!" she had laughed long and heartily.

And Jillian had told her elderly employer, making a joke of it, of how her lively tongue had been forged in steel in battles with her two older brothers. Of the care-for-nobody wastrel who had been her husband, she was more reticent, not liking to recall their fierce verbal battles.

Unfortunately, this most congenial employer of fourteen months had expired, forcing Jillian to make do by taking the less satisfactory position as governess in the Jenkins' household. And it was that position which had led to her present predicament.

The inn door opened and light from within the cozy-looking establishment briefly flooded the muddy yard. Jillian saw two burly figures wrapped in oilskins walking toward the stage. She hoped that one of the men was the coachman and that they would be on their way at last. The two figures did indeed turn toward the coach, but one of them came round to the side of the vehicle, opened the door, and lurched in, spattering mud from his boots on the hem of her cloak and liberally wetting the other passengers as he flung off his oilskin and stored it on the rack above Jillian's head. Damp, cold rainwater dripped onto her bonnet and cloak.

"Would you have the goodness, sir, to remove your cloak from above my head. It is thoroughly wet and, as you can no doubt see, dripping all over me. I shall be soaked through soon." Jillian could not prevent herself from addressing a complete stranger in her best governess voice after his utterly thoughtless act of placing his drenched rain-slicker above her head.

The tall, rather large man had been trying to seat himself in the small space left to him by the other gentleman's bulky bag, but he turned at her words and looked down at Jillian out of bleary, bloodshot eyes. She noticed that he had to bend his head so that he would not collide with the roof of the vehicle.

"'Tis nought but a bit of fine English rain-water—good for the complexion, it is," the man said in a rather slurred Scottish burr. "But if 'tis inconveniencing ye, lassie, 'tis sorry I am, then, that ye're such a delicate flower of Sassenach womanhood."

Jillian was outraged. To be spoken to in such a way was the outside of enough. And by a grinning idiot of a stranger, too!

The man obliged her by reaching to remove the oilskin, but the coach lurched forward into motion just as he moved. He leaned heavily against her knees and braced himself by placing his large hands on either side of her head against the rear wall of the vehicle, almost touching the sides of her bonnet as he did so. The giant grinned down at her. His very white teeth gleamed in a tanned face made even darker by several days growth of black beard. Brandy fumes reached her nostrils, and she delicately twitched her nose as she glared into black eyes ringed with fatigue only inches above her own.

"Jack Mackinnon, some say 'Mad Jack,' at your service, ma'am."

"I do not converse with strangers. Kindly remove yourself to your own seat at once, sir."

The impudent fellow continued to lean against her and stare down into her face. "Why, 'tis just a bonnie wee thing ye are. Too pretty to be so fierce, even if ye're trying to hide in ye're impossible headgear," he remarked, flicking her straw bonnet with a careless finger as his detestable grin grew even wider.

Jillian flushed and quickly looked away. The man was a bounder. An unshaven, drunk, rude, shabbily dressed rogue. She looked to the well-dressed gentleman for assistance but saw that he was regarding the stranger with narrow-eyed suspicion. His hand was clenched rigidly round his valise as he clasped it tightly to his side.

The large man continued to grin down at Jillian for a minute then turned and stuffed his wet cloak down the side of the seat. "Might I trouble ye to remove yer portmanteau, sir," he said as he turned to the other occupant of his bench. There was that in his voice that made it more of a command than a request. "'Tis a great lot of room I'll be needing, ye ken, laddie." He gestured at himself.

An idea seemed to strike the impudent stranger. "Unless ye'd be so obliging as to change seats with me, lass." He turned to Jillian again. She would not look up at him nor answer him. "Nay, then, I didna doubt that ye would not." He raised his black eyebrow as he turned once more to the finely dressed gentleman who grudgingly removed the heavy valise to his lap. It seemed he would not even part with it to the extent of putting it in one of the overhead racks.

Though she kept her face averted, Jillian slanted her eyes to watch as the disheveled stranger—McKane or McKeon or whatever he had said his name was—sat down heavily and stretched out his long, well-muscled legs. They immediately collided with those of the fat woman across from him. She screeched and stopped her muttering.

"Here, then. Not enough room for the both of our limbs, sir. Change places with me, missy. Yer just a bit of a thing," the elderly woman said to Jillian even as she heaved herself upward. Jillian had no choice but to slide herself along to the end of the bench seat. When the woman sat again, Jillian found herself squashed against the side of the coach. Her look of outrage was not missed by the inebriated gentleman who again grinned at her, showing his very white teeth in his tired, unshaven face. He pulled his legs up slightly to make room for her, but Jillian resigned herself to extreme discomfort as she turned to gaze out into the blackness beyond the coach window once more.

"Well, lassie, ye shall jist have to make do with this less than elegantly equipped coachy," Mackinnon remarked to her in that Scottish drawl that she detested already. Jillian raised her brows at his impertinence. "Though 'tis plain enough, ye're used to more genteel modes of travel. I do na ken why ye chose this one." Jillian didn't deign to answer him, turning away and giving him a good look at her determined little chin set in her rather gamine profile. Little did she realize how her pouting lips appealed to her tormentor.

She darted one final glance at the well-dressed

gentleman only to see that he took no interest in her comfort or lack thereof. It seemed he would not come to her aid against the ill-mannered, drunken stranger. So much for a champion in that quarter, she grumbled to herself. Jillian's only consolation was that there was not enough room in the coach for actual physical assault on her person by the large, castaway brute. She glanced at her bête noire again and saw that his well-worn hat had been pushed down over his tired, dark eyes and a low snore seemed to be issuing forth along with brandy fumes from his partially opened lips—and rather finely carved lips they were, too, she couldn't help remarking. She took a more careful inventory of the man.

He was big, yes, but well-formed. His thighs, hard and well-muscled when they had pressed against her knees, had not an ounce of flab on them. Shoulders, seemingly a mile wide, rested against the dirty squabs of the old coach. His tattered greatcoat of an indeterminate dark color was open to reveal travel-worn tan riding breeches and a jacket of olive green. The shirt he wore in such a casual style may once have been white, but now it was a grimy gray and, to complete his inelegant toilette, there was an equally grimy cravat knotted loosely round his neck. She could see that the leather boots on his large feet as they were stretched toward her were well-made but worn. They hadn't seen polish in many a day, she judged. Yes, he was altogether a rather heedless character, a thoroughly disguised ne'er-do-well, if she were any judge.

Jillian was glad now of the crowd of people in the stagecoach, however uncongenial they might be. She gave a delicate shudder as the thought crossed her mind that she could be cooped up in here alone with the fiendish lout and subject to who-knew-what sort of dissolute behavior. She had had quite enough of that with Reg, and she wasn't about to let herself be subject to a man's ill treatment again.

She was disturbed in her thoughts by the creature opposite her giving a sigh and shifting his position so that his long legs stretched out all the way to her side of the coach. Jillian found that her legs were effectively trapped between the stranger's own. She would have thought that his legs would be relaxed in sleep, but they seemed to clasp her limbs with a latent strength. She tried to squirm free, but her movement seemed to provoke only a tightening and slight rubbing motion of his legs against hers.

She peeped suspiciously at him in the gloom of the old coach. His head lay on one shoulder, his eyes and a good bit of his face were hidden by his hat, but his mouth remained partially open, and she could still detect a slight snoring breath issuing forth. Her eyes were on his firm chin where she was fascinated to note a decided cleft when she thought she spied a movement. Had she imagined it, or had he indeed run his tongue round his wide, firm lips in a lazy but perfectly conscious manner? She quickly looked away and missed the slight, satisfied smile he could not conceal.

Jillian smoothed her worn gloves over her hands as she tried to ignore the rogue. She sat as perfectly still as the motion of the old coach lumbering and skidding along the steep, rocky road would allow. The driver seemed to be setting an exceedingly slow pace; she began to worry that she would miss her connection in Exeter at the rate they were progressing. Then, considering the severe limitation of her funds, heaven only knew what she would do for food and shelter until the next Mail Coach departed for London. She unpinned her watch and tried to read the time in the light of the one dim lantern that gave scant illumination to the inside of the coach. She thought the hands of her timepiece were just coming onto midnight when a rather loud blast of thunder caused the coach to lurch to one side.

Jillian was startled. The rain had slackened off an hour or so earlier, and now rather watery moonlight streamed in through the dirty windows. There were several more short, loud bangs in quick succession—too close to be thunder.

Suddenly they were all plunged into chaos.

Chapter 2

Jillian gripped her reticule tightly in her hands. Before she could so much as scream, the doors of the old coach were thrown open and a band of masked highwaymen were upon them. "Out wit yer, me fine ladies and gents. Now!"

The horses were plunging and rearing and neighing deafeningly as she and the other occupants of the coach were dragged, none too gently, out of the rocking vehicle and flung out into the mire of the steep, rain-slickened roadway.

The smell of gunpowder hung in the damp air as two of the masked men held long horse pistols, gleaming silver in the moonlight, on the five stagecoach passengers. Jillian could see that another of their cohorts sat on a large dappled horse pointing a rifle at the coach driver and the guard on the box. The guard, in great danger of being pitched to the ground at any moment by the rearing of the coach horses, held his hands high in the air, his old-fashioned blunderbuss lying useless on the ground where he had thrown it at the shouted command of the mounted highwayman. The driver was desperately trying to bring his terrified team under control.

The stout woman was screeching and kicking and calling on the Lord above to curse all robbers and thieves. Jillian found herself pushed to the ground as she saw the well-dressed gentleman thrust back into the coach and his valise confiscated. She lay disheveled where she had been thrown in the mud and mire of the road; her bonnet was hanging by the strings round her neck. There was noise and confusion all around, and she found it hard to make out her surroundings in the murky night with only the moon for illumination. Clouds intermittently scudded across its surface, dimming what scant light it provided.

The drowsy farmer was hit on the head with the butt of a pistol as he unknowingly staggered into one of the highwaymen. Jillian thought it doubtful whether the old man had come fully awake long enough to grasp what was happening before he was rendered completely unconscious.

Jillian turned her head just in time to see that one of the masked men was about to perform a similar office for another passenger—the Scot, her drunken tormentor from the coach. She was astounded to see the mad jack of a fellow suddenly kick out with his foot, hook the highwayman about the legs, and send him flying heavily to the ground. My God, the Scot had a gun in his hand! Where had he gotten it? Even as she watched, horrified, he scrambled to his feet and dove for cover in the heavy undergrowth of bracken at the side of the road.

Three shots rang out. Two were fired after the running, diving man, and one came back toward the robbers from the Scot's gun, unfortunately missing its mark. Then Jillian heard a muffled cry come from the direction where the stranger had disappeared, followed by the sound of something heavy rolling down the sharply inclined hillside, sending showers of small stones crashing down with it. The highwaymen had evidently hit the Scot, who had then fallen over the side of the steep cliff.

Two of their attackers stood looking down into the gully, peering into the darkness beyond trying to spot the escapee. One of them fired his gun down into the void for good measure. Jillian covered her ears and bit her lip.

"Ye've done for 'im, Dan'l," said one of the men, an excessively evil-looking character with large, hairy hands and a walleye that gleamed white in the moonlight.

"What h'about them other morts, Sam?" The men glanced over to where Jillian was rising from her knees near the old woman and the unconscious farmer.

"Leave 'em 'ere. H'its miles afore the next town." The fat woman was cowering and moaning beside the inert body of the farmer. Jillian could see that the fourth member of the gang, who had remained mounted throughout, still held a rifle pointed at the coachman and guard. The team had been brought under some control and were sidling and stamping in the road, heavy steam issuing from their nostrils in the chilly night air. She assumed there was also someone inside the coach guarding the well-dressed gentleman and his precious valise. Had the villains been after that bag and whatever valuables it contained, she wondered, even as her teeth chattered with the cold and the fear of what would happen next.

"That gentry mort there's a mighty tasty

armful," leered the man called Sam, pointing in Jillian's direction. "Cast yer peepers at 'er 'air, Dan'l. Damme, ain't never seen the like afore. Might 'ave a use for 'er afore the night's over." Her disheveled appearance, with her honey-colored hair loosened from its braid in the turmoil and now shining in the moonlight, had attracted his attention. Jillian grabbed at the ribbons of her bedraggled headgear and tried to tuck her hair back up underneath it as she pulled the straw bonnet onto her head again.

"Naw. Capt'n wants them bloody papers. Quick like. 'E'll be in a devil of a temper, else."

"Still and all, think ole Sam'd like a taste o' that morsel." And the half-masked walleyed man started over to where Jillian sat in the mud.

Sam gave a low whistle of appreciation as he bent down and grasped her elbow and pulled her to her feet. Jillian staggered against him; then, as she saw his wet and glistening gap-toothed mouth descending toward her lips, she summoned up every bit of her courage and strength, and shoved him away, screaming, "Don't you dare to touch me, you vile, filthy villain!"

The now-snarling highwayman grabbed Jillian roughly again and gave her a mighty shake in the moment before a hulking shape came hurdling out of the darkness and knocked Sam to the ground, sending him sprawling beneath the wheels of the coach.

It was the Scot! They had not killed him! How had he survived? Jillian's heart hammered against her ribs as Mackinnon moved to stand in front of her. His hat was gone and a trickle of blood came from his forehead where one of the bullets had grazed him. He put one of his hands behind his

30

back and grasped Jillian's arm to push her quickly toward the edge of the roadway, shielding her with his body the whole time.

"Keep your filthy hands off the lady, or I'll have your cobbler's awls before I see you dangling from the nubbing cheat, you lecherous old gallow's bait," her rescuer growled out menacingly to the walleyed man.

"Ho, yer will, will yer now guv'nor?" Sam picked himself up and grinned under his mask as he grasped the horse pistol stuffed through his belt. He spat, "We'll see about that, guv'nor, we'll jist see what them peepers of yern'll see when yer 'onor's snuffed it."

Jillian, peering over the Scot's shoulder, could only describe the look on Sam's half-covered face as Satanic. He continued to grin as he slowly cocked his long silver pistol and aimed it straight at the Scot's heart.

A shot split the still night air, and Jillian felt the man who stood in front of her stagger back against her and groan. Oh God, he had been hit!

The Scot dropped his hold on her arm even as blood poured out from the gunshot wound somewhere on his left side. Even thus sorely wounded he somehow managed to clasp Jillian round the waist and press her tightly against his right side as he continued to back them both to the edge of a steep incline at the side of the road.

"Leave go o' the gentry mort, guv, or ole Sam'll give ye another taste o' 'is lead."

"Oh, let go of me, please, before they kill you," Jillian pleaded, half-crying.

With a half salute and a crooked smile on his now deathly white face, the mad rogue whispered against her ear, "Anything to oblige a lady." Then

31

he released her—and toppled over in a heap at her feet. Jillian braced herself not to faint as her knees buckled under her and she sank down beside him.

The two highwaymen stood over the body of Jack Mackinnon, peering down at him in the darkness. The one called Daniel bent down to examine the man. "Ye've kilt 'im, for sartin, this time, Sam. Ain't the right cove, neither."

Daniel jumped up with a frightened look on his face. "Let's get out o' 'ere," he pleaded shrilly as Sam shoved the body to the edge of the deep gully with the toe of his boot, gave a mighty heave, and sent a lifeless Jack rolling over and over down the hill.

Jillian's stomach lurched nastily as she heard the body tumbling down through the rough bracken. There could be no doubt that he was dead this time. So much for his ill-timed gallantry, she thought.

Sam turned to her and leered as Jillian tried to crawl away from him in the mud and found herself slithering downward into the gully that had swallowed Jack Mackinnon's lifeless body. Her teeth were chattering again. She was icy cold with the certainty of her fate at the hands of the murderous, walleyed villain. There was but one thought in her benumbed brain, to escape some way, any way. She must escape or hope that a bullet would end her terror. The other was unthinkable!

Sam reached a hand down to help her up. "Come along up, now, missy. Old Sam'll warm yer blood for ye."

A terrified Jillian closed her eyes and pushed backward with all her might until she was slipping through the undercover of bracken. Then she panicked as she heard Sam's curse as he tried to come after her without losing his footing. "Bloody 'ell, woman, ye'll fall to yer death!" He was almost upon her. Jillian let go of her hold on the fronds of the bracken and felt herself fall over the edge of the gully to go tumbling down and down and down.

"Oy, gar-damn it! Wher't she go?" Sam yelled to his fellow highwaymen.

"Leave 'er, Sam. 'Er's dead now, most like. Let's get the bloody 'ell out o' 'ere," Daniel repeated urgently in a shaking, frightened voice.

When Jillian came to after swimming through layers and layers of pain, she found herself at the bottom of a deep ravine lying only inches away from a huge boulder. She shuddered as she realized that she must have narrowly missed crashing into the neolithic stone. It seemed that her heavy cloak was entangled in a small sapling that was bent to the ground with her weight. The little tree had saved her from certain death had she indeed collided with the prehistoric block of granite left behind by some long-ago ice age.

Jillian surmised that she had been so dizzy and frightened as she fell that she had passed out even before tumbling to her present resting place. Every muscle in her body screamed in agony as she tried to move, and her hands and face were lacerated and bleeding. She had lost her bonnet in her end-over-end descent down the hill, and her hair had come loose and was streaming wildly around her face.

How long she had been unconscious, Jillian hadn't a clue. She lay still, all strength drained from her battered body, listening for sounds of pursuit from above. All was stillness. The rain had completely stopped, and the stars were out in force in the now-clear sky. She heard the trickling noise of a small stream gurgling its way among the rocks nearby as she listened intently for sounds of life in the silent night. She was surprised to find that she still gripped her reticule in one hand and, miracle of miracles, she still had shoes on both her feet. Her clothes must be torn to ribbons, she thought. But no! Her cloak, her shabby, worn, unfashionable, wonderful, beautiful, thick cloak had saved her, she knew. The heavy woolen garment now encrusted with mud had afforded some protection from the stones and rough undergrowth of the hillside and now was her only protection from the elements. She supposed if she had to die, she would prefer to do so here. The prospect was infinitely preferable to submitting to the embraces of that vile animal of a highwayman.

"Arrhhhh . . ." A muffled moan came suddenly out of the darkness causing Jillian's hair to stand on end.

There it was again! And quite close by, too. Was it some animal about to attack her? She bit down painfully on her lip, trying to suppress the scream of terror that rose in her throat.

It came once more. Low and . . . *human*, Jillian realized with a different kind of fear. It was a man's cry of pain that she heard. Somehow she forced her protesting muscles to obey her brain's command to move. She was up on her knees, then sat still a moment until her head stopped spinning. She looked carefully about her and listened again for the sound. It came soon, stifled somewhat now, but quite nearby.

Jillian put her hand on the rough surface of the boulder to brace herself as she stood up slowly and

34

looked to her left. The sound definitely seemed to be coming from her left. She tried to see in the dim moonlight, and there, not four feet away in a small depression in the ground lay her tormentor and her savior . . . the drunken madman of a Scotsman.

So the highwaymen had failed a second time to put a period to the lout's existence. She knew not whether to be glad or sorry.

Carefully, biting her lip to prevent a cry of her own pain from escaping her, she made her way as silently as possible to the wounded man and knelt beside him.

"Sir. Sir? Can you hear me?" she whispered. "Where did they shoot you? Where are you hurt?" Nothing issued from his lips except low moans. She put her ear close to his lips as she thought he was trying to speak to her, but all she heard were mumbled incoherent phrases that made no sense.

"Must get back . . . found the code . . . London, must get to London . . . tell John . . . have to stop. . . ." He continued to mumble low, unintelligible fragments of sentences in his delirium.

Jillian shook the man gently but could not rouse him to consciousness. She set to work to try to help. "Cannot you give me any idea of how to help you?" she cried. "You may die—all through your own stupid fault, you foolish madman. You should have let them knock you out. They just would have left you in the road," she scolded helplessly, trying not to think what would have become of herself if he had chosen that cowardly path and saved his own skin. "I have little idea of what to do, you know." She kept up a steady monologue to give herself courage as she worked.

Jillian stripped off her sodden, torn gloves and

gingerly laid aside the man's greatcoat and jacket, thankful that both were open. Her fingers were shaking too much to deal with buttons. There was little light, but enough for her to see that the whole of one side of his shirt was soaked in something dark and wet—blood from the gunshot wound, she realized as she pulled back, repelled. She had never dealt with a wounded man before. She had never dealt with a wounded *anything* before.

"I hope you're not quite the scoundrel you seemed in the coach, Sir Scot, since it seems I'm to be your nurse. Heaven help me, I've never had any experience of this," she animadverted as she tried to pull away his jacket, none too gently it seemed, for she jarred him into consciousness.

"Then heaven help *me*, sweetheart," he said breathlessly.

Jillian jumped back. "You've come to," she almost screeched as she looked down into his pain-filled eyes that nevertheless held a glint of amusement as he gazed up at her.

"Very observant, sweetheart. I don't know how you got here, but thank all the saints in heaven you have arrived. Help me out of this shirt, sweeting." His voice was a thread and the Scottish burr seemed to have disappeared from his speech, but there was still mocking laughter in his words.

"Where are you wounded? Can you tell?" Jillian was all business as she realized the necessity of aiding the wounded man, gentleman or no.

"All over after that fall. I think my head's broke." He raised his right hand to the crown of his head where a large knot had formed.

"Where did they shoot you, man?" Jillian's temper was almost gone. Patience had never been one of her virtues, and added to her own pain and fear was the knowledge that she was responsible for this man's life. She owed him some recompense after he had saved her earlier from a fate worse than death.

"All the evidence points to my left shoulder," he joked. "I don't think the villain hit anything vital—he wasn't a good enough shot." Jack lifted his right hand and felt under the material of his shirt. "Yes. I think the bullet has gone clean through the flesh. No bones hit. That's one less job for you, sweetheart. You won't have to dig the lead out." He pulled out sticky fingers and wiped them on his torn and filthy shirt. "He seems to have spilled enough of my claret to serve an entire banquet, though."

How could the man be laughing at such a time? Jillian wondered. He couldn't still be drunk. Surely such a fall after being shot would have sobered up the most deeply castaway fellow. A cloud that had been covering the moon drifted away just then leaving Mackinnon's face bathed in moonlight. Jillian thought that she had never seen anyone so parchment white, despite the stubble on his unshaven cheeks.

"Look, I know you find this . . . me . . . distasteful, but, please, ma'am, I need your help. It has stopped bleeding, thank the Lord, but the wound needs to be bound up. I'm too weak to do it myself. Can you manage?" he asked seriously and soberly.

"Of course. I'm not a mewling weakling, sir." And Jillian set to work, gripping her lips tightly together to pull away the material of his shirt. She remembered her small embroidery scissors in her reticule and had them out instantly. She cut away the material of the shirt then sat back on her haunches to think what to do next.

"Bind it up," Mackinnon said in a tone of command.

"One moment, sir. There is a stream nearby. I must bathe the wound first."

"What do you have to carry water in, woman?"

She stood up and emptied the contents of the reticule on the ground. "This." She was off in the direction of the gurgling stream as fast as her protesting muscles would allow. She quickly located the water, filled the reticule with the ice-cold water and hurried back before it could leak out. She had taken the precaution of soaking her handkerchief, too, and used it to sop away the mass of blood and to clean the wound. She knelt again to her task.

Jack kept his lips tightly closed as the pain hit him anew. "Here, tear away part of my shirt and bind it up," he said when she had finished cleaning the area.

"That shirt! It's filthy. You would have a festering wound, for sure." She stood up, turned her back to him, lifted the front of her skirt, and proceeded to rip away a portion of her petticoat. When she turned around, she observed him grinning at her again.

"You're just like the Cheshire cat, sir. One can see your teeth glowing in the dark even if the rest of you is invisible."

"I didn't think you could be so charitable, sweetheart," he laughed as she bent to her task. The smell of brandy had dissipated, and there was a not unattractive musty smell emanating from the gentleman's person. He didn't smell dirty and unwashed as she had assumed, and Jillian even thought she detected the lingering scent of some long ago used cologne. Perhaps he was not quite the ill-mannered, lowlife vagabond he had appeared on first impression.

"Sweetheart, there's a flask in my greatcoat pocket. Get it."

Her first impression was immediately reinstated. "You don't mean to start drinking now!" Jillian was incensed.

"You're quick on the draw, are you not, my little spitfire? Pour some of the brandy over the wound to cleanse it before you bind it up. 'Twill serve to prevent it from festering, you know. There's a good girl."

A furious Jillian flounced over to the greatcoat which had been flung aside and retrieved the bottle. She bit down on a groan as her aching muscles protested her sudden movement. She returned to kneel beside him and proceeded to pour the contents of the flask over the wound before his right hand reached to grab her wrist tightly. "That's enough. You may give the rest to me."

He roused briefly to remark sardonically, "'Tis a waste of good whiskey to be a' pourin' it over m'body. Down m'gullet would give me more relief, me lass."

"It's of no use trying that Scottish burr on me, you humbug. You've abandoned it once too often for it to be anything but a sham," she said severely. She could see that his eyes were laughing at her again which caused her to tighten her lips primly.

"I knew you would wish to drink it," she said nastily as he greedily gulped the last dregs of the strong-smelling spirits.

"Then you'll have the satisfaction of being proven right, won't you." He sighed and fell back panting after uttering this last, and Jillian realized that the wound was causing him a good deal of pain despite his banter. Perhaps she should not begrudge him the relief that the spirits would bring.

She began to make a pad with a piece of her torn petticoat and a long strip of binding with another portion. Her fingers were deft as she went about her task even though she lacked experience. She didn't pause to think about the touch of the man's warm skin beneath her fingertips. Nor did she dwell on the sight of his broad, dark-haired chest as it was bared to her interested view.

He seemed to break into a sweat as she worked, and a new worry beset her. Fever. And they were exposed to all the elements in this godforsaken place. At least there was a bit of shelter against the wind here in this crevice against the edge of the hill they had tumbled down. When she finished tightening her makeshift bandage and had buttoned his shirt and jacket over his chest again, Jillian made her way to the stream once more and filled the empty flask with water and brought it to him to drink.

She wiped the sweat from his forehead with her freshly dipped handkerchief. He seemed to have weakened in the last few minutes. It was with a great effort that he looked up at her out of pain-glazed eyes and spoke again. "It's cold here. We must have some cover if we are to survive this night. Bring my greatcoat here for cover. See if you can break off some branches of those shrubs and put them over the coat. Then lie down here with me."

"How dare you, you libertine!" Jillian recoiled from the man she had been treating so tenderly only moments before.

"You can die if you like, sweetheart, but please cover me before you undertake your suicide." Jillian was astounded that the man could actually *joke* under such circumstances.

But the teasing mood lasted only briefly. When she didn't move, he reached over and grabbed her wrist again. "Listen to me, girl," he said harshly above his labored breathing. "I am like to die and so are you, exposed on the moor as we are. I have no amorous intentions in mind. I'm afraid I would be incapable of them at the moment anyway, even if I were so inclined. Put aside your foolish notions and do as I say. Quickly, before the mist comes down and we lose sight of one another if you move so much as ten feet away." He fell back against the ground panting heavily but had breath for one last command. "Be careful of the gorse! It pricks like the very devil."

Fuming to herself, Jillian moved to do as he asked, ordered rather. Well, she reasoned, she wasn't ready to strike out on her own in the middle of nowhere, and besides, however odious the man was, she could not leave a fellow creature to die if some effort on her part could prevent it. It was better for them both to live. No one would ever know of the compromising situation—how could they? And she did believe that he was incapable of assaulting her, though he remained quite capable of insulting her at every turn.

Jillian spread his muddy greatcoat over him, then removed her own torn and dirty cloak and spread it out too before arranging the branches she had collected with much damage to her already-scratched fingers and hands on top of the two garments as best she could. Then she sat down beside him. It seemed that he slept . . . or more likely had lapsed into unconsciousness again.

She shivered in the cold, damp air as she took off her spencer and wadded it into a pillow for her head, then slowly lowered her own bruised body down to lie under the blanket she had made. She tried not to lie right up against the man, but the lure of his warmth drew her protesting, aching body into close contact with her untrustworthy patient.

Jillian had been sleeping soundly for what must have been two or three hours when she was awakened by a low moaning in her ear. The scamp had decided to use her breast as a pillow! she seethed. But now he was very hot and seemed to be in great pain.

He was sweating heavily, and when she jarred him in her attempt to sit up, he stirred briefly and asked for water. She reached out for the full flask from where she lay and offered it to him. He drank greedily then lay back again breathing shallowly. "I hate to leave you alone, ma'am, at this very interesting juncture," he said as he relaxed against her breast again, "but needs must."

Jillian realized that he had fainted. "Oh, you provoking man," she shook him slightly with her hand on his back, "don't die!"

Unsuccessful in her attempts to rouse him, Jillian lay back, afraid to move him. She did not know if she would find a dead man half covering her body in the morning, but for now she was grateful for the warmth he provided in the freezing temperatures. Forcing herself to put all her fears for his safety, as well as the horror and discomfort of their situation to the back of her mind, she closed her eyes and tried to will herself to sleep.

Chapter 3

Jillian awoke to bright sunshine and stiff limbs, thankful at least to be alive. She sniffed the air and noticed immediately that it was considerably warmer. Her patient was yet asleep. He still lay over half her body, but his breathing seemed easy. Gingerly she placed the tips of her fingers against his forehead and uttered a fervent prayer—he didn't seem to be in a fever. Her sore muscles and the man covering her prevented her from moving her body, but she could move her head. She gritted her teeth as she stretched her sore neck muscles, then stopped abruptly. A distinct impression that they were being watched raised the hairs on the back of her neck. Biting her lip with fear, she slowly turned her head to the right . . . and let out a piercing scream when she saw two pairs of eyes peering at them over the edge of the slight depression they lay in.

Mackinnon sat up groggily saying, "What the— Oww!" as Jillian flung her arms around him and buried her head against his good shoulder.

"What's the matter, sweetheart?" he said, slightly slurring his words in his weakened and sleepy state.

"Th . . . there's . . . someone looking at us. Oh! Are they still there?" She was shaking and still hiding her face against him as he held her with his good right arm.

He looked up and beheld their observers—two grazing sheep wondering who had invaded their private preserve. A large grin split his unshaven face. "Shoo," he said, and the animals took themselves off, wagging their tails behind them.

Jillian looked up. "'Shoo'? What did you mean, 'Shoo'?" she questioned him suspiciously.

A deep, rumbling laugh shook him. "Oh, long-forgotten bucolic joys! Come, my Phoebe, let us survey our kingdom and meet our subjects."

"Oh, you horrid man! How can you tease at such a time?"

"You're not afraid of a pair of sheep, are you, after braving a night with a desperate rascal like me?"

She looked over his shoulder and observed that sheep dotted the hillside round about them. "Oh," she said again, and outrage warred with embarrassment in her expression. Observing her, he laughed again as his arm came round her, and he hugged her to himself. "Shall I slay them for you, Lady Dulcinea?"

Jillian disentangled her arms from about him, pushed herself away, and stood up. "Ugh! You stink, Sir Rogue," she said to cover her embarrassment, but truly she was glad that he was alive . . . and he seemed much improved considering the state he had been in just a few short hours ago. They weren't out of the woods yet—ah, off the moor, she amended—but at least she thought they had a chance.

"It's good, honest sweat, sweetheart. A man's

smell. Me thinks that my brave nurse is afraid of me," he teased easily as his warm brown eyes twinkled up at her. They held a gleam that Jillian didn't trust. "Come here. No? I told you you were afraid," he said provocatively. He left off his nonsense after a moment and lay back down again with a stifled groan.

Jillian looked down at him, worry and irritation flitting across her open, delicate features. A very disreputable-looking half smile quirked his mouth as he looked up at her quizzically while he settled himself back down again with his good right arm behind his head. The beard on his unshaven face had darkened with a night's growth. He scratched at his chin awkwardly with his left hand even as she watched, then closed his eyes and sighed. Jillian continued to observe him—only a nurse's natural interest in her patient, she assured herself.

The dark circles under his eyes were more pronounced this morning in his pale, drawn face—and no wonder, she thought sympathetically.

She could see now, without his slouching hat to cover it, that his rather long hair was black, and thickly textured as it curled almost to his collar. He didn't seem quite as old as she had presumed earlier on the stage. There was an almost boyish aspect to the man, but he looked extremely careworn and uncomfortable at the moment.

There was also a thin streak of blood across the side of his forehead where she assumed the first bullet had grazed him. Just when she felt some pity for the man, he looked up again, crinkled his eyes at her, and smiled a most roguish smile. "What a night, sweetheart! Thought I'd died and gone to heaven when I realized what a supple pillow I was enjoying. I can't recall ever sleeping on anything

45

more, ah, well-cushioned, shall we say."

"Oh, you shameless cad!" Jillian colored up as she turned away from him and forced her stiff muscles to carry her several yards to the gurgling stream where she filled the flask again and wrung out her much-abused handkerchief, using it to cleanse her face as best she might. Then she ran her fingers through the tangles in her hair and recalled that there was a comb in the contents of her reticule. "Oh, botheration," she exclaimed fretfully, remembering that she had spilled everything out on the ground the night before in her rush to care for the provoking man. Now she would have to find the scattered contents that included her last remaining sovereign and few shillings, the only money she would be able to lay her hands on for quite some time.

She rung out the handkerchief and brought it back to the makeshift bed where Mackinnon still lay quietly. He was stretched out again, looking worn and worried. But when he saw her, he smiled and his eyes crinkled in just such a way that Jillian found very disturbing. She didn't trust him an inch.

"Ah, my nurse returns. I feared I had been abandoned to my fate. A just one, I'm sure you would agree, but not one I could contemplate with any degree of complacency."

She offered him a drink of the cool stream water from the refilled flask. He took it gratefully and sipped as he watched the sunlight play over her tangled golden hair where it streamed down about her shoulders.

She shook her head at him, vowing to keep her tongue firmly between her teeth if he should continue to aggravate her. One unruly tongue betwixt the two of them was one too many. She bent to look at his bandaged arm again, gently pulling the shirt aside and trying not to disturb her handiwork. As she leaned down, her hair fell in a curtain round her shoulders and brushed against his chest. She brushed it back impatiently.

"The wound looks to be not too bad this morning," she said, critically, looking at his shoulder.

"Yes, I think it is only a flesh wound and should heal quickly after your expert ministrations, O my little angel of mercy."

"What is your name, again, sirrah? In all the excitement, I'm afraid I did not quite catch it last night."

"Your most humble servant, Jack Mackinnon, at your service, ma'am," he twirled his hand at her and tilted his head slightly forward in a mock bow, grimacing at the pain in his temples as he did so. He had forgotten that he had taken a severe knock to his crown in his fall.

"Oh, Mackinnon, is it?"

"Jack," he corrected, smiling crookedly so that she got a glimpse of the cleft in his chin and noticed for the first time one slightly chipped front tooth in an otherwise dazzlingly white, even smile.

"And yours, sweetheart?"

"Jillian St. Erney . . . Mrs. St. Erney to you," she said firmly. "And I object to being called 'sweetheart.'"

"I shall call you Jill," the rogue decided.

Jillian clamped her lips firmly together to smother the retort that sprang to them and pushed down just a little too hard against Jack's wounded shoulder. "Oww," he shouted. "Where's my gentle sweetheart? . . . Cat got your tongue, eh? I ought to be grateful if last night's harangue was a foretaste of its barbed shafts. St. Erney, is it then? Well, well, well. I suppose you were Reginald St. Erney's wife."

"You knew my husband!"

"Oh, of a surety. A wild blade. Got himself killed for a wager, didn't he. And none too soon, heh? . . . Oh, excuse me, Jill. I apologize. That was not very handsome of me. You must make some provision for my weakened state. I'm still a little out of my head. No telling what outrageous things I may say—or do—not being totally *compos mentis*, you understand," he said meekly. Too meekly, Jillian judged. She maintained a stony silence in the face of so much provocation as she used the wet handkerchief to cleanse his forehead.

She had almost finished her task when she became aware of his breathing sounding less easy than before. "Is that not better?"

"More to the left," he said.

"The left?" Jillian questioned as she lifted up slightly away from him.

"Ah, perfect," he said.

She observed that his face was glowing with color after being so pale only moments before. She put her hand to his brow. "What's wrong? Have you a fever? You're very flushed all of a sudden."

Jack sighed gustily. "It's the view."

"The view?"

"Ummm."

Jillian looked down and saw that several buttons of her dress were missing, undoubtedly lost in her wild tumble the night before, and that the ribbon tied under her breasts had come undone. He had an excellent view of her well-endowed bosom!

She clasped her hand to her chest and sat up abruptly, chastising him roundly the while. "You villain! Unprincipled, lecherous rake! Wretched, wretched man! How can you be so shameless when I am trying my best to help you!"

"What! Castigated for shameless behavior when all I'm doing is lying here enjoying the view." He raised his eyes skyward in mock appeal, then his grin flashed again and he wagged his black eyebrows up and down suggestively. "But if it's shameless behavior you expect from me, sweetheart, who am I to disappoint you?" Before Jillian knew what he was about, Jack leaned slightly forward, entangled his right hand in her flowing hair, and pulled her down. The rascal then kissed her breast through the outside of her dress before she could pull away from him.

Jillian felt ready to scream with outrage as she managed to disentangle her hair and push him away. She jumped to her feet and stormed at him, "What am I going to do with you, you infuriating blackguard. Leave you here to die, I suppose, or must I continue to suffer your insults?" With that rather inadequate expression of her feelings, she flounced away. She picked up her crumpled spencer from the ground where it had served the office of pillow, continuing to mutter under her breath the while.

He looked at her sheepishly, false contrition writ large on his face. "Do not be distressed, sweetheart. Your sweet, ah, appendages were just too luscious for a starving man to resist. Perhaps if we could find some food my appetite would be appeased. . . . It's only when I'm hungry that I'm dangerous, you know," he said outrageously, humor lurking in the depths of those drooping brown-black eyes.

"For such a big man, you have a remarkably tiny mind," Jillian said as she shook out her ruined, wrinkled spencer and put it on, buttoning it to the chin. Although equally soiled and torn, it was considerably more modest than the upper portion of her ruined dress and effectively hid the torn bodice.

"Oh, ho. A shrew! Ye gods have landed me with a veritable shrew!" and the abominable Jack Mackinnon dared to laugh at her—a wonderful, full-bodied, infectious laugh. She was beside herself with anger at the vexatious creature.

"Now, Jill, I know you don't want to come near me again, sweetheart, but my legs are so cramped from sleeping in this ditch and my shoulder so stiff that I can't arise without your help. Come," he said holding out his hand to her. "I promise to behave." When she still did not turn in his direction, he joked, "I am yet half dead, you know."

Biting back a grin of her own, she turned and grudgingly helped him to his feet, then gazed at him suspiciously when his hand seemed to tighten unnecessarily on her waist as he took a few tentative steps to shake the cramps out of his muscles. "There we are, sweeting. I think we could both use some privacy to make our morning ablutions."

He carefully took himself off to the stream, stumbling only a few times. Jillian was surprised at his sensible attitude for a change. She admonished herself for standing like a stock watching him instead of going about the task of gathering the contents of her reticule. She set about making herself somewhat more tidy by first plaiting her hair again. As she had nothing to pin it up with,

50

she let it hang in one long braid down her back.

When Jillian returned a few minutes later to the giant boulder that marked their previous night's sleeping place, she found Jack leaning against the stone, soaking up the warmth from the morning sun. Long, thick dark lashes spread themselves in a semicircle below his closed eyes. Despite the rogue's unshaven state and the shaggy hair falling over his forehead, Jillian beheld before her a remarkably handsome man. Even the disreputable state of his clothing that made him look a veritable beggar didn't detract from some essential quality in the man she couldn't identify for the moment.

Jillian had stopped some little way from where Mackinnon rested, and now she put her head on one side and frankly assessed the man. Though not as heavyset as she had assumed the night before, she thought he was well above average in height. It must have been his wide shoulders beneath his large greatcoat that had deceived her in the stage-coach when he had loomed over her so threateningly. She could see that his long legs, outlined in the torn and dirty riding trousers he wore, were indeed well-muscled at thigh and calf. Overall his physique was not at all bulky, but rather he was surprisingly slender in the lower torso. Why, his hips were as slim as a boy's she thought in amazement. And she blushed as she remembered easily spanning his narrow waist with her arms earlier that morning as she hid her face against his neck.

Jillian shook off her reverie and took herself severely to task. It wouldn't do to conceive any admiration for the detestable scamp, even in her innermost thoughts. Yes, he undoubtedly thought himself a fine figure of a fellow, she scoffed to herself, and was no doubt a raging success with the ladies, too—his kind always were.

Anyway, he seemed almost miraculously improved this morning. He certainly looked healthy enough to survive any number of bullet wounds. But her lack of experience in such matters caused her to bite her lip in worry—not only about his health, but about their situation, lost on the open moor with no food, drink, or shelter. The possibility of the return of the highwaymen, too, was never far from her mind.

"What is our next course of action, then, sir?" Putting her worries aside, Jillian approached nearer and addressed her companion brightly, all trace of her earlier rancor dissipated.

Jack opened his eyes and bit back a leering grin and suggestive retort just in time.

"Much as I welcome the opportunity to spend time alone with you, sweetheart, I can foresee certain difficulties in that plan."

Jillian just snorted. "Where are we and what are we to do next? We need food and shelter and you must have a doctor to look at your shoulder."

"Well, my dear, it appears we have been abandoned to our fate. Your protectors have deserted you—no slumberous farmer and half-wit fishwife stayed around to hunt for you, did they? They are probably back in Yelverton by this time. Perhaps they will organize a rescue party, do you think? Can you not just see it?" He laughed and met Jillian's cold stare, then reached out and pulled her braid forward from behind her back, letting his hand run down its golden brown length before giving it a yank.

She flicked her head back and jerked her hair out of his hand. "Mackinnon!" she said threateningly with her hands on her hips.

"To answer your first question, I judge we are somewhere on Dartmoor—near the Higher White Tor, if my schoolboy geography serves me correctly."

"Very funny, Mackinnon. How far from Exeter are we?"

"Exeter!" Jack turned his eyes to the heavens. "Ye gods, the woman thinks we are near Exeter, if you please. We were not halfway across the moor before we were attacked last night. Surely you noticed when we passed near the new prison that Prinny had built for French prisoners of war at Princetown. I judge that our masked friends intercepted us about five miles beyond Two Bridges."

"How can you know all that when you were sleeping the whole time?"

He raised a skeptical brow at her.

"Well, you were certainly snoring, at any rate," she said uncomfortably.

"I'm gratified to see that I had so much of your attention. But I snore when I'm awake, too, as you'll discover for yourself one of these days."

A thought suddenly struck her. "You knew we would be attacked, did you not? You had your gun in your hand when we were stopped! You were prepared," she accused, pointing a finger at him.

And then she knew. "They were after you! What are you, Mackinnon? A thief. Did you swindle them and they took the wrong man away?"

"Tsk. What a lurid imagination it has," he tried to divert her.

"It's of no use trying to deny it. I can see it; 'tis as plain as a pikestaff. You're on the run from something. Phony Scottish accent, pretending to be asleep. . . . A rare greenhead you must take me for.

Ohhh. I've just saved the life of a dangerous criminal. And now I'm stuck with him here in the middle of God knows where." It was her turn to raise pleading eyes skyward and beat her small fists impotently against the rock.

"Yes," he leered, "you've landed yourself in desperate company, my dear. I'm a dangerous man, Mrs. St. Erney. Who knows when my fiendish nature may get the better of me." He waggled his eyebrows at her provocatively. "I can't promise not to attack you at first opportunity."

And that's too near the truth for my own comfort, he thought guiltily. For all the girl tried to hide behind a stern manner and unattractive clothes, he found his companion a decidedly luscious little baggage with her small, curvaceous figure, large sherry-colored eyes, and that long, glorious honey-colored hair that reached to the middle of her back. Her lips were wide and sensual, her complexion, with the lightest dusting of freckles across her nose and cheeks, was soft and fresh; a strong nose and determined little chin detracted not one whit from her loveliness. The lady's small stature on first glance made her look no more than a young girl but could not belie her womanly charms for one who looked closely.

Jillian had turned away from him, trying to win the battle over her temper, Jack guessed wisely, as he tried to tear his gaze from those pouting lips and teach himself not to long to reach out and touch her poor, lacerated cheeks. What a courageous little woman she was, he thought admiringly. Most ladies of his acquaintance—with one notable exception, he amended fondly, thinking of Dolly—would have had the vapors ten times over to endure just one half of what Jill had taken in her stride. Yet here she was carrying on like a regular trooper. Life with Reginald St. Erney must have dealt her some hard knocks, too, yet her trials and tribulations had not cowed her one bit, but served instead to forge a strong, determined, competent—if somewhat contentious—little character. His luck was definitely in when he had tumbled down that hill with her, he smiled crookedly to himself.

The sun that had been shining down so brightly moments before suddenly disappeared behind a cloud. They both glanced up to see heavy, black clouds threatening to spill their contents shortly. Jillian ran to gather up her mud-caked cloak and Mackinnon's equally filthy greatcoat. She returned to see that her irrepressible patient was suddenly all business.

"We must find some sort of shelter, Jill. I am obliged to ask you to help me walk on across that enclosed field yonder. That direction would seem to present our best hope as the field itself has been cultivated and enclosed. It must belong to some farmer hereabouts. But, I warn you, we must be careful. Those brigands may still be hunting for me." He laughed as he saw her grimace. Unfortunately, his light bantering words had much truth in them. He was a man on a secret mission and there were plenty of desperate cutthroats on his trail, men who would pay well to insure his failure. His life was easily forfeit, but he must have a care for her. His enemies would not stop at hurting a woman, either, and he began to rack his brain for a way to send Jill away from him out of the danger that her continued presence in his company would surely bring.

Those cork-brained miscreants of the night

before had badly bungled their mission if they had been looking for him. But perhaps they were not part of the network he knew to be working in this area and instead were only ordinary highwaymen looking for a few sovereigns and some baubles. But no—they hadn't attempted robbery. They seemed intent on the other gentleman who had shared the coach—the shifty-eyed dandy had clutched his valise as if it were worth his very life. Jack was abstracted as he puzzled over the events of the previous evening.

"Are you sure you feel strong enough to walk any distance, Mackinnon? There is a modicum of shelter here under the overhang of the cliff."

At Jill's question and inquiring look as she came to help him walk on across the field, Jack shook his head briefly and smiled. "Just wool-gathering, sweetheart. Speaking of which, perhaps we shall find the farmer who owns all these sheep." He gestured toward the scattered flocks on the hillside. But he knew that herds were often left to graze on the open moorland for weeks at a time without attention, and he was not sanguine that they would find human habitation.

"It's no good staying here, sweeting. We must find some sort of protection to avoid a thorough soaking. I'm in no condition to face the elements much longer, though I know you would be ready to brave anything, being such an intrepid creature and as strong as an ox to boot." At this blatant attempt to get a rise out of her, she took the bait and blazed up at him from under his shoulder where she supported him, "You, sir, are an insufferable tease and an unrepentant scoundrel."

"Well, it stands to reason. You must be inordinately robust for your size, a veritable strapping

56

little pocket Amazon, if you can bear my weight."
He laughed slightly, but Jillian could perceive
that he was perhaps somewhat embarrassed at
having to lean so heavily on her.

"I may be little, Mackinnon, but I am not
weak!"

"No, no. Little and *fierce*, my Hermia." He
grinned down at her again. He could only hope
that perhaps they would find a crude sheep shelter
that would accommodate them until the worst of
the weather passed. Food, however, was an entirely
different problem and one that was becoming
more urgent by the minute, if his growling
stomach were anything to go by.

Chapter 4

After wading through waves of yellow broom, oceans of pale green fern and emerald bracken, and a regular sea of heather—purple, lilac, and even some of the rare white variety—Jack and Jillian came to the edge of a rather close-cropped field surrounded by trees. Interspersed among the Contorta pines and Sitka and Norway spruce were a few large home oaks that had been damaged in the previous night's storm. Several broken limbs lay in their path, making walking difficult.

"Let us rest here a moment, sweetheart." Jack was trying to conceal his labored breathing. Jillian, too, was exhausted. Each was aching in body but unflagging in spirit and unwilling to let the other know of their physical weariness.

"I think if you would hand me one of those broken branches there, I might be able to fashion a kind of walking stick for myself that would ease some of my weight off your poor shoulders." Jack pointed to a likely looking oak branch. "Much as I dislike to break physical contact. . . ." He winked at her as he lifted his arm from her shoulder.

"What a good idea, Mackinnon," Jillian panted

as she moved to do his bidding.

Jack sat to rest on a low stone wall at the edge of the field and proceeded to strip the leaves and twigs off the limb until he had a relatively sturdy-looking cane. He breathed easier as he stood up and was able to lean on his rough crutch rather than on his companion. "Damnation!" he cursed involuntarily, "but I feel weak as a kitten. Sorry, sweeting, I'm not used to admitting to physical weakness," he smiled apologetically. Jillian did not complain, but he knew the going was hard enough without her having to bear him along like a baby.

As they trudged across the stony expanse, the wind picked up making conversation below a shout impossible. Jillian supported Mackinnon with an arm round his waist. He quickly tired and though he made an effort to put more of his weight on his walking stick and tried not to lean too heavily on her, he was weak and shaky from loss of blood and lack of food and soon sagged against her thin shoulder once more. He felt his meager strength draining away.

They came up to the top of a small rise just as the first drops of rain hit them, driven hard in their faces by the fierce wind. From their vantage point they could see the heavy curtains of rain swirling up from the valleys below coming nearer and nearer to them and knew that soon even the distant tors would be shrouded in rain and mist. The need to find shelter was urgent.

Jack squinted into the distance and thought he could detect a small hut, unless it was only another outcropping of the famous Dartmoor granite tors that deceived him by its regular shape. He raised his voice above the wind and shouted to Jill, "Over there."

She noted the object he pointed to and increased their pace. As they came nearer, they were relieved to see that it was a sort of shelter, however inadequate. It appeared to be some sort of shed for the sheep that roamed freely thereabouts. It had been placed so that it faced a nearby cliff and the wind and rain were effectively blocked from its entrance. They entered the tumble-down structure and saw that there were hens about the place as well as a few straggling sheep. But best of all, to Jack's eyes, was a straw-filled rack above the dirt floor that evidently held extra food for the sheep. His rain-drenched face split into a wide smile.

"Up you go, sweetheart."

"What! You cannot mean you expect me to climb up *there!*"

"It's the warmest, and I daresay the cleanest, spot in this barn. I think we can rest there quite comfortably."

"And how do you plan to climb up, Mackinnon, with the use of only one hand and arm?"

"Oh, no doubt I'll manage. You appear to be as strong as Atlas—and he held up the world, you know. If I can't make it on my own, I'm sure you will manage to heave me up." His mouth twisted up at one corner in the maddening way he had that was sure to raise her hackles.

"You expect us both to share that tiny space! You must be mad if you think I'm going up there with you!"

"Afraid, sweeting?"

"Prudent, sir. I have a care for my reputation, even if you do not."

"Ye gods! The woman has a care for her 'reputation.' Here in the middle of nowhere, a storm breaking all around her, chased by desperate bandits, without vittles and drink—she thinks a wounded, half-starved, three-quarters dead, rather shy gentleman is about to take advantage of her virtue!" Jack shook his head in sad disappointment at her lack of spirit.

"Where is my fine, courageous nurse of last night, then? The woman who slept beside me and kept me warm and comfortable all night? Gone with the coming of day, it seems. Must we wait for night to fall before she becomes reasonable again?" he raised his eyes to heaven in mock appeal as he teased her unmercifully. "Come, Jill. I thought you were made of sterner stuff."

Jillian gave him one smouldering look before she stepped smartly away from him, stood on the edge of a manger filled with sheep fodder, and boosted herself up into the rack of sweet-smelling straw above. Jack stood grinning as he watched her, admiring her spirit—and her tidy ankles as they were revealed when she hoisted her skirt up for the jump. He then stood on the same manger and was able to pull himself up onto the low rack with his one good arm. As he rested the elbow of his left arm on the uneven boards of the rack, a sharp pain shot through his wounded shoulder, and he was unable to prevent himself from uttering a cry of pain.

Jillian, all solicitation, was immediately at his side and helped him settle himself on the straw. The storm broke outside with a crash and she couldn't help flinching, although she managed not to throw herself at him as she had done when she had been frightened by their ovine onlookers of the morning.

"Rain, rain, go away," he mocked. "Jack and Jill want to play." She gave him an old-fashioned look and turned up her nose, trying to snub him. Her action only made him want to shout with laughter—the little enchantress was incapable of looking severe, no matter how hard she tried. That was not to say that she was incapable of giving one a sharp set-down with her acid tongue, he reflected with wry amusement.

After they settled themselves as comfortably as possible, he on his greatcoat and she on her cloak, Jillian could not prevent her curiosity from getting the better of her judgment for once. "How did you get away the first time they shot at you last night, Mackinnon, when you dived into the undergrowth? I distinctly heard the noise of a body falling down that hill. I was sure the villains had killed you."

His eyes gleamed at her interest. "A simple trick, sweetheart. I kicked a large stone loose and sent it crashing down. Naturally, the bungling swine thought it was me they heard falling. The noise provided sufficient cover for me to move far enough away so that they couldn't see me or hear my movements in the darkness."

"But why did you come back again and try to save me? You could have easily made your escape. Our attackers didn't seem bent on murder then."

"No, only ravishment, as I recall. I've heard that some women consider it a fate worse than death." He turned his head slightly to look into her face more closely.

Jillian flushed. "Yes, 'tis true. But why did you save *me?*"

"Just saving you for myself, I guess."

"Ohhh! Must you consider *everything* a joke!"

"You think I'd be concerned to save my own hide before anyone else's? A pretty opinion you've formed of me during our, ah, intimate acquaintance. . . . Well, sweeting, if you want the truth— I've been called Mad Jack Mackinnon for long enough. 'Twas just living up to my name.''

Jillian shook her head at the unquenchable foolishness of the man, then tried another tack. "What were you doing on that stagecoach in the first place, Mackinnon?"

"I was running away from home." He leered wolfishly.

"Will you never be serious? . . . No, I can see that you will not. How could I even for a moment have expected it."

"Oh, I can be as grave as the tomb, sweetheart. I'll prove it by asking what foolishness was it that prompted you to be traveling by yourself in the middle of the night without so much as your maid to accompany you? To catch the Mail in Exeter for London, was it?

"No answer, heh? A St. Erney, after all, can't be without all resources for comfortable, respectable travel. Hmm. And dressed like someone's companion or a governess, too. What have you been up to since Reg died, Jill?''

A crack of lightning flashed alarmingly near, followed by a long, loud roll of thunder. Jillian shuddered, and Mackinnon moved to put his right arm around her. "There, there, sweetheart. Nothing to be frightened of. Just Hera throwing a few pots and pans at poor old Zeus's head. Surely you can sympathize with her. A jealous wife, angry at her husband."

She tried to move away, "Oh, you are despicable! How dare you suggest such a thing. I was never jealous of Reginald in my life." Jack tightened his hold.

He smiled, satisfied, "Oh? . . . No, I don't suppose he was worth the effort."

"I don't choose to discuss my former life with you." She turned her face from him, giving him a tempting view of those pouting lips of hers.

"No, quite boring. Let's discuss your present life." He moved to bring her closer to him again. "Nothing like a tumble in the hay, now and again, is there?" And his lips took hers in a sudden light kiss.

The touch of his warm lips on hers sent Jillian skittering away. "Oh, you rake! I might have known you wouldn't behave as a gentleman." She ran the back of her hand across her mouth and moved as far from him as possible in the confined space.

"Yes, so you might, so you might." He smiled knowingly at her as he leaned back with his right arm behind his head and tried to settle himself for some rest.

He refused to admit how much his shoulder pained him. Devil take it, but they were in a damnable coil! He couldn't see his way clear out of their predicament until his arm healed somewhat. At least it seemed to be a clean wound, he reflected with some of his characteristic optimism. It could have been worse . . . much worse.

God, but he was starving, though! His stomach rumbled mightily at the thought. And food wasn't all he was hungry for, he admitted to himself with a sigh. He would just have to keep his hands off the lovely little termagant he had been stranded with, but it would be hard . . . damnably hard, he sighed again.

Tired and battered as they both were, it was not surprising that both soon fell asleep on the dry, sweet-smelling hay. Jillian awoke sometime later to peer out into a murky, still-damp day. It had grown considerably colder since the morning. Jack stirred, and she heard an ominous cracking sound.

"Ach, you fiend," she yelled. "You've destroyed our dinner!" Jack raised up to find that he had rolled over on an egg and cracked it. A messy yellow glob spread over the seat of his already severely stained trousers.

"Damn!" He looked genuinely dismayed for the first time in their brief acquaintance. Jillian couldn't repress a slight giggle at his predicament, though she sobered immediately when her own stomach began to rumble, reminding her that it had been many hours since she had had any food.

"Sorry, sweetheart," he said in accents slightly blurred from sleep. He felt somewhat dazed and decidedly shaky as the sharp ache in his shoulder brought him to full consciousness.

"I am sorry to have to suggest this, Jill love, but I think that you will have to scout around for something for us to eat. Perhaps you'll find a friendly farmhouse as you reconnoiter and all our problems will be solved. I'm afraid I'm not going to be up to moving until I absolutely must." He spoke seriously for once.

"I'll be glad to avoid your company for awhile, Mackinnon."

"Hey, sweetheart. I'm not forcing you to stay with me, you know. I assumed you stayed out of the goodness of your heart and the sweetness of

66

your nature." He cocked an eyebrow at her as one side of his mouth curved upward.

"You flatter yourself, Sir Rogue. You and your scurrilous tongue can take themselves to perdition for all I care. Only the direst of necessities prevents me from walking out of here and not coming back."

"Ah, my old sweetheart is herself again. I knew the sweetness would wear off soon and we would be back to the sour. I shall miss your honeyed converse while you're away. Come back to me soon, my heart."

"Go to the devil, Mackinnon, and while you're about it, take your remarkably foolish palaver with you!" Jillian wrapped herself as well as she could in her cloak and carefully climbed down from the rack, disdaining the offer of Jack's good hand to assist her.

"Only if you'll come with me."

The man was completely irrepressible and utterly maddening, Jillian thought disgustedly. "While I'm gone, why don't you have a talk with yourself, Mackinnon, and decide to reform your manners—or I just may decide to abandon you to your fate here among the sheep and fowl where you belong."

She could see the white flash of his familiar grin in the gloom of the little shed as she left.

Chapter 5

Jillian came running and shouting back to the shed about half an hour later. "Mackinnon, Mackinnon! I've found something!" She paused when she came into the sheep hut and put her hand up to lean against the rough-hewn wall while she caught her breath and stilled her fast-beating heart.

"What have you found, Jill, love? Food and shelter, I dare to hope." Jack had been dozing again, but roused at the sound of her voice calling to him.

"Yes." She still panted heavily.

"What is it? And where—how far away?" Impatience began to grow in him.

"A small cottage—well, one room really. No one seems to be about, but the door is not locked. There are a few supplies. Let's hurry before it gets dark or starts to rain again." She looked up at the still threatening sky to note black clouds hanging low on the hillside.

"You've done well, sweetheart. I should like to take you on campaigns with me."

"You needn't start your nonsense again." She

pokered up immediately. "I'm only aiding you because I must. If you hadn't been shot I would have found my way alone, I assure you."

"And here I thought you were staying for the pleasure of my company. You wound me, sweetheart. Really you do."

"Come on, Mackinnon, before the storm breaks again. We've no time to spare for brangling now."

"I'm coming. I'm coming, my little taskmaster. But first I think it wise to catch and kill one of these chickens."

"Ugh. Must we?"

"If you want to eat, we must."

With great aversion, she helped him catch a fat hen, but wouldn't have anything to do with the killing. She averted her eyes as he managed to wring its neck with his one good hand. She discovered two more eggs, carefully wrapped them in her handkerchief, and put them in her pocket.

Jillian found Mackinnon weaker than he had been earlier in the day. At first she was suspicious that he was shamming it but found on closer observation that he was gritting his teeth in earnest and making an effort not to groan. The shoulder was bad then. One more problem laid in their dish.

The walk was uphill along the edge of the same meandering stream they had slept near the night before. Undoubtedly the little rill was one of any number of small tributaries that fed into the River Dart as that body of water swelled and carved its winding course across the moor to form the large river that had its outlet far to the south in Dartmouth.

Jack and Jill were both exhausted when they reached the austere, one-roomed cottage. The door creaked on its hinges as they entered. It was a question of who carried whom by the time they collapsed inside the door.

"I don't know about you, sweetheart, but I'm fagged half to death."

"You're not a featherweight by any means, Mackinnon," Jillian panted as she sat next to him on the floor.

"Well do I know it. I much fear that it will take more than one scrawny chicken to fill this empty pit where my stomach used to be."

"Oh, no, Mackinnon. I'm not going back to that shed, so don't even think it," she warned him sternly.

Although moderately better than their previous sheltering place, the building was designed for rugged usage not creature comfort. The cottage was made of uninviting, rough-hewn gray stone, obviously granite collected from the region. The floor was of wooden planking and there was a crude fireplace. Implements were minimal: a tin plate and cup, a knife, a large pot for cooking, a few worn blankets spread on a narrow bed, and one straight-backed chair with a broken leg leaning against the wall comprised the few meager contents of their sheltering place.

There were no windows, and the light had grown so poor by the time they reached the cabin that they had to leave the door open until they could find a way to light the few logs and sticks piled in the fireplace.

"One piece of luck, at least. Someone's thoughtfully left us some firewood. I should hate to have to hunt around outside in this weather for fuel," commented Jillian as she searched around the edge of the fireplace looking for a flint. She smiled when she found it and held it up like a prize to show Mackinnon. He smiled weakly as he sank down on the bed and covered his eyes with his good arm. "I picked myself a prize nurse, didn't I? She carried me here and now she's going to cook my dinner."

Thankfully the logs were dry enough to catch immediately when Jillian struck the flint against them. Then she closed the door against the wind and rain that had picked up again outside.

"Well, Mackinnon, I hope you can recover enough energy to pluck this chicken, for I'm sure it is beyond me, no matter how hungry I am."

"I believe I've already fulfilled my part in this enterprise by hunting down and slaughtering our dinner, bloodying myself in the process. Surely now 'tis the woman's place to do the rest. Boil the thing feathers and all, if you must."

"The climb has made you light-headed, I see," she commented as she swept past him, pot in hand, to make her way to the little stream to collect enough water to cook their dinner.

"Little minx," he remarked to her retreating back. When she returned, they managed between them the unpleasant task of defeathering the plump fowl.

An hour later saw them greedily gnawing at the bones of the chicken they had boiled. They had to sit on the floor and share the one plate, but at least Jillian had found the stubs of two candles and they had some light to guide them. The flicking flames of the log fire served to provide a little more illumination and quite a bit of warmth.

Mackinnon had slept while Jillian cooked the bird, and he had awakened much refreshed. He wasn't even feeling any particular pain in his shoulder; it was sore, but the pulling, tearing sensation had subsided. His naturally buoyant spirits rose, and he began to derive some enjoyment from their situation.

"This is the best meal I've ever had," Jack asserted when he had finished his half of the chicken and had had his fill of fresh spring water from the tankard. He lay back on the hard floor and flashed a beaming smile up at Jill.

"Oh, you say the most ridiculous, absurd things, you silly man."

"No. It's true. I've never been so hungry. Therefore, this food tastes better than anything I've ever eaten before. And since I'm sharing it with you, that makes it all the more enjoyable."

"Stop that! Stop trying to flummery me, Mackinnon. I don't want any more of your nonsense and humbug."

"Why do you think I'm trying to flummery you? Here I am with a beautiful woman who saved my life, who continues to nurse a crotchety, wounded patient and favor me with her company—even though she hates men—and she can't accept a simple compliment."

"I do not hate men," Jillian said in a subdued voice.

"Don't you, little one. I should if I had had to live with Reginald St. Erney for any length of time."

Jillian didn't deign to answer, turning away instead to stare into the fire.

Jack watched the light play over her face for awhile. He ran his hand over his scratchy chin as he regarded her with a gleam in his eye. "You present quite a temptation, you know, sweetheart."

"Me!" she scoffed. "What rot you talk. I know I'm nothing much to look at. I'm rather small and plain—not beautiful at all. I have nothing to recommend me to men. You're just a practiced seducer alone with a defenseless female. I'm like that chicken we had for dinner. You've nothing else to satisfy your appetite for the moment, so you make do with what's at hand."

"Now who told you that pack of lies about your not being beautiful—Reg?" he guessed accurately.

She turned her head away from him again. He sat up and reached to wipe away a speck of food from her chin. Allowing his hand to linger, he turned her face toward him as he gently stroked her face with his thumb.

"Listen to me, Jill. No matter what anyone else has ever told you, you are quite, quite lovely. . . . You're right. I do have experience, and what I tell you is true. You have a beautiful face—a man could drown in your warm hazel eyes."

He transferred his good right hand to stroke her hair. "I have never seen such thick, lustrous hair— I love its soft, golden color. And my dear, you have quite a trim little figure, you know. So what if you lack inches—you make up for them in curves." Here he slid his hand down the side of her bosom.

"As for your lips—they cry out for a man's touch." He bent forward and gently touched his mouth to hers. She did not draw back immediately, so he allowed his lips to play over hers for a moment, sucking in the honey nectar of her. But when he dared to run the tip of his tongue over her tightly closed mouth, she pulled back spitting at him, "You are contemptible. You admit to being a practiced rake, a hardened seducer of innocent virtue. Ugh. You are repulsive. I can't stand for

74

you to come near me. Why do you persist in such shameless behavior?"

Jack sighed and sat back, "I forgot to mention your one flaw—your barbed tongue. It lashes one most vilely, you know. But then some men can't help but grasp the nettle, hoping against hope, I assume, that eventually they will become inured to its pricks."

"If it's my tongue that preserves my virtue, then I'm glad of it."

"Deuce take it, little shrew, you are a very wasp for stinging set-downs."

"A wasp! I knew you would be back to insulting me soon. Well, sir, if I'm a wasp, best beware my sting and don't provoke me."

"And I know where you carry your stinger."

She raised her brows at him. "I'm sure an uncouth lout like you will make some ill-bred, vulgar joke of this. You seem to be incapable of any civilized, polite conversation. Where were you bred, Mackinnon? In a stable?"

"Yes, it's in your tongue, alright."

"Back to my tongue again!"

"Where else would a wasp carry her stinger—in her tail?" Jack, restraining his warm laughter with much difficulty, shot her a provocative look from under his eyebrows. If Jillian had dared to look closely, she would have seen wicked little devils dancing all the way back in the depths of his mocking brown eyes. She was so easy to bait, 'twas almost unfair of him he knew, but the sport of it was too delicious to resist.

"My tail! Whatever do you mean, you odious man? . . . Oh! How dare you say such a thing! I warn you, Mackinnon, I will not bear your insults a moment longer!" Jillian flushed darkly as she jumped up and moved jerkily away from him. But Jack was up in the same instant and moved forward and caught her with his good right arm. He ran his hand over her derrière. "Too gentle a maid—too soft and round to carry a stinger here."

Before she knew what he was about, he leaned forward and said, "Perhaps it's in the tongue after all. I'll pluck it out, shall I?" He whispered before he bent his full lips to hers and kissed her deeply.

Jillian was too shocked to struggle for a moment. She had been through too much in the last four and twenty hours and could not resist leaning into his warm body for a moment—for comfort . . . and something else she couldn't name. Her senses returned too swiftly for the both of them and she pulled back scolding him, "You, you, you . . . vile, lecherous, debauched brute! How dare you? How dare you take advantage of me, you unfeeling reprobate! . . . Ohhh! I don't know the words capable of describing your shameless, wretched, heartless behavior. You are no gentleman!"

Jack couldn't help shouting with laughter at her severe but quite unconvincing reprimand. She had enjoyed that kiss as much as he had. "I can see that I shall just have to keep that wagging tongue of yours busy with other sport if I'm to avoid a blistering set-down at every turn."

"Don't you dare to laugh at me." Jill was in such a rage with him, and anger at herself for her unthinking response, that she reacted physically. She lifted her small foot and kicked him in the shin, then trod down hard on his toe. Jack gave a startled "Ummph" and grabbed the offended digit, straining his wounded shoulder and nearly falling over in the process.

"Damn," he said as the pain shot through his shoulder like a knife. He fell back on the bed, exhausted but satisfied—their play had been worth the price. He flashed a wide smile at Jillian's stiff back. To see his little shrew in a passion was worth enduring her insults, he decided. Her complexion positively glowed and her eyes flashed with beautiful, dangerous lights. She didn't realize that every time they came to cuffs she presented more of a temptation than ever before. He vowed to himself that soon he would tame his little termagant and claim her for his very own.

Jillian sulked for the next hour. Jack rested quietly on the bed, recruiting his strength, then picked himself up, slung his greatcoat over his shoulder, and took himself outside briefly. When he returned, he removed his coat, jacket, neck-cloth, and boots then settled himself on the bed under the one meager blanket she had left him with his greatcoat on top for extra warmth.

"Umm. A *much* more comfortable bed than the one we shared last night, sweeting. Coming?"

"You must be mad!"

"A mad Jack and a bad Jack and a heedless jack of a lad. 'A mad-cap ruffian and a swearing Jack / That thinks with oaths to face the matter out,' Aye, the very gent, sweetheart. Mad Jack Mackinnon at your service.

"Jill, you can't sleep sitting against that wall. Come, my dear, lie here by me. It's warm . . . and you wouldn't believe how agreeable this old mattress is after our previous makeshift arrangements."

He raised up slightly to see a decidedly stubborn tilt to her chin as she turned her head away from him. She had been sitting combing out her hair, and now it formed a glorious mantle about her shoulders as it caught the light from the dying fire and gleamed in the otherwise darkened room.

"Right. Have it your own way." Jack settled himself for sleep. His arm was not aching so much and with a full stomach, warmth, and shelter, he was feeling quite drowsy. He lifted one eyelid briefly to see Jill still huddled against the wall with the other two blankets.

"Jill," he said dangerously, "if I have to get out of this bed and come over there and carry you back, you're going to regret it. Now be sensible and come to bed, sweetheart."

"I might have known that you would soon be threatening me."

"Fustian! But do not doubt that I will do as I say."

"No. For a wounded man with the use of only one arm you have amazing strength when you've a mind to use it."

"Just wait until I have the use of both arms," he grinned, unrepentant.

"I know I can't trust you, Mackinnon. You don't have to remind me of the fact."

"I'm too worn out to assault you, tonight, my lovely one. I think your virtue will be safe for a few hours more. The only thing you have to fear is being awakened by my snoring." I won't guarantee to stay away from you tomorrow, though. You present too much of an enticement for a man of my appetites to withstand, he added to himself.

It was too cold and uncomfortable to stay where she was for long, so Jillian put her scruples aside

78

and reluctantly came to the bed. "I'm too tired to argue." She took off her shoes but carefully kept her spencer buttoned over her gown should he be tempted to pull the same trick again he had attempted this morning.

"Move over, Mackinnon." Jack immediately moved over as far as he could to make room for her on the narrow cot, smiling into the darkness with contentment as he did so. Jillian snuggled down into the warmth where he had lain and sighed as her tired, aching limbs settled against him on the soft mattress. Warmth was better than words, at least for the time being.

"Sweet dreams, Mrs. St. Erney." She could hear the laughter in his voice, but she was too near sleep to take exception to his mode of address.

Chapter 6

They both slept deeply and woke late the next morning to the sound of incessant rain beating down against the roof of their abode. Jillian was embarrassed to find herself cuddled up against Mackinnon's chest, but she was so warm and comfortable that she couldn't bring herself to move her sore body and aching limbs which had stiffened up considerably overnight. She kept her eyes closed and tried not to think about the man's body pressed to hers.

Reg had never slept in the same room, much less the same bed, with her in all their married life. This was the first time she had actually shared a night's sleep with a man in the same bed, she thought with some dismay—and a very virile man he was, too. And she couldn't trust him an inch.

She wouldn't think about that. Nor would she think about her compromising situation. If she thought about those things, she would have to get up and leave the heavenly warmth to step out into a cold, damp room. She listened instead to the rain washing over the cottage and regretted that the fire had died down overnight. It would be her job to build one up again, she supposed. Thank goodness whomever had inhabited the cottage before had left a supply of branches and twigs inside out of the wet. Her mind dwelt on the complications of the day ahead. It would be next to impossible to strike out across the moor on foot in such weather. And even as her stomach gurgled, she wondered however they were to find something to eat.

She shivered with the cold. Her bedfellow seemed to be breathing evenly and she assumed that he slept still. She untensed and let her body relax against his into sleep once more.

Jack awoke several minutes later with a drowsy sense of contentment. He smiled to himself as he felt the little body curled so trustingly against him. Jill was still asleep, then. Good. He wanted to savor the peace and quiet and the sensation of having her all to himself. God, but she was a tempting little armful. He would have to go carefully, so as not to frighten the girl—or to bring her anger and wrath down on his head. It was hard, damnably hard, not to tease her though.

What a lovely little bundle of womanhood she was, never mind her hot temper and the cutting retorts she let fly from that sharp tongue of hers. Reginald St. Erney had been the worst kind of rake, Jack remembered from one or two nasty encounters with the man, heedlessly cruel and insensible of the harm he caused others—and himself. With his penchant for dangerous living, he had gone to the devil with all possible speed.

Jill undoubtedly had nightmarish memories of her former husband. Jack shuddered and grimaced as unbidden thoughts of what she must have had to endure found their way into his mind. His hand tightened into a fist as he caressed her shoulder.

Never, never would he let any harm come to her again, Jack swore.

Oh, but she felt good against him. He could detect the scent of the subtle perfume that still clung to her torn clothing. What a little ragamuffin she had looked when they awoke in the ditch yesterday with her clothes all dirty and torn and nasty scratches on her face and hands, and her glorious honey-colored hair in an untidy tangle. He had wanted to hug and kiss her right then, and he couldn't for the life of him resist teasing her. She seemed to have the ability to provoke him in any number of ways.

He ran his hand down her arm. She stirred, then stiffened. "Unhand me, Mackinnon," she said crossly.

"Whatever you say, sweetheart. I was only trying to warm your cold arm, you know. You will insist on throwing off the covers in your sleep. Tsk. So unwise of you. We don't want you coming down with the ague on top of my ah, er, incapacity, now do we?"

Jillian disdained to answer him as she forced her tired limbs to move and got up out of the bed with great but concealed regret—for its warmth, of course. It was freezing in the cabin. She threw on her cloak and made her stiff way to the fireplace where she placed more logs in the hearth and felt around for the flint.

"There's enough chicken broth left to serve as breakfast, I suppose," she remarked prosaically. "I shall just heat it up."

"Trying to change the subject, eh?" She turned to see Mackinnon laughing at her as he lay cozily in the bed, his right arm behind his head and his knees bent up under the blankets. She resented the fact that he was still warm and comfortable and she was forced to wait on him.

"As you're always assuring me that you're much less dangerous when you have a full stomach, I think it a prudent policy to feed you as often as may be."

"Touché, my dear. What about the eggs you collected yesterday? I don't think thin soup is going to be enough to satisfy my appetite. You were sleeping soundly until my stomach started grumbling. Didn't you hear it? That must have been what woke you."

"No. It was your pawing me that woke me, as you well know. Get up, Mackinnon, and help me cook. I'm not your servant, you know."

"No, no, sweetheart, 'tis I who am slave to you. For you hold my heart in chains, you know."

"I'd like to cut out that black devil's heart of yours, Mackinnon. So best beware!"

Jack raised his brows and asked in all innocence, "Dear me! Are you *that* hungry, sweetheart? Sounds most unappetizing to me, but then there's no accounting for tastes."

Jillian choked and turned away to stifle her laughter. When she had regained some semblance of composure she said, "Wha—what nonsense!"

"Ah, no, my dear. You enslaved me with one glance—sharp and nasty as it was—from your beautiful wide eyes. I must have a closer look at them sometime. Those green and gold flecks all mixed in the warm brown quite fascinate me."

"Will you be sensible!"

"Funny the sparks they can shoot sometimes, though," he winked at her. She wanted to throw something at him. Instead she turned her back on him and hunted for another pot to cook eggs in.

She found that she had to go outside to get more water from the stream and couldn't help grumbling under her breath at the fate of women forced to wait on men. 'Twas most unfair.

Jillian was surprised to see Mackinnon up standing near the hearth when she returned. His right arm was thrust through the sleeve of his bottle green jacket and his left arm was hanging loosely at his side with the jacket slung over the wounded shoulder. He looked a real vagabond with his scruffy black-bearded face and ruffled hair, dressed in his dirty, torn garments as he was.

Jack greeted her cheerfully. "Look what I have discovered," he said proudly, holding up a rusty old canister of tea which he had found on a tall shelf unnoticed in last night's gloom. "Do you have any spare water to make us a cup of tea?"

"You can get your own water and make your own tea. I'm not your slave to run outside in the rain at your every whim."

"Don't bite my head off. . . . I'm glad to have this warning that you are grumpy when you wake up in the morning. I console myself that one of us can keep his temper, though. It makes up for the other's crosspatchity mood."

She tightened her lips and lowered her eyebrows at him, knowing that he was being deliberately provoking.

"Oh, you won't find me digging in my heels at making the tea. I'm not so high in the instep as all that, you know." He opened the lid and sniffed the tea. "It smells fresh, at least. Maybe you'll be your usual sweet self after you have a cup of this brew?" he raised his brow in innocent query, succumbing once more to the irresistible urge to raise her hackles.

"More of your nonsense!" she spat back. "I thought you were pretending to be Scottish yesterday, but now you're pitching the gammon so hard and fast one would think you'd kissed the Blarney Stone when you were still in leading strings. Sure it wasn't an *Irish* brogue you were trying to imitate?"

He just stood looking at her with a decided twinkle in his eye and smiled boyishly. "You're on to me, then. There's no pulling the wool over your eyes, is there, sweeting. I'm just trying to worm my way into your good graces, after all."

"Oh, I've already realized that you're a worm, Mackinnon."

"Another hit direct, sweetheart. I left myself wide open for that one, didn't I." Jack bit back a smile at her quick retort. "You leave me sparring for wind. Think I'll take myself out of range until you cool down."

As he made for the door, Jillian couldn't help calling after him, "It's raining quite hard, you know. Best put your greatcoat over your head," in motherly fashion. She was immediately irritated with herself for taking so much interest.

Heavy, dark, rain-laden clouds sat right down on the moor making it much too wet and misty to find their way back to civilization that day. They spent the morning taking turns napping in the small bed and in intermittent desultory conversation as they heard the rain beat down on the roof of their shelter. Mackinnon slept soundly for several hours and seemed disinclined to indulge his penchant for bedeviling her much when he was awake. Jillian thought he was brooding on their enforced imprisonment in the little cottage.

During one lull in the rain and lift of the mist, Jillian made her way across the field to the lean-to where she met several damp sheep who stared at her warily as she went about the task of hunting up eggs for dinner. She tried to catch a chicken, but every time she approached one of the alarmed birds, it would flap its wings and squawk loudly, causing Jillian to back off. Just when she had admitted defeat, one silly old hen took off at her approach and crashed into the door head first. It lay dead at her feet like a gift from heaven. Jillian smiled in triumph and anticipated telling the story to her companion with great glee.

Although the wound to his shoulder had proved less serious than he had first thought, Jack was disappointed to find himself still feeling far from robust physically. He was bruised and sore from his tumble, and the loss of blood from his wound had weakened him considerably. He knew that no discomfort would stop them from leaving the next day, however, rain or no. They would starve else! And after hiding out for two days there was less chance the highwaymen would be searching for him, he reasoned—if he had been their quarry in the first place.

Jack fretted while Jill was gone and was surprised that he did so. He who took most things in his carefree stride worried that a passing cloud of fog would descend quickly making it impossible for Jill to find her way back.

They again took turns resting in the bed when she did return, quite safely and not too wet, proudly fishing out six eggs from her pocket and producing the dead hen which she gladly handed over to Jack for plucking. Then as she changed the bandage on his arm with a fresh piece of her petticoat, she tried to find out what he planned to do to get them safely off the moor, how they would find their way to the next town, where they would aim to walk to, but he was noncommittal, turning her queries aside with quizzing remarks.

"'Tis healing already, Mackinnon. You'll be in prime twig in next to no time," Jillian said as she saw the pucker of flesh where the jagged edges of the wound joined together. There was no sign of fresh bleeding to worry her either. "We shall be able to leave this hovel tomorrow. You do mean to aim for the closest town, do you not?" she questioned closely.

"Are you *that* anxious to be rid of me? Too much of a handful for you, heh?" he roasted her. Jillian looked at him reproachfully as she finished her handiwork with the bandage, longing to tell him that she could handle him in a minute. "I find you beyond redemption, sir," she said instead.

"Have you no ambition toward reforming my disreputable character, then?"

"'Twould be a lifetime's work to reform you, I fear. Do you take me for a Methodist, sir, to dedicate myself to such an impossible task?"

"Dear me, no. I take you for a most determined little baggage and a most beautiful and desirable woman to boot. If you find the task daunting, though, I can only say I thought you made of sterner stuff."

She sniffed at his persistent attempts to raise her hackles. "Next time I find myself running short of wit, Mackinnon, I shall make sure to visit your store. You are so well-stocked you never seem to run out."

"I'm glad there's something of mine you covet, sweetheart."

Some hours later as they worked together to prepare their evening meal, Jack fingered his unshaven chin and remarked, "It's a wonder you can put up with this ugly mug of mine. Perhaps that's what's been making you so cross all day."

"How absurd you are!" Jillian scoffed. "'Tis not your person I take exception to. 'Tis your mode of conversation, that unruly tongue of yours, and your shameless persistence in taking liberties with my person that I find odiously unbearable."

"Ah, do I detect a note of admiration hidden in that catalogue of my faults? Can it be possible you find me attractive, then?" he twitted her.

"You flatter yourself, you impossible man! I've just told you that I hate you!"

"No, have you? I'm an incurable sinner by your account. Well, I have every confidence in your judgment of my manners and morals. You are not behindhand to admit that there is no hope for me. One who is as sweet-tempered and soft-spoken as yourself is a scrupulous judge of such things. But I was asking for your judgment of my physical appearance. You think there's no hope for me in competing with you in that category either, then?"

"More of your nonsensical rubbish. You may be an impossible rakeshell, sir, but I have no illusions about my own appearance. I know I'm no raving beauty . . . just a regular plain Jane, I vow."

"Now that's where you're wrong, Jill, as I've

told you before. 'Tis unlike you to be fishing for compliments.''

She disdained to enter into another branglement but concentrated on her cooking, such as it was. They had to make do with a meager meal of boiled fowl once again, but with the added luxury of eggs and tea, they both began to feel more replete. Jack remarked that he had finally lost ''that hollow feeling'' and could put aside his fears that the next strong wind would blow them both away.

Later in the evening they faced the dilemma of the previous night—how would they both sleep in the same bed? ''Now, don't start to argue, my termagant. I will have to sleep on the floor and risk fever setting in to my wound if you won't be sensible and come to bed.'' She looked unconvinced.

''You will be safe. After all, I behaved last night. That should be all the proof you need that I'm trustworthy.''

''I wouldn't trust you as far as I could throw you, Mackinnon. You were assaulting me when I awoke this morning.''

''Assaulting you! Why, I was only stroking your cold arm to warm you up,'' he smirked. To do no more than run his hand along her arm and breathe in the delicious scent of her lovely hair had required all his willpower—and of course his lack of strength in his weakened state had made a fair contribution to his lack of action—but he wasn't about to make such a damning admission to Jill at this juncture.

''Perhaps I don't fancy you, sweetheart. Have you considered that?'' he winked. He couldn't resist casting his bait once more before her nose. It was so amusing to see her rise to the fly every time.

"You! You would fancy one of those sheep in the field if it were dressed in skirts, Mackinnon!"

"Dear me! You think I'm an animal lover? Or are you saying that I'm not discriminating. How insulting—both to me and to yourself."

"*Will you kindly be serious,* you muttonheaded makebait," Jillian said in low, ominous accents.

"Yes, ma'am. Right away, ma'am. Serious she wants and serious she'll get. No, I won't attack you. I want to go to sleep. We'll have to walk out of here tomorrow no matter what the weather—we shall die of hunger else. So come to bed, mistress crab. Arm yourself with one of the logs from the fireplace for protection, if you must. I don't have the strength to fight with you further tonight. I'm tired of arguing. I'm tired period. Good night." So saying, Jack rolled over onto his back and closed his eyes.

Jillian was taken aback. She had never known him come close to losing his temper before, despite all their misadventures, and it was a daunting experience. She crept to the bed and lay down carefully, trying not to touch any part of his body.

Several hours later Jillian awoke to find herself cradled against Mackinnon's good shoulder and was again attracted by the very faint musky smell of cologne. The crisp ends of his hair curled softly against her cheek. He was breathing evenly, with none of the moans of that first frightful night to disturb his sleep or hers.

She wondered again what sort of scandal broth she had landed herself in. She supposed if no one knew of their enforced sojourn together, there would be none the wiser. She hoped the incorrigible creature she found herself tied to for the moment would make no difficulty when it came to a parting of the ways and that he would promise not to mention their scandalous behavior in sleeping together—no, no, sharing a bed merely— on three successive occasions.

Trouble was, for all her protests to the contrary, she found him a dangerously attractive man, handsome in that raffish sort of way that set some women's pulses to racing—and she knew not a single thing about him. She supposed he was some sort of minor criminal, on the run from the law, the way he wanted to keep out of sight and not take a chance on getting a ride back to Two Bridges or on to Moretonhampstead by walking along the road. He seemed to think it safer to hide out here on the moor until his shoulder recovered somewhat. The thought crossed her mind that he was hiding out from his creditors. Perhaps he had cheated someone at cards and they were after him, she imagined luridly, remembering Reg.

Whatever his reasons for remaining out of sight, she could not stay with him after the morrow. She would not have the excuse that he was dangerously wounded, nor could she use the rain and terrible weather as a pretext. She would have to strike out on the road and hope that she would come upon a traveler in some sort of conveyance who would agree to take her up.

She snuggled closer and couldn't resist lightly kissing his rough unshaven cheek. No man had ever told her she was beautiful before, even if he was just trying to turn her up sweet. Certainly not her husband, who had taken one look at the small, gauche eighteen-year-old she had been when her brothers had lost her to him for a bet and laughed,

"Why, 'tis a very child. How old are you, girl, twelve? or not so much. You'll never grow into a beauty, that's sure. How could my father think a baby like you would hold me. Why, you're all bones, girl. 'Tis a woman I want, and 'tis sure I'll have before this night's over."

He had taken her, it was true, but only when he was too drunk to even think straight. It had been unpleasant in the extreme—he had repeated the repulsive act few times in their four-year marriage—and then only when he was drunk, as he invariably was. He was frequently from home, and when he returned it was only to boast about his conquests among the wives of his fellow officers and the muslin company. She didn't care; she was grateful that his attentions were turned elsewhere. He had moved about with his cavalry unit a great deal and gone to London whenever he had leave. She supposed that they had not lived together for more than six months all told in those four horrible years. She had actually felt relief when he had died, though sorry that a young life had been so wasted.

Her frequent quarrels with her brothers and Reginald over the years had formed her into the outspoken woman she was. In her untenable situation in the Jenkins' household she had great difficulty mastering the urge to tell the girls and their mother a few home truths. And so it was her explosion two days previously—was it only two days ago!—that had been the start of this madcap adventure. As a consequence, here she was . . . with she knew not whom, she knew not where, she knew not why, and, for the moment, she knew not why she should care.

Chapter 7

Jillian must have fallen asleep again because she thought she was dreaming an especially pleasant dream—her own special dream where she was with a man who treated her with the utmost tenderness, who worshipped her and made love to her with great gentleness. The dream was becoming almost too real. She could feel the phantom's lips kissing her with increasing fervor and she was responding, opening her mouth to his probing tongue. He was holding her with his arm and leg over her body, pressing her down hard onto the mattress. She could feel his breath, warm and rapid on her cheek. She was responding to his kiss as she had never done to her husband's—indeed, Reg had barely done more than peck her on the mouth once or twice before he went on to do other things—unpleasant things—to her.

But this was wonderful, kissing like this, having a man's hand caressing her waist, her hips, her breasts—good heavens! His hand was beneath her dress on her bare skin. Jillian awoke with a start and pushed Mackinnon off her. She leaped out of the bed and pulled her disordered clothing round her.

"I knew it! I knew I was a fool to trust you, Mackinnon! You can't be trusted one inch, yet I was so tired I forgot what a beastly libertine you are!"

"So was I dreaming . . . dreaming that someone was kissing me—could it have been you? You happened to be there at any rate and I did what came naturally. Well, you know I wouldn't deliberately give you my head for washing again . . ."

"So . . . you were half asleep—dreaming—and you thought I was someone else, did you? Who?"

"Yes—I mean no." He looked at her helplessly. "Give me a clue, Jill?" he grinned lopsidedly.

"You admit it! You're so accustomed to having a woman in your bed every night you thought nothing of using *me* in such a way—your convenient! Bah."

"You think me a rake. To admit otherwise would spoil your image of me, now wouldn't it? I wouldn't want to disillusion you," he leered.

"You take fiendish delight in antagonizing me, don't you? You are the most provoking creature alive and test the limits of my endurance."

"As you do mine, sweetheart."

"If I had a small sword about me I'd have your liver and lights!"

He shuddered playfully, put his hand over his face, and peeped at her through his fingers. "Such a bloodthirsty little spitfire. I suspect that you're just hungry again. Most unappetizing organs those, though, you know," he roasted her.

Jillian turned her back on him and beat her fists impotently against the stone wall, resisting the urge to crown him. She knew she was screeching like a fishwife.

"I didn't mean to 'assault' you, you know. And I

think, love, you were enjoying it as much as I was. Come on back to bed, sweeting."

"Oh, if it isn't just like a man to think that *that* is fun. It's horrible and disgusting. How dare you suggest that I would enjoy such a repulsive act!"

"What's this then? Was Reg such a bad lover that he gave you a disgust of lovemaking? . . . I can see by your expression that he was. Poor Jill! I can teach you better than that. You will like it with me, sweetheart, I guarantee. You liked what we were doing just now as much as I did."

She kept her back to him and went over to the fireplace to try to coax the few remaining sticks and twigs into some sort of fire.

"Won't answer, hmm? I would like to get my hands on Reg St. Erney so that I could wring his neck. Too bad he's broken it already. How could he fail to see what a hot-blooded, little beauty you are, just made for such sport."

She turned around red-faced and furiously spat at him, "Stifle it, Mackinnon. I swear I will abandon you if I hear another word on this subject. My relations with my deceased husband are no concern of yours. You are to keep your hands off me and keep your mouth shut. Just because I'm a widow you think to take advantage of me. Well, I have news for you! I'm not a woman of easy virtue as you seem to think.

"I've had enough of your insinuations, lewd suggestions, and ribald comments, and I've had enough of you pawing me. I know I'm not attractive—just convenient. But I won't have it! Do you hear me." She stamped her foot. "I hate what happens between a man and a woman. So just leave me alone!" Her voice had risen in volume as she railed at him, becoming ever more shrill until she was shouting at the top of her lungs. Then Jillian surprised herself exceedingly by bursting into tears; she ran out of the cabin wearing only her woolen dress and thin spencer with no cloak to protect her from the damp and the cold outside.

"Bloody hell, woman! Come back here!" Jack, swearing mightily, awkwardly got to his feet and started after her, until he remembered that his feet were bare. "God damn you to hell, Reginald St. Erney, for what you've done to that beautiful girl!" Sharp pain shot through his left arm from the sudden movement, and he halted in the doorway, worried that Jill would indeed do something silly. At least the rain had stopped and a watery sun was showing through the clouds, he noted as he glanced upward through the open door.

Now why couldn't he restrain himself just a bit when he was around her? Jack asked himself, still swearing at his own lack of control. But he had been dreaming of holding a warm, little body against his own, and somehow he had started kissing her in his sleep, despite his good intentions not to frighten the girl. Knowing full well that their compromising situation of the first night had made it imperative that they marry as soon as he could contrive it, he did not want to do anything that might make her balk at the idea.

Jill had become too precious to him in the last two days for him to do anything that would truly give her a disgust for him. And knowing her—and himself—Jack knew that their future relations were likely to be stormy at the best of times. He smiled in anticipation, then quickly sobered. His quirky personality and lack of amorous activity for months—and her very desirable proximity—

had led him to abandon his good intentions and almost take her—with her cooperation, mind—then and there. How he was to restrain himself until he got her and himself safe again, he did not know.

He sat on the floor and held his head in his hands as he pondered the difficulties that lay before them. She didn't know the half of it. He had to deliver the documents that were hidden in the heel of his boot before many days had passed or his superiors would have his head for sure. And then he must get back to Plymouth to relieve his colleague John, who had remained behind to watch their quarry. It had been difficult enough to get this far. He couldn't fail now. And those swine-hearted vermin who had attacked the coach would be out looking for him once their leader realized they had taken the wrong man. Perhaps they would think he really had been killed. He had to get Jill away. He was feeling stronger today—if only the damn weather would cooperate!

Jillian returned, restored from her embarrassment and determined to act sensibly, after a brisk walk to the sheep hut to look for more eggs. She found Jack freshly washed and shaved. He had found an old razor and some soap pushed to the back of the tall shelf where he had discovered the tea and had been to the stream to collect water so that he could make a lather and shave off his several days' growth of rather heavy, dark beard. Jillian was taken aback at the appearance he presented. Without the stubble he didn't look like a hedgebird after all. And his eyes and face had lost some of their tired, strained look.

Despite the unkempt state of his clothing, she beheld before her a young and darkly good-looking man. Jack turned to see her silhouetted in the doorway. She was aware of his overwhelming masculinity as never before when he regarded her out of those flashing dark eyes with a lopsided smile turning up his very sensual lips. She was suddenly shy before him. Then Jillian did a thing completely foreign to her nature—she lost her tongue.

Jack's eyes were alight with mischief as he said, "I'm glad you've come to your senses, Mrs. St. Erney, although a long walk on the damp moor in just those thin clothes wasn't the wisest thing you could have done this morning. Won't you come in and be seated now. I have a cup of tea all ready for you. You see, I don't expect you to wait on me hand and foot all the time. I even found the two remaining eggs you collected yesterday and have boiled them up for our breakfast. Have you got some more there? Good. We can boil them up, too, and take them with us when we set out. I hope you don't object to boiled eggs?"

She shook her head as she continued to gape at him.

"Won't you be seated, then?" He had stuffed some rags under the uneven leg of the chair and she sat down abruptly.

"What's the matter, Jill. Cat got your tongue? Oh, yes, I remember—I plucked it out for you."

Her complexion went fiery red and she averted her eyes. He handed her the tin plate with the egg on it while holding his own in his hand. "Ouch. This is hot." He blew on it for a minute before peeling it.

"Good Lord, woman. What's the matter now?

You're not still in a miff
you decided not to speak
because I twitted you about
must know that I have quite a
own." God! I want to kiss you,
eyes fell to her tightly compr
swollen from his attentions of the
hazel eyes looked huge in her worried
long hair hung about her shoulde ... not yet
braided this morning. Jack's heart did a flip-flop
in his breast as he regarded his recalcitrant love.
He resorted to words instead of actions to bring her
round.

"Oh, well. If you won't come down from the
boughs, I guess I'll just enjoy the peace and quiet."
Jack ate the peeled egg in two bites.

"We will need to discuss our plan of action for
the day, you know. Or will you be content to
follow the orders I plan to give? It will be *such* a
comfort not to have to argue over everything, don't
you agree?" he said, deliberately inviting her ire.

Jillian's head swung around and she regarded
him fiercely out of narrowed eyes. He was looking
at her with such expectancy that she couldn't help
laughing. "Jack Mackinnon, you are an incorrigible rogue. How am I to put up with you for
another day?"

"Ah, she called me *Jack*. We're making progress.
And I hope you'll agree to put up with me for
many days yet, sweetheart."

"Mackinnon, I hope you plan to tell me exactly
why we have been so careful to avoid being
detected and why we can't just make our way back
to the main road and walk along it where we could
beg a lift when someone happens by with some
sort of conveyance. We could either go on to More-

...ack to Yelverton or to that other ...tioned—Two Bridges, was it? If we ...k, it would be closer to make our way ...o Two Bridges than to go on to Moreton-...ampstead, anyway, would it not?"

When there was no response as he pondered how much to reveal—or conceal—in answering her question, Jillian continued suspiciously, "I trust you really aren't wanted by the law, are you? There's something decidedly smokey about you, Mackinnon."

"It's my hair. I singed it trying to dry it over the hearth while you were out."

"You're impossible!"

"No, no. I just tried to wash my hair and generally tidy myself up a bit. Remember you told me how repulsive I was. I thought I had better clean up a bit."

"You *are* wanted by the law!"

"No, no. It's not that."

"Well, why must you be so secretive, then? Cannot you just tell me what you were doing on that stagecoach?"

Jack hedged his answers, leading her on a merry dance of a cat chasing its own tail with his round-aboutation. He determined not to tell Jill for her own protection that his business was highly dangerous and indeed secretive. Yet it rankled that she should really believe he was engaged in criminal activity. Could she not see the truth of his character, as he did hers? In any event, it was essential to win her cooperation in order to get her safely off the moor without giving her a clue as to his real mission.

"I knew it was too good to hope to get away without coming to cuffs with you, little shrew,"

Jack sighed. They had wasted half an hour circling round one another in futile verbal games, each determined not to let the other get the better of the argument. Finally, with their few belongings packed and the flask refilled with fresh water, they were able to set out across the stony hills of Dartmoor.

The air was cool but not frosty as they set forth. A pleasant fresh scent hung on the slight breeze and tickled Jillian's nose as she walked. They found that their outer garments were adequate protection against the chill as long as it did not come on to rain again. Jillian was glad to see that Mackinnon was able to bend his left arm sufficiently to get it into the sleeve of his greatcoat instead of just letting the garment drape over his shoulder. He assured her that the wound was healing miraculously well—all due to her ministrations, of course—and that the shoulder was only a trifle sore still. She didn't believe the half of it, of course, but could only admire his fortitude.

The rain, and more importantly, the mist held off as they trudged along. Soon Jillian realized that they were walking along a low side track that followed the main road but at a safe distance from the high thoroughfare that wound its way across the very top of the desolate moors.

The sweeping panorama of moorland spread out before her in all its bleak beauty took Jillian's breath away. The wide expanse of uninhabited hills and valleys made her feel that she and the man who trudged beside her were the only two people on earth. The undulations in the mysterious, windswept, almost treeless land, topped in many cases by soaring craggy granite tors on the hilltops, reminded her that long-ago geological forces had swept through this area, leaving permanent scars on the wild, lonely landscape. As she gazed to the valleys that lay between the hills, she could see that their wooded streams offered slightly more hospitable places of habitation for man and beast. The only other evidence of life she could detect were a few sheep grazing on the hillside and a herd of free-roaming, shaggy Dartmoor ponies congregated around one of the high tors, looking as though someone had painted them into the scene.

And then she saw the hawk. Silently riding the swirling currents of air above their heads, the beautiful bird of prey eyed them with disinterest and continued to scan the surrounding hills for a rabbit or other small rodent. Jillian shivered as she watched it, taking it as an omen of danger ahead.

She shook off her pensive mood as Jack pointed out a circle of stones in the distance that marked a Bronze Age settlement. Jillian could not contain her look of surprise as he talked on, informing her that not only had the Saxons, Danes, and Normans had a presence on Dartmoor but that the Roman army of occupation itself had at one time made its presence felt in the area. The thriving cathedral and market town of Exeter, at the mouth of the River Exe just to their northeast, had been a Roman encampment, he explained.

"I wouldn't have taken you for a historian, Mackinnon," Jillian remarked.

"Impressed you, have I, sweetheart? There are a lot of things about me you don't know," he winked at her with his brown eyes full of playful, twinkling lights.

"No, and I don't want to know those particular things either."

"Hmm. Suit yourself then. I thought earlier today you would have liked nothing better than to put me through a grand inquisition."

Jillian scoffed—she knew he was not prepared to tell her anything of import, but would only taunt and tease and go on in a most improper manner to allude to things better left out of polite conversation. She told him roundly that she was too tired for his peculiar form of "conversation."

And she was not just giving him a set-down, she reflected grimly. The pull on the back of her calf muscles had become a constant, nagging pain after an hour or so of hard walking over the stony ground. Outcrops of granite rocks and a crisscross pattern of small gullies in the ground caused her to have to watch her feet and use caution at every step. And the constant rise and fall of the winding hillside path under her feet put an almost unbearable strain on not just the muscles of her legs but on her entire body as well. She had still not recovered from the bumps and bruises of her tumble down the hill the night they had been attacked on the coach, she reflected wearily.

Wispy clouds flew by under a pale blue sky pushed along by a breeze that had picked up considerably in the last half an hour. It was enough to cause Jillian's ears to freeze, then tingle. She felt thoroughly cross and out of sorts.

"Why can't we walk along the road, Mackinnon? The surface seems somewhat more evenly graded up there. It would be easier going, would it not?" Jill asked when her ankles were almost too weary to carry her another step. "And we might meet with someone who could help us find food and shelter."

"'Tis far safer to keep ourselves somewhat

hidden. We can make for cover a little farther down, if needs be. Trust me, Jill, trust me."

"Ha! An impossibility. You know that I do not. Stop trying to fob me off and tell me why we must be so cautious. I'm not a child. I know you're on the run from something."

Jack gave her a sideways glance and admitted, "I fear those villains who attacked the stage the other night will come back and try to find me."

"Aha!" she exclaimed triumphantly. "They *were* after you, then."

"Alas, you are too acute for me."

"Why, why, why? Can you not tell me why?"

"It's too dangerous for you to know. Ignorance is bliss for you, sweeting."

"Ignorance of who you are and what you're running from is not bliss, I assure you."

"Let's talk about what you're running from for a change."

Jillian turned up her nose and tightened her lips. "I'm going to find another situation as a companion."

"What! Companion to some old dragon! Why, you're just a girl. Why would you want to be at the beck and call of some old harridan? If it's a position as companion you want, I know of one that's open," he said suggestively.

"Your insinuation is offensive, Mackinnon, and well you know it," she snapped hotly.

The glint of a smile touched his lips at her retort. "Surely even the St. Erneys take care of their own."

"Ah, but I am not 'one of their own.' I choose to make my own way. 'Twas merely that my last position as governess to two young lad—ah, girls soon to make their come-out was unsuitable to one of my years and temperament."

He had a hard time containing his mirth as he looked at the girl beside him pretending to be so stricken in years. "Couldn't stick it, hey? I don't blame you. Unbiddable were they? Knowing your 'temperament,' my little vixen, I imagine you gave them a taste of your tongue at its most stringent. You're *much* too young to be a governess to two young ladies on the verge of making their comeout, in any case."

"I'll have you know that I'm four and twenty, sirrah."

"Oho, so much? Such a great age for such a little person! Dear me! Here I am at nine and twenty and verily a youth, so you've no call to pull rank on me, you see. You were still in the nursery when I was a great tubby toddler, tearing through the grounds outside when you could only sit in your pram and suck your thumb."

"You're mad, Mackinnon!"

"As the midsummer moon. Come, there's a cure for my madness, you know," he said beguilingly.

"Anything to bring a return of sanity so that you will tell me how you plan to get us to the nearest town without walking for the next three days. . . . What is it?"

"Come kiss me sweet and twenty-four and we'll all the pleasures prove. For why be planning when we can be loving?"

"Ohhh! I might have known you would say something ridiculously improper!"

"Ridiculous? Improper? You call poetry ridiculous and improper? Where is your soul, woman? Where is your passion, my hot-tempered little fury?" Jillian glared at him, disdaining to answer and give him yet more fuel for his quizzing games.

107

Jack laughed and continued his nonsense, "But you know, Jill, you are not such an age that you should be ready to throw over the chance to make your bow in London, to dance and make merry with the other ladies, young *and* old, in the market for a husband. Lord St. Erney would not begrudge you a chance to take your rightful place in society. Surely he's made provision for his son's widow. The St. Erneys do take some pride in their position in the *ton*, in spite of what Reg's behavior may have lead you to believe."

"What foolishness!" she scolded. "I am a widow who was married for four years. I did not find the state of matrimony at all satisfactory, in any case, and would be loath to embark on such a course again, no matter what the financial temptation. I choose to earn my living in my own way, and your unsolicited, not to mention impertinent, opinion has no bearing on the matter."

"What! Can it be that you did not find wedded bliss with Reg? Well, damme, what a surprise! However ill-fated your first venture was, I advise you to try again . . . with someone more practiced in the arts of, ah, lovemaking, shall we say, and more suited to dealing with one of your, ah, eccentric disposition."

Her sherry-colored eyes flashed with temper at his ribbing, and she longed to strike out at him with her hand and wipe that lopsided grin off his face. It irritated her beyond endurance. "My eccentric disposition! What the devil do you mean by that, Mackinnon?"

"Well, I was temporizing. I wouldn't wish to call you headstrong, nor a contentious, quarrelsome, hotheaded nag. No, that would never do. You might strike me, and in my wounded condition I could not be answerable for the consequences."

"You see fit to amuse yourself at my expense, sir. Well, I hope you are vastly entertained, then, for I am too old and tired to spar with you any longer. These games of yours have worn me out, you provoking reprobate."

He wanted to shout with laughter when she put on a prim face and pretended to be some aging spinster—she who looked no older than eighteen with her small stature and girlish features.

"And I advise you to leave off your attempts at matchmaking. You needn't be afraid that I shall demand restitution of *you* after your licentious behavior during this enforced sojourn together. You needn't fear to have your leg caught in Parson's mousetrap, I can assure you. I've had quite enough of your company as it is."

"Are you turning down my proposal, Jill? How unflattering—you haven't even heard it yet."

"To think that you would consider doing the right thing is ridiculous. And besides . . . I wouldn't marry you if you were the last man on earth. I detest you, Mackinnon!"

"What? Do my ears deceive me? You plan to overlook our compromising situation. Hmm. I think I shall demand that you make an honest man of me," Jack said with a diabolical smirk. "I shall never be able to hold my head up again, else."

"You must have windmills in your head if you think we should suit. Why, we'd tear one another limb from limb inside a fortnight!"

"Ah. You think living with me would be too much for you?" he baited.

She rose to it. "No such a thing. I could handle you in a snap." And so saying she snapped her

109

fingers together.

"You think me too frippery a fellow, then?"

"How can I think you anything but a black-hearted scoundrel when you won't tell me who you are or what you're up to?"

"Up to? Why, just trying to make myself agreeable, madam shrew. But I'm having the devil's own work trying to insinuate myself into your good graces so that you'll look upon my suit more favorably, sweetheart." He stopped and struck a pose, bending down on one knee and raising his folded hands in supplication. "Behold your broken-hearted swain, trying to win the favor of his hard-hearted lady."

Jillian was hard put not to laugh at his nonsense. She bit down hard on her lip and turned her head away, swinging her hair over her shoulder as she did so, hitting Jack in the chest with her long braid as he rose to his feet.

God! How he longed to run his fingers through her long, honey-colored tresses, Jack thought as he smiled at his successful attempts to make her laugh and distract her from their tiring walk. He wished she had not bound her hair up so tightly in that infernal braid today. On second thoughts, perhaps it was better so. He had been distracted long enough.

They stopped to rest on a hillside where Jack could watch the road but near enough to a grove of trees to take cover if need be. Jack lay back on the stony ground and shaded his eyes against the bright sky while he focused his attention on the horizon. Jillian sat on a large flat boulder encrusted with spongy moss and watched as the swallows twittered and swooped low over the ground while the skylarks flew seemingly straight up into the air briefly before settling again on the upper branches of the plentiful prickly gorse and yellow-flowered broom. The sweet, liquid notes of the larks' distinctive song lulled her into humming along with them as she reached down to pick some of the white heather springing up beneath her feet. She had been surprised to find the rare plant on the moor, growing here and there among its more common purple and lilac cousins. She reached over and put a sprig in a buttonhole of Jack's greatcoat. "White heather for luck," she smiled at him, and he turned toward her and smiled his heart-stopping smile. Her heart lurched in her breast as she gazed at her handsome tormentor; she dropped her eyes and tried to catch her breath.

"You think we need it then?" His low-timbred voice affected her strongly.

"Oh, assuredly, sir, if we're to reach civilization without further mishap." Jillian turned aside to hide her blush and hoped that the sudden strange feeling in the pit of her stomach was caused by hunger. "We've had enough *bad* luck in the last three days to last a lifetime."

"What! You would call meeting each other bad luck? I would rather call it the best turn fortune has ever done me."

Jillian swallowed against a suddenly constricted throat and would not look at him. Trouble was, she thought grumpily, he had the disconcerting trick of sounding sincere even when she knew he was only amusing himself, playing this wicked game of flirtation with her. She was at a loss as to how to protect herself against his dangerous charm.

A fine mist descended on them while they sat silent, each afraid of breaking into the other's thoughts. They looked up to see that the sky seemed to be clouding over again. Both were wishing for more substantial fare and, more urgently, warm shelter as they quickly demolished the last of the eggs and rose to be on their way.

"Ahrrr. Goo' day to 'ee. 'Oo be 'ee then?" They turned, startled, at the sound of the thick Devon country accent to see a white-haired, wizened old man leaning on a shepherd's crook staring at them curiously out of bright, birdlike eyes.

Jillian spoke first. "Good day to you, sir. Can you tell us where we may seek food and accommodation hereabouts? We have been stranded here—" Jack interrupted before she could get further and reveal the true state of affairs.

"Old grandfather, we were set upon and robbed two days ago. Our stagecoach was attacked by a band of four or five ruffians and the coach and all our goods were taken. I was shot in the shoulder, and my wife and I were left for dead on the moor." A furious look from Jillian as Jack pronounced them man and wife almost overset him as he glanced toward her then back at the shepherd.

"Do you know of a gang of highwaymen hereabouts who set upon unwary travelers? We were certainly not warned when we left Plymouth that there were robbers and cutthroats abroad on the moor."

The bent-over creature held a hand to his ear as

Jack spoke. He appeared not to have heard much of what was said but evidently the gist of the matter penetrated his deafness. "Robbed, wus 'ee."

Jack nodded and shouted, "Can you tell us where we may find shelter nearby for a night?"

"Ain't got me gray mare to lend 'ee, today," the old man cackled. "Widder Manaton, over to Widecombe way will take 'ee in. Tell 'er ol' Uncle Tom Cobbley sent 'ee."

After some confusion—the old man's accent was nearly impossible to decipher—Jack was able to ascertain the way to the good widow's cottage. It appeared to be about half a mile away to the east and perhaps slightly south of where they were. It would mean a longer walk to Moretonhampstead on the morrow if Jack stuck to his plan to get there on foot. He thought perhaps he would try to hitch them a ride on a wagon or some other farm vehicle on its way to market, if the opportunity presented itself. Surely someone trustworthy would be going their way, he thought optimistically. Jillian had clearly had enough, and he felt near to collapse himself. Three days on the moor without sufficient food and barely adequate shelter together with the bullet he had taken in his shoulder had put a pretty sizeable dent in his heretofore iron constitution. There had been no sign in the past three days of further pursuit by the highwaymen. Perhaps they had not realized their mistake in not taking him, after all, and all his extra caution had been for nought.

The old grandfather seemed impervious to the elements as he took himself back to his flock. Jack and Jillian started off down the hill in the opposite direction.

"Looks like the end of our idyll, sweetheart,"

Jack remarked.

"Your thoughts have certainly been idle, Mackinnon. Though your scurrilous tongue hasn't. How dare you tell that old shepherd we were married, you blackguard!" Jillian stopped, hands on hips, all too ready to berate him again.

He put his arm up protectively over his face to ward off her furious assault. "Was I to let him think we had been stranded alone with no chaperon for you? I thought you would be pleased by my quick thinking."

"Quick thinking, indeed. You just want to further compromise me!"

"No, no, sweetheart. I'm afraid the teasing gods of mischance have accomplished that task already. It's their way of amusing themselves, playing with the lives of humans, you know. After all, they have not much to do up there on Olympus but sit around eating nectar and drinking mead."

"Don't you dare laugh! You always think to amuse yourself at my predicament." Jillian clenched her small fists impotently against her side. "Ohh! How could I have been so unfortunate as to have been on that accursed coach? Why, in the name of all justice, did I chance to end up with *you!*"

"Just good luck on your part, sweetheart. Unless you put it down to incredible foresight and uncommonly good judgment."

Chapter 8

It was just starting to spit with rain, and the mist was becoming heavier as Jack and Jillian wearily trudged down a winding path that led to the picturesque little hamlet of Widecombe-in-the-Moor, set like a rough-cut jewel in a lush, green valley. Jack spotted a plume of smoke just before they rounded a bend in the road. "Ah, human habitation at last!" he exclaimed happily, increasing his pace as his feet squelched over the soggy path, tugging Jillian by the hand behind him.

They found the farmhouse the old man had described just on the outskirts of the small village as they descended rather steeply through a fold in the high granite ridges surrounding the valley. The sight of the pretty little hamlet with its tall granite church tower and its promise of warmth, decent food, and shelter was all that Jillian had been longing for. She was more thankful than she could say to be walking downhill and back into the comforts of civilization she was sure were to be found in the tiny place. Jack smiled as he noted her sigh of relief and began to sing the old folk song about Widecombe Fair as he strolled up the primrose-lined path to the door of the little cottage that fit the shepherd's description.

Tom Pearse, Tom Pearse, lend me your gray mare
  All along, down along, out along, lee.
For I want for to go to Widdicombe Fair . . .

A small woman in a large white mobcap peeped round her door in answer to Mackinnon's insistent knock. "Mrs. Manaton?" Jack questioned easily with a smile pasted across his handsome rogue's face that would have charmed the birds from the trees, Jillian thought disgustedly.

"Aye, 'at be me, young'un." The widow was a jolly, plump little soul with a round red face and an accent as thick as Devon cream. "My stars, ye'er a handsum one, ain't ye." Her merry eyes danced and she shook like a jelly as she laughed up into Jack's face.

"Mac . . . Cade. My name is Jack MacCade." He hesitated over giving his correct name, Jillian saw. Instantly her suspicions of him soared astronomically. "My wife and I," Jack glanced at Jill as he identified her and saw that she was resigned to this mode of introduction, "were robbed and stranded on the moor. I was shot in the shoulder when a band of rascally highwaymen attacked our coach, demanded that we get down and hand over all valuables. Our coachman was forced to drive away at gunpoint. The coach, the horses, and all our luggage and money were taken. We've already spent one night in a small shelter we were fortunate enough to find on the moor. Then this morning we came across the old grandfather, er, old Uncle Tom Cobbley I believe he said his name was, that sees to the flock on the Moretonhampstead road, and he suggested we could find shelter with you until I can arrange for transportation into the town. I'm afraid that I can pay very little as those blasted cutthroats took just about everything, even my wife's wedding ring." Jack improvised quickly and smoothly with an aplomb that Jillian concluded came from long practice in the art of deception.

"Ol' Uncle Tom, were it? Oh, ye purr laddie and lassie. Come ye in, come ye in. Ye both be soaked through. Get ye to the furr." And she fussed over them and saw that they were settled in front of a comfortable fire in her little front parlor while she bustled about taking away their muddy outer garments and promising to bring them hot tea and crusts of bread and butter straight away.

Jack smirked over at Jill in what she considered to be a smugly self-satisfied manner. "Well, aren't you going to congratulate me? I think we've landed in heaven—and Mrs. M. is just such a red-cheeked cherub to insure our happiness in this paradise." Jillian turned her shoulder to him, refusing to give him the satisfaction of congratulating him for his quick-witted, resourceful cleverness.

"Anywhere I land with *you* is sure to be quite the opposite."

"Jill, Jill. We've got shelter, warmth," he gestured to the fire, "and the promise of as much food as we can eat. What more could you want?"

Making a great effort, she managed to keep from voicing a hot retort about wishing to be free from his vexatious company. Being obliged to witness his cozening ways with the widow had ruffled her uneven temper, but in truth she was extremely glad of their abode. She sank into the cozy chair

117

before the much-welcomed fire, sighing thank-fully. "Humph," she thought to herself, "the gammon-pitching creature thinks it's all due to his fascinating charm that we have landed in such a snug place." And she had the lowering feeling that it was.

"I see you are doing an admirable job of keeping your temper firmly in check even though you are longing to come to cuffs with me, sweetheart." Jack dared to wink at her as he settled his long frame on the floor near her chair and lay at his ease on two cushions Mrs. Manaton had thoughtfully provided before busily scurrying out again to prepare the tea. The irrepressible wretch was laughing at her as usual.

She could not resist the temptation to chide her shameless companion for being such an accomplished liar. "Does having such monstrous tales at the tip of your tongue always make you so cocksure of your welcome wherever you go, Mackinnon?"

"Now, now, Jill. Mind your manners, wife. What would the good widow think to hear you saying such things of your beloved spouse? Tsk."

"I shall not allow you to goad me, you coxcomb. 'Twould be a waste of my limited energy to take you to task for your preposterous sham and outrageous faradiddles. I think it shameful to try to pull the wool over poor Mrs. Manaton's eyes in such a way." She stretched out her weary legs to warm them before the grate and thought that the only thing that could have been more agreeable at that particular moment was to have been spared the company of her tormentor.

Mrs. Manaton bustled in to serve her unlooked for, but fascinating, guests a more substantial tea than she had promised, bringing sandwiches, cheese, cake, and fruit along with a large pot of the steaming hot brew. She served them as they rested and warmed themselves before the cozy fire in her tiny parlor. She was positively bursting with curiosity about the two young people who seemed to be from another world and who, to her sentimental eyes, seemed so very much in love.

"'Ere ye be, surr." She handed Jack a large tankard of ale.

"Ah, home-brewed! A drink fit for a king. How can I thank you, my dear Mrs. Manaton? I've been dying for a drink this age," Jack exclaimed as the lady handed him the liquid potation. "Behold in me your devoted slave, madam." He bowed his head exaggeratedly and toasted the good housewife with his tankard, stopping just short of blowing the blushing woman a kiss.

The widow laughed with delight, obviously charmed by his nonsense. "Git along wit ye, Mr. MacCade. As if Emma Manaton didn't ken what a fine figure of a laddie like ye would be athirstin' for," she said as she poured a cup of the strong, hot tea for Jillian.

Jillian could only shake her head at Jack's blandishments—telling the woman he would forever be her devoted slave, indeed! Her incorrigible companion certainly knew how to pour on the sauce when he wanted to turn someone up sweet, as she knew to her cost.

Mrs. Manaton seemed delighted to have two people to fuss over and mother . . . and such an interesting pair as they were, too. She had never seen a more handsome gentleman, and his quiet little wife was a bit of an odd little soul—pretty, though. Clearly quality, they were, she could see

119

in a twinkling.

As soon as the hospitable housewife had judged that her tired guests had satisfied their appetites somewhat, she called Jillian out of the room and took her up the narrow staircase that divided the parlor from the kitchen to a little room under the eaves. There she smilingly held out a round gown of faded blue poplin to Jillian. "H'it was m'-daughter's dress afore she was married," Mrs. Manaton said. "H'it may be small enough to fit ye, me dear, and it's pleased I'd be if it was of any use to ye, Mrs. MacCade."

Said daughter must have been about ten years old when she grew out of the schoolgirl's dress, Jillian thought despairingly as she tried to pull the tight garment down over her hips. It fell considerably short of her ankles, but it was clean and dry and in a good state of repair in contrast to her dirty, tattered dress. Jillian thanked the good lady for her kind offices and was glad to shed her disreputable garments, letting Mrs. Manaton take them away for laundering.

When Mrs. Manaton left, Jillian took off her clothing and washed as best she might with the warm water left behind in a large white porcelain ewer decorated with pink roses. Her thoughtful hostess had even left a fresh bar of sweet-smelling soap, she noticed thankfully as she picked it up and dipped it in the water to form a good lather. When she had dried off and redonned the small but perfectly clean dress, and combed out and repinned her hair, she was ready to descend downstairs again, feeling somewhat refreshed.

She found that the competent matron had also found a shirt of her deceased husband's for Jack to wear. The late Mr. Manaton must have been a large man, indeed, for the shirt was yards too big for Mackinnon despite his own not insubstantial height and chest width. Jillian had to bite back a laugh when she saw her supposed spouse. Mrs. Manaton was fussing about him as though he were a little boy. She couldn't seem to keep her eyes or hands off such a fine specimen of manhood. She patted him several times on the shoulder, sometimes choosing the left, causing Mackinnon to wince. But he gritted his teeth and gallantly made no complaint.

Having provided all that she could in terms of refreshment, fresh, clean clothes, and a warm place for them to rest themselves, the energetic widow busied herself in the small kitchen preparing a huge meal of everything her larder had to offer.

"Just off for a wash, sweetheart," Jack informed Jill when she returned to the parlor. "Do you wish to lend me your assistance?" he arched a brow at her.

"You can no longer hope to be successful with that gambit, you know. I'm on to your games now," she scoffed, but then added, "I shall rebind your shoulder for you, Mackinnon, if you wish, *after* you have completed your ablutions."

"Kind of you to offer, sweetheart, but I will manage on my own this time. Why don't you rest?" He quirked a brow at her. "By the bye, did I mention that you look ravishing in that, ah, dress. Yes, indeed. Quite, quite ravishing." He exited on this parting shot.

Jillian disregarded his taunt even as she took his advice about resting. The heat of the room together with the comfortable chair she was seated in soon enabled her to doze off quite happily. She must have snoozed for quite some time, for when she awoke with a start it was to find Mackinnon bending over her chair shaking her gently by the shoulder. "Time to wake up, sleepyhead. You have slept the day away and, though I am loath to disturb your rest, I think you should see what awaits us in the kitchen." Jillian could see his dancing brown eyes were alight with eager anticipation.

"Mrs. Manaton has prepared a kingly feast just for us, sweeting. I hope you're not too fagged to eat. I swear, my belly has been howling for the past hour or more, despite our lavish tea when we arrived. I will gladly eat your portion, too, if you can't manage to drag yourself from your comfy chair to the table." He quirked an eyebrow at her.

"Don't you dare eat any of my portion, Mackinnon. I'm so hungry I could eat a whole roast pig." Jillian was on her feet without more ado.

"You'll have to settle for roast capon, smoked ham, and lamb stew, I'm afraid." He smiled widely at her look of amazement.

When she got to the table, Jillian saw that for once Mackinnon hadn't exaggerated. In addition to the meat dishes, there were roast potatoes, a variety of braised greens, caramelized carrots, a huge white loaf, and a slab of butter that would have lasted her a week at home. The table was set with a beautiful white damask cloth and a hodgepodge of china dishes that lent an air of gaiety to the small, ill-lit room. Mrs. Manaton had only a brace of pewter candlesticks to provide illumination.

Jillian turned to her left to see that there was a varied assortment of preserved fruits and sweets, as well, set out on an elaborately carved oaken sideboard, including a rhubarb and apple pie that had her mouth watering already. A large pitcher of thick yellow cream was set next to the pie. Jillian surmised that Mrs. Manaton must have raided her neighbors' larders as well as her own to assemble such a feast in such short order. She frowned as she considered that she and Mackinnon would be the talk of the village. She could only hope that no one there had connections in London where they might spread the gossip.

Mrs. Manaton also had produced an old bottle of claret that immediately caught Jack's interest. He was able to congratulate his hostess on its quality, and she blushingly admitted that her husband had had a case of it in payment for a bit of carving he had done for "a great lord down to Dartmouth way." Her dear departed had been a woodcarver of note in the district, she related proudly, in addition to owning a herd of sheep that grazed on the moor.

All three made a hearty meal of it indeed. Jack, talking as fast as he ate, spun a wildly implausible tale about how he and Jill came to be traveling across the moor in the first place for the gullible Mrs. Manaton, who was all solicitous attention. He couldn't have wanted a more attentive and admiring audience, Jillian snorted to herself. The scamp used his cajolery to wheedle himself into the widow's good graces with the mere flick of an eyelid in her direction. The broadly smiling old woman hung on his every word and was ready to refill his plate as fast as he emptied it as well as to ply him with a second bottle of the precious claret!

Quite thoroughly sated, Jillian was so tired by the end of the meal that she could no longer keep her eyes open. Mrs. Manaton recommended that she rest herself in the parlor while she lit a fire in the spare bedchamber.

"I shall just help Mrs. Manaton finish this most excellent bottle of claret," Jack said with his most conning smile. The widow blushed and declined his request that she join him, but Mackinnon was insistent.

Jillian, weary of watching Mackinnon play off his tricks on the unsuspecting woman, took herself to the parlor and was soon asleep in the one comfortable chair the room afforded. She woke sometime later in a room lit only by firelight. She heard no sound of activity in the house and moved to open the parlor door. She picked up the small candlestick left for her near the stairs and made her way up the narrow passageway. She opened the door to the spare bedchamber only to find Jack up to his neck in soapy lather in an old-fashioned tin hip bath.

"Ah, there you are at last, sweetheart. Come in, my dear," he said, anticipation lighting his dark eyes.

"I might have known such a rapscallion as you would—" Jillian began but was stopped when Mrs. Manaton bustled up behind her and handed her a large towel and two extra blankets for the bed.

"'Ere ye be, me dearie. Was ye asleep in yon parlor? Yer good 'usband's 'ad a 'ot wash."

"So I see," Jillian said scathingly as she walked into the room and set the towel and blankets on the bed. Mrs. Manaton asked if Jillian wished to bathe as well and upon being assured that she had washed adequately with the hot water so kindly provided earlier in the evening, the ever-helpful housewife handed her a large man's nightshirt that she explained had belonged to her dearly departed spouse. "It will fit Mr. MacCade to a turn, see if it don't."

The tireless matron pointed out the ornately carved fourposter bed that took up three-quarters of the room and assured them that the mattress was a proper good 'un and that the bedframe was sturdy enough to bear any amount of weight. Here her eyes shifted appreciatively to Jack's broad shoulders visible above the suds. He winked back at her, in what Jillian could only call bold as brass fashion, from his watery station.

Mr. Manaton had built the bed out of strong oak, the widow went on to tell them, and spent many hours carving a detailed headboard just to please their only daughter. She herself, Mrs. Manaton added proudly, was responsible for the tatted lace hangings that covered the bright pink quilted spread. Jillian was dutifully, if somewhat weakly, admiring of the couple's handiwork.

With that the friendly woman pulled the door to and bid them a good night, a sunbeam of a smile lighting up her little round face as she added that she would empty the hip bath on the morrow.

"Mrs. Manaton has seen to your every need, it seems," Jillian said tartly. Jack grinned up at her devilishly from the tub.

"Oh, not to my *every* need, sweetheart," he said wickedly. "Just hand me that towel and night-shirt and I shall get out of here."

Jillian, knowing the abominable man was past redemption, hunched her shoulders resignedly and did as she was requested. Her sensibilities had been battered down to such an extent in the last three days that she was inured to his shameless way of carrying on. She couldn't help darting her eyes to his wound to see that it looked red and raw but not infected. Not lost to all modesty, she then turned her back on him. "I shall just take two of these blankets and sleep in the parlor, Mackinnon."

"Now, now, my dear. You don't wish to offend Mrs. Manaton after all her indefatigable hospitality, do you? She would think there was something decidedly smoky going on if she were to find you in the parlor." She hesitated with her hand on the doorknob at his words and tried to close her ears to the sounds he made sloshing around in the bath.

"There *is* something decidedly smoky going on, Mackinnon."

"Come now, sweeting, it will not be a novel experience sharing a bed with me, after all. You should be used to it by now. . . . I know that *I* could not get to sleep without my cozy little bed partner. Mrs. Manaton will have let the fire die down in the parlor, you know," he reminded her as further enticement to stay with him. "It will be *much* warmer in here." There were sounds of Jack getting out of the bath. Jillian made a low-voiced protest under her breath as she stood rigid, her back still turned away from him.

"Piqued at me again?" Jack asked playfully as he wound a large towel around himself.

"I most certainly did not," Jillian answered indignantly, setting her hands on her hips.

Jack let out a roar of laughter. "Oh, sweetheart! Never was a man more misunderstood," he said when he could speak again, wiping tears of laughter from his eyes. "No, no. Don't be in a taking. I enjoy being peeked at by you," he chuckled again. "You may turn around now, Miss Prim and

126

Proper. Your counterfeit husband is properly attired in his nightshirt—and how wonderful it feels to be clean again. You need have no worries that I will not sleep like a top, either, after that enormous meal we've just consumed. No internal rumblings to disturb our slumber.''

Afraid that he would override her scruples, yet wanting to be convinced, Jillian turned to see him standing in a long white nightshirt that almost reached his ankles, his aspect almost cherubic. Jack yawned and stretched. "I feel quite relaxed— almost human for the first time in days.''

"And so you should feel *relaxed*—you consumed almost two bottles of claret. It would be a miracle if you aren't quite foxed.''

"No, no. Mrs. Manaton put back her fair share with ease—didn't you notice?'' he laughed at her with just that warm look in his eye and smile turning up one corner of his mouth that Jillian found impossible to resist.

"How is your shoulder? Would you like me to dress it?'' she asked, then blushed as she realized that it would be an embarrassing undertaking with him in his nightshirt.

"Healing nicely, thank you. And if we're to talk of dressing, I think it's time for you to don this magnificent nightrail our good lady has left for you,'' Jack pointed to an ancient satin and lace confection lying on the bed that might have been the poor woman's wedding garment, "and join me here.'' He patted the bed. "Ah, I must've died and gone to heaven!'' Jack exclaimed as he climbed into the big bed with its deep, soft feather mattress and snuggled down under the covers even as Jillian watched.

"I think you mistake your place of abode,

Mackinnon. They wouldn't let you in there," Jillian roasted him with a smile of her own.

He bit back a laugh. "You had better don this incredible night garment, my dear, else my eyes will close and I'll be left with the sight of you in that dress."

"And what is amiss with this dress, pray?"

"Oh, there's nothing *wrong* with it, love. It's bursting at the seams is all. I put it down to you having eaten virtually a whole sheep at dinner. Don't think that I *object*, however, for it's made your sweet, er, curves more tempting than ever."

"Why will you insist on saying that I tempt you? I know 'tis only because there are no other women around."

"No, no—there's Mrs. Manaton. I wonder you could forget. Dear me! What a shocking memory you have, my dear."

"You wouldn't have to use much of your cajolery to talk her into sharing a bed with you—she couldn't take her eyes off you at dinner. I feared she would gobble you up."

"Oho! The green-eyed monster rears its ugly head. Jealous, sweetheart?"

Jillian disdained to answer him but took a pillow and all but one blanket from the bed and piled them into a heap on the hard floor in the small space left by the hip tub and the enormous bed itself.

"If you aren't gentleman enough to sleep on the floor, then I suppose I will have to do so." She took off her shoes and lay down as Jack sank into the deep, fluffy mattress and uttered several sighs of contentment. "Suit yourself. I'm too worn out to come to blows with you tonight, delightful as our

128

MORE PASSION AND ADVENTURE AWAIT... YOUR TRIP TO A BIG ADVENTUROUS WORLD BEGINS WHEN YOU ACCEPT YOUR FIRST 4 NOVELS ABSOLUTELY *FREE* (AN $18.00 VALUE)

Accept your Free gift and start to experience more of the passion and adventure you like in a historical romance novel. Each Zebra novel is filled with proud men, spirited women and tempestuous love that you'll remember long after you turn the last page.

Zebra Historical Romances are the finest novels of their kind. They are written by authors who really know how to weave tales of romance and adventure in the historical settings you love. You'll feel like you've actually gone back in time with the thrilling stories that each Zebra novel offers.

GET YOUR FREE GIFT WITH THE START OF YOUR HOME SUBSCRIPTION

Our readers tell us that these books sell out very fast in book stores and often they miss the newest titles. So Zebra has made arrangements for you to receive the four newest novels published each month.

You'll be guaranteed that you'll never miss a title, and home delivery is so convenient. And to show you just how easy it is to get Zebra Historical Romances, we'll send you your first 4 books absolutely FREE! Our gift to you just for trying our home subscription service.

BIG SAVINGS AND FREE HOME DELIVERY

Each month, you'll receive the four newest titles as soon as they are published. You'll probably receive them even before the bookstores do. What's more, you may preview these exciting novels free for 10 days. If you like them as much as we think you will, just pay the low preferred subscriber's price of just $3.75 each. *You'll save $3.00 each month off the publisher's price.* AND, your savings are even greater because there are never any shipping, handling or other hidden charges—FREE Home Delivery. Of course you can return any shipment within 10 days for full credit, no questions asked. There is no minimum number of books you must buy.

4 FREE BOOKS

TO GET YOUR 4 FREE BOOKS WORTH $18.00 — MAIL IN THE FREE BOOK CERTIFICATE T O D A Y

Fill in the Free Book Certificate below, and we'll send your FREE BOOKS to you as soon as we receive it.

If the certificate is missing below, write to: Zebra Home Subscription Service, Inc., P.O. Box 5214, 120 Brighton Road, Clifton, New Jersey 07015-5214.

FREE BOOK CERTIFICATE

4 FREE BOOKS

ZEBRA HOME SUBSCRIPTION SERVICE, INC.

YES! Please start my subscription to Zebra Historical Romances and send me my first 4 books absolutely FREE. I understand that each month I may preview four new Zebra Historical Romances free for 10 days. If I'm not satisfied with them, I may return the four books within 10 days and owe nothing. Otherwise, I will pay the low preferred subscriber's price of just $3.75 each; a total of $15.00, a savings off the publisher's price of $3.00. I may return any shipment and I may cancel this subscription at any time. There is no obligation to buy any shipment and there are no shipping, handling or other hidden charges. Regardless of what I decide, the four free books are mine to keep.

NAME

ADDRESS _____ APT _____

CITY _____ STATE ____ ZIP ____
(   )
TELEPHONE

SIGNATURE _____ (if under 18, parent or guardian must sign)

Terms, offer and prices subject to change without notice. Subscription subject to acceptance by Zebra Books. Zebra Books reserves the right to reject any order or cancel any subscription.

rows always are. . . ." After several minutes he murmured sleepily, "Sure you won't join me? No? Well, good night, Mrs. St. Erney. The floorboards are not the bedfellows I would choose. I hope you enjoy them and get some rest. We have a long walk before us tomorrow—if you're sure you'll be up to it," he added challengingly.

Jillian pretended to sleep. Her toes touched the metal edge of the now freezing cold tin hip bath and her head was almost smack up against the wall at the side of the room while her back was wedged against the footboard of the bed. She dared not move, although she was wretchedly uncomfortable and longed to toss and turn until she found an easier position. She couldn't bear the thought of giving Mackinnon the satisfaction of being right—again.

She waited until she heard his deep, even breathing, making sure he was asleep, before she attempted to lie more restfully. Then she tried shifting her position first one way, then another. As soon as she tried to lie on her side, her shoulder would ache. If she lay straight, she felt the floor through the thin blanket along all points of her body. Curling up was no better.

The fire in the small hearth had quickly turned to embers and soon she was icy cold as well as mortally uncomfortable. Jillian acknowledged defeat and tiptoed to the bed, dragging her make-shift bedding with her. As carefully as she could, she arranged the extra blankets over the bed and slipped under the covering. To her dismay the mattress gave a mighty squeak and sagged in the middle—so much for their hostess's boast. She found herself rolled up against the warm body of her nemesis. But miraculously he did no more than give a rather loud snore. She decided that he was so tired it would take an earthquake to wake him.

Jillian sighed and settled to sleep. Jack grinned a satisfied grin into the darkness.

Chapter 9

"It's amazing how the time passes—not to mention the miles—when one is enjoying an agreeable discussion with a wizened person of advanced years, is it not?" Jack couldn't resist twitting Jillian as they walked along a sunlit road not far from the outskirts of Moretonhampstead.

Mrs. Manaton had seen them off with much motherly fuss and good cheer, mixed with apologies for their mode of transportation, as she saw them mounted onto the back of a hay wain. Jack had bestowed a parting kiss on the cheek of the kind dame and called her his 'Lady Bountiful,' causing the old woman to blush fiercely and pat him on the wrong shoulder saying, "Go on with ye, then. Yer lad's full o' nonsense, missus." She winked at Jillian.

The widow had arranged for them to be given a lift in the cumbrous farm vehicle for most of the way to the busy market town of Moretonhampstead. The shy, tongue-tied young lad who was their driver had let them off on the main route to the town just before he turned off a side track that would take him and his cargo to the little village of

131

North Bovey.

His two passengers, enjoying the feel of their freshly laundered clothes, had lain back against the sweet-smelling hay, drowsing for most of the way. Mackinnon hummed in an off-key way under his breath. There was too much noise as the wheels rumbled along the ancient track for either of them to attempt conversation.

Jillian was almost glad to abandon the wagon, despite the long walk still in front of them. Her teeth had rattled in her head at every bump and rut in the track, and as Mackinnon helped her down from the wagon, she was momentarily giddy from the cessation of the rocking motion she had experienced for the last two hours and more and had rested against his broad chest for a few moments. She quickly regained her senses and moved away from the comforting arms that had held her steady and strode out along the path.

The afternoon was pleasant as they walked, although Jack was feeling decidedly peckish almost as soon as they alit from the wagon. He denied himself the luxury of pausing to eat immediately as he wanted to cover a bit more distance before they stopped to rest and consume the enormous picnic Mrs. Manaton had prepared for them. She had sent them on their way with her hugs crushing their bodies and her good wishes and hopes for a safe journey ringing in their ears along with a prediction for Jill: "This time next spring, ye're sure to 'ave a wee 'un in yer arms, me dearie. Yer man's strong enow to give ye many a babe." Jillian had flushed brightly under the delighted smile of the old woman.

Now as they made their way over a rough bit of ground, they could see the wild granite tors outlined against the clear blue sky. There was a faint breeze but not a sign of the rain clouds that had bedeviled them for the last three days. The distinctive cry of the skylarks could be heard as they wheeled and turned overhead. Jack dared to link his fingers through Jillian's as he helped her over a pile of stones in their path and didn't release her hand when she was safely over the uneven turf. The sweet scent of wild roses in bloom was heavy in the air. He breathed deeply of the crisp moorland air and wished they had time for dalliance.

Jack hoped the weather wold hold until they reached Moretonhampstead. He planned to settle Jill into a respectable inn while he made contact with his superiors. Then he would escort her to London if he could. If not, he would see that she reached the city safely and in some comfort. In addition to alerting his superiors that he had the code they desperately wanted, he needed to contact them about an equally pressing personal matter—the need was urgent. They must forward him some of the ready immediately. He was distinctly light in the pocket, and he doubted that Jill had much more than two coins to rub together in her reticule. He would just have to adopt his lord-of-the-manor aspect with any landlord who doubted his word and refused to extend credit. His lips curved upward as he thought how such a performance from himself would astound Jill. She had yet to see him come the great man.

As they trudged along, Jack felt a telltale prickling along the hairs at the back of his neck. He looked around uneasily several times until his nervousness transmitted itself to his companion. Jillian finally asked, "What's the matter now? You're as edgy as a cat on hot tiles."

"Oh, I'm looking for a likely spot to rest for a bit. Let us head off the road and commune with nature for some little while."

"We've been *communing* with nature for the last four days, Mackinnon. I want to *commune* with civilization for a change—as soon as may be."

"Would you not welcome the opportunity to put your feet up for a few minutes and help me make some inroads into this delightful picnic luncheon our Lady Bountiful has prepared for us?" He tried to calm Jillian's suspicions. Unless it became absolutely necessary, he would not alert her to the danger that might await them.

"What a whisker! Do you think to hoax me so easily, sir. You've spotted something—or some-*one*—haven't you?" When he didn't answer immediately, she began to scold. "Come, Mackinnon, I have a right to know. I'm not a child."

"No, you're certainly not," he said with an appreciative wink.

"Well, then, what is the matter? Why are you suddenly so tense and watchful?"

"I'm not quite sure," he answered seriously, "but I would like to get out of this open ground for a bit. I may be wrong, but I have a feeling we are being followed. Let's head for those trees over there." He pointed to a stand of copper beech trees that would take them farther from the road. He grabbed Jillian's hand again, not gently this time but in a hard clasp. He hurried them along until they were almost running. As they approached the beeches they could see a sort of structure through a clearing, surrounded by a hedge of yew. Jack threw the picnic basket into the hedge as he passed it. As they came closer they could see that the building resembled a chapel. The small chapel appeared to be placed in the center of a small graveyard. Jack looked around as they came up to the chapel and noticed a newly dug grave near the edge of the clearing. He guided Jillian to the pit.

"You jump into that ditch while I gather up some leaves and loose dirt."

"Now I know you've taken leave of your senses! That's not a *ditch*, Mackinnon, it's a grave!"

He paid no heed to her railing as he quickly gathered up a large armful of leaves and threw them into the depression. He hurriedly repeated the action three times, then jumped down into the pungent, freshly dug earth. "Come on down, sweetheart. Now!"

"You're mad!"

"While you stand there, you're quite visible to anyone who may have been following us. You may wish to chance it, but I do not." So saying he reached a hand up and grabbed her ankle and toppled her over on top of himself into the cavity. Leaves cushioned their fall. She began to screech at him again so that he clapped a hand over her mouth whispering, "Shhh. Listen." Her eyes widened behind his hand as she heard a man's voice shouting, "They 'uns went o'er ta 'ere, Sam."

Jack released her and pushed her as far down into the foliage as he could, then burrowed down after her, trying to cover them both with the debris he had thrown in. They heard footsteps crashing through the undergrowth and voices calling to one another coming nearer.

Jack's hard, muscular body was covering Jill's and the damp, moldy leaves were sticking to her

135

face making it difficult to breath, but for once she didn't mind his high-handed ways that put her into such close contact with his large masculine frame. She was very frightened, and his weight and warmth provided some measure of comfort to her shaking body and jangling nerves. The now very familiar scent of him was like balm to her disordered senses. Indeed, she thought it was the only thing that kept her from fainting dead away.

The voices of the men seemed even closer as they called to one another. "Where't the hell they git to, Dan'l," yelled one of them. The harsh, grating voice sounded sickeningly familiar to Jillian's perceptive ears.

"Maybe in this 'ere church, Sam," shouted the other.

To judge by the sounds they were making, the men seemed to be conducting a thorough search of the little chapel. Though Jillian longed to speak, she was afraid to even whisper into Jack's ear, even though it was only inches from her lips. He seemed to be breathing calmly and evenly. She could not know that his every strained nerve, every heightened sense, was highly attuned to a possible attack.

His shoulder was still weak, but Jack thought he could manage to land a blow or two with his right fist. He thought there were only two men, but he couldn't be certain. For once he was hardly aware of the curvaceous little body beneath his own pressed tightly to him at every point.

The footsteps came to the edge of their hiding place. "''Ere. A grave. Some pur blighter's cocked up 'is toes, then, and gone to the devil.'' Jillian clamped her chattering teeth together and held her breath.

"Let's get out of 'ere, Sam. Don't like grave-yards. There be ghosties aboot, me granny says."

"Ee, man, don't ye be afeared. This 'ere lead in me pistol'll blow a 'ole a yard wide in any o' yer damn ghosties."

"Me fingers is itchin'. Somethin's acrawlin' up the back o' me neck. Don't like it 'ere, Sam."

"Where'd they vanish to, then, Dan'l?"

"Over that way, I reckon. Down by that stream there. Don't know as 'ow's it 'us the right cove this time, anyways."

"Ye go on down this 'ere path, Dan'l. I'll creep round the back 'o this 'ere church. And keep yer damn peepers peeled fer that big cove, not fer yer damn ghosties!"

The men seemed to be moving away. Jack let out a breath he didn't realize he was holding and relaxed his tense muscles. Suddenly he was aware of Jill trembling beneath him.

"It's alright. They've gone for now, love. . . . I'm afraid we must remain here a little while longer in case they should double back," Jack whispered against her cheek as relief flowed through him.

Jillian reached up and put her arms about his neck and sighed into his shoulder, letting go of her fear for the moment. Her action prompted him to seek her lips as he reached to comfort and reassure her with a kiss. He kissed her gently at first, then, as he felt her lips soften in response to his touch, a warmth flooded his body and he began kissing her in earnest. The supercharged emotions of the last few minutes had heightened their senses and, as fear dissipated, passion rose rapidly to take it place in the hearts of both.

Jack's hands were at her breasts urg

pushing aside the material there as his mouth opened over hers and his tongue began working its magic behind her parted lips. His hands moved down to her thighs as his mouth followed the curve of her neck down to her breasts. His legs were pushing between hers with some urgency when the sound of a gunshot reverberated in the air. Those fool highwaymen had likely shot a sheep, Jack thought, irritated and frustrated beyond measure.

However, he could not but be thankful when Jillian pushed him away, although not as fiercely as was her wont. It was too dangerous to continue their sport here. He noticed that her breathing was distinctly disordered as she reviled him. "How dare you embrace me! Let go of me at once, you vile seducer!" she hissed. Mackinnon grinned down at her as she still held him about the neck whereas he had let go of her already. Jillian squirmed back from him as far as she was able— which was to say not more than two inches. "How could you be so profane as to touch me in such a place? A tomb. . . . Ugh."

Still breathing heavily, Jack too pulled back, whispering, "Andrew Marvell would agree with you, sweetheart, for he wrote, 'The grave's a fine and private place, but none, I think, do there embrace.'" It wouldn't do to have that gang of desperate ruffians come back and find them thus. He cursed himself for his carelessness. Damn it, his shrew was just too appealing for a man to resist

_ _ _ moment of extreme danger.

_ _ _lmed somewhat, he whispered,

_ _ _nnon would say rather 'tis a

_ _ _brace—to show you my true love

_ _ _art and unite us again in even

such a cold chamber."

"To speak of such things here! Must you always be so depraved? You're forever shamming, pretending what you feel for me is love when 'tis only lust, I know."

"Why, sweetheart, I swear by this sacred place—" he began. Jillian sat up and tossed her head. Jack put up a cautioning hand, reminding her of the danger, and she lay back down again. "No? Well, by this hand, then, or the moon. . . ." When he couldn't get a rise out of her, he goaded, "It's your turn, sweetheart. Have you forgotten your line about the 'inconstant moon'?"

She ignored his playacting and said instead, "These are the highwaymen who attacked us come back again looking for you. Tell me the truth, Mackinnon. What are you hiding from me? Who *are* you?"

"Romeo," Jack quipped glibly.

Jillian groaned and responded with a tart riposte. "You're too old to be Romeo, Mackinnon. You've confused yourself with his father, old Montague—not the hero at all but one of the villains of the piece."

"Oww, ouch, ohh," he wailed.

"What's the matter? Is your shoulder wound bothering you?" She was quickly all solicitation.

"My wounds are bothering me all right. All these pricks and stings from your pointed tongue have stabbed me all over."

She turned a murderous look on him. "One of these days, Mackinnon, I shall plant you a facer." She shook her small fist at him.

"Come, don't be so *grave*, sweetheart." He plagued her unmercifully as he kissed that same little fist shaking in his face. "It's just that our play is so enjoyable, you know. I can't resist stealing scene after scene—not that you aren't a magnificent heroine in your own right." He goaded her with more outrageous nonsense until she quite forgot the danger they had been in. And, try though she might, Jillian could get no more than irreverent quips from Jack for the rest of their sojourn.

It was dusk when they trudged into the little market town of Moretonhampstead on the north-eastern edge of Dartmoor. The square tower of its fifteenth-century granite church had been their guide post for the last hour. They were tired, hungry, out of temper with one another, and each had worries the other was unaware of.

Jillian was afraid that somehow word would get around that she had been alone for several nights with an unprincipled social outcast. Ha! she caught herself up short—if he had been the most respectable of men that would still not excuse her behavior in the eyes of polite society. She feared that she would never be able to get another respectable position. How she was to get to London now that her money was gone was another pressing problem. Jillian bit her bottom lip as she realized that she would have to rely on this same unprincipled scoundrel to advance her a certain sum. And to top it all, both her shoes now had holes in the bottoms and had rubbed vicious blisters on the soles of her feet.

Jack had money worries, too. He had very little blunt left to sustain himself and Jill until he could get in touch with his cohorts. He had to deliver the letter he had secreted in his boot to a certain office in London before too many more days passed for it to be of maximum use to his superiors, and he had

140

to get himself and Jill safe away from the vicinity of those who still hunted for him and his precious information.

When they finally entered the little town, after waiting for an hour in their moldy hiding place before Mackinnon judged it safe to leave, they passed some finely constructed granite almshouses whose architectural highlights, including modified gothic arches, had brought admiring tourists from miles around to see them. The two foot-sore travelers were much too weary to note these widely praised local landmarks as they dragged themselves to the edge of a low stone wall and sat to rest.

"I don't know about you, sweetheart, but I'm ready to eat a whole cow," said Jack as he surveyed the buildings ahead for a likely inn. "I wish we had the direction of another Mrs. Manaton."

"I don't care about food. I just want to rest."

"Don't care about food! You must be lightheaded. Here, let me carry your reticule; it must be too heavy for you."

"You are the most nonsensical man who has ever crossed my path!"

"You tumbled after *me*, remember." They sat for some minutes in silence as dusk fell about them. Jack spoke. "Do you wish to wait here while I arrange accommodation, or shall you come with me?"

"I think we should part company right here, Mackinnon."

"Now, sweetheart, don't start another argument. I'm much too fagged to fight now. Sheath your pointed tongue and be sensible. How much money have you?"

Chapter 10

The solidly built and well-proportioned White Hart Inn had stood in the main square of Moretonhampstead for over two-hundred years. The graceful portico supporting a statue of a large white hind was of some local interest, both architecturally and historically. The inn had been established as a posting house for the Plymouth to London mail coaches during the reign of George I, and a more luxurious accommodation was not to be found for miles around. What Mackinnon didn't know when he chose it as the likeliest place to seek rooms for himself and Jillian was that it was a meeting place for the French officer prisoners on parole from the gaol at Princetown and was known to be frequented by French agents. This piece of information would likely have given him some pause.

"I expected you to congratulate me for my resourcefulness in procuring you a room in such a respectable establishment," a harried Jack tried to placate his nagging companion as he closed the door to their room and pocketed the key.

"You had no right, do you hear me, no *right,* to tell the innkeeper we were married. You should have insisted on two rooms!" Jillian shouted at poor Jack's head.

"But, sweetheart, I have told you, it's market day tomorrow and the inns are full up. There are no more rooms to be had. We were damn lucky— pardon me—we were uncommonly fortunate to procure even one. The farmer had already sold his cow and was on his way home. He was arguing with the innkeeper as I came in, refusing to pay for a room he no longer needed. I immediately said that I would pay the shot. Looking as we do in our tatters, both in need of fresh clothes and a wash, I had to show the man my blunt as it was before he would so much as consider letting us pass under his portal.

"We need a comfortable room to rest in. I'm exhausted. I don't know about you, my shrew, but I look forward to sleeping in this soft bed here," Jack sat on the bed and sank back against the pillows as he spoke. "I am sure I shall fall asleep immediately. You need have no worries."

"That's what you said last night. That's what you always say, and somehow I always *do* manage to have to fight you off."

"Last night! What did I do last night? I don't recall you fighting me off."

Jillian did not wish to answer, not wanting to admit that he had been right about how uncomfortable she would be in attempting to sleep on the floor. She refused to give him the satisfaction.

"You can't be so out of frame as to rip up at me for that quite brotherly kiss I pressed on you when we awoke this morning, can you? Why, 'twas the

144

merest trifle. Not worth getting yourself worked up about—especially when I was so proud of myself for showing such restraint!"

"You're an ill-bred, ungentlemanly, lying bounder!"

"I see I have given you my head for washing again. Well, I wouldn't want you to fall behindhand in your insults."

Jack closed his eyes as he lay on the coverlet. He tried another tack. "I never thought to see light dawn on the day that you turned missish on me, though."

"Missish! I am no such thing!"

"No? Well, then, there is no problem with us continuing to share our, ah, sleeping arrangements as we have done for the past four nights. I think I shall just have a nap now, before I order our dinner. I need to recover from the lashing I've received from your tongue today. I'll be better able to spar with you when I'm well-rested. Sure you won't join me?"

"You can have a nap now—enjoy it while you may—but I assure you, you won't be sleeping in that bed tonight. Indeed, you won't be sleeping in this *room* tonight!"

"All right, my headstrong little shrew, I hate to remind you of this, but whose blunt is paying for this room, anyway?" Jack didn't even open his eyes as he spoke, which action Jill perceived as a further cause of insult on top of injury. "Perhaps you'd prefer to seek shelter in those fine new almshouses we passed as we came into town," he suggested with a straight face.

"You're not a gentleman, Mackinnon."

"Never claimed to be," he responded with stillclosed eyes. "You can do as you like, my little screech owl, but I intend to sleep right here."

Jillian went in search of a Ladies Withdrawing Room in order to refresh herself, and when she returned to the room she found that Mackinnon had left. She had no real hope that he actually would sleep elsewhere, so she expected his return at any moment. At first she did not dare to lie on the bed, but as the minutes passed and still there was no sign of her tormentor, she was sorely tempted to lie herself down on the invitingly wide bed. Her eyelids closed of their own volition as she gave in to the temptation. She was soon fast asleep.

Jillian awoke to total darkness and wondered where Mackinnon had taken himself off to. She struck a flint and lit the candlestick on the bedstand. The anger rolled up in her, first simmering, then coming to a full boil as she marked this further treachery of the maddening man. How dare he leave her all alone like this! Then she began to worry. Her stomach was growling so loudly she put her hands up to her ears to block out the sound. She took them down again when she thought she heard a scratching at the door. Thinking it Mackinnon, she leapt up off the bed and threw the door open, ready to give him the rough side of her tongue.

"Where have you be—" she screeched before realizing that a lad stood there holding a tray of food.

"Gent said to bring you vittles at eight, missus." The young inn servant sheepishly handed her the tray.

"Where is Mac, er, the 'gent'? Is he downstairs in the taproom getting foxed?"

"Nay, missus. Don't know where gent is. Left, 'e did. Know 'e ain't in the taproom, though." The lad's gap-toothed grin was knowing as he snickered, "nor below stairs neither."

Jillian tried to pull herself together. Surely Mackinnon wouldn't just abandon her. "Well, thank you for delivering the food. I'm sure Mac . . . er, Mr. Mackinnon will return shortly."

The servant scratched his head. "Thought your man said 'is 'andle were MacCade."

Jack made his way back to the inn with a spring in his step, feeling lighter of heart than he had for some days. His typical devil-may-care air had returned in full measure. He had been able to get a message out to his contact in Exeter, though he had had to use just about all the rest of his meager supply of the ready to do so. It wouldn't be long now before he and Jill were rescued—possibly even by the end of the next day. The young stable boy he had paid to take the message swore the nag he was riding was as fast as the wind.

Well, he thought, it would be a pity in some ways if his friends arrived before morning. He grinned wickedly. It would be *interesting* to spend one more night with Jill. Not that he intended this to be their last night in bed together. No, not by a long shot, but it was probably the last opportunity he would have to tease her about it before informing her of his honorable intentions. Letting down his guard as he thought about the pleasures in store for the two of them and about how much he would enjoy drawing out their little farce for maximum entertainment to himself, he began to hum lightly as he approached the inn. Usually alert under all circumstances, Jack had allowed his habitual caution to desert him, and he didn't glimpse the figure slinking along in the dark shadows on the opposite side of the street, following him.

The figure took note when Mackinnon entered the inn, gave him some minutes to get to his room, then went round to the kitchen door and asked to speak with a very accommodating serving wench with whom he was intimately acquainted. The man stood back in the shadows as the wench came to the door. She stepped outside, bent toward the man and, spoke with him for some minutes, then accepted the coin he pressed into her hand, smiling saucily at his retreating back before returning to her duties inside.

Jillian sat on the bed tensely waiting for Mackinnon to return. It must be past ten o'clock already, she thought, and he had left no message. She should just rest, she knew. It would be a blessing, she told herself, if the blasted rake had indeed abandoned her. At least he had paid the shot for the room and a substantial meal for her already. She jumped to her feet and gave a little squeak as a key sounded in the lock. The door handle turned, and Jack walked in.

"Where have you been?" she demanded, advancing on him with clenched fists.

"Have you been worried, sweetheart? How flattering." He took her balled fists in his two hands and rubbed the backs of her slender fingers with his thumbs. "I trust you have eaten your fill . . . and you can't complain that I didn't give you ample opportunity to rest all alone in 'our' bed without my, ah, stimulating presence."

"You haven't answered my question, damn you, Mackinnon. I won't be put off. Where have you been? What devilment have you been up to now?"

"Some things a man must keep private, you know, sweetheart," he answered wickedly.

She pulled her hands out of his grasp and pounded them against her side before turning and flouncing away. "You are a fiend!"

"Ah," he sighed melodramatically, "you're going to peel another strip off my hide, I can see by that particularly sparkling light in your eyes. They've gone almost completely green, you know."

"I'm not only going to peel your hide, Mackinnon, but tan it as well, if you don't stop bedeviling me!"

"Dear me! Sounds exciting! Tan away then, vixen. Shall I bare it for you? I should have thought that such an undertaking would upset your tender sensibilities." He smiled devilishly as he began to strip off his clothes. His neckcloth followed his greatcoat, jacket, and shoes to the floor. When he began unbuttoning his shirt, Jillian shrieked in protest. "What do you think you're doing now?"

"Now, now. Don't fly into a temper, little termagant. You know I intend to sleep in that bed. And I intend to be comfortable for a change. You can't expect me to sleep in these wretched clothes one more night, despite Mrs. Manaton's kind offices in laundering them. They are disgusting and repulsive as you've said yourself—and highly uncomfortable to a man such as myself who is used to sleeping in, ah, shall we say the bare minimum?" In his never-ending attempts to provoke her, he had the pleasure of looking at the sparkling eyes, flushed cheeks, and heaving bosom of his winsome little love. If he couldn't kiss her then the next best way to arouse her passions was to tease her, he had learned from the moment of making her acquaintance.

"I want you to get out of here, Mackinnon. Now."

"What! I can't believe my ears. Not two minutes ago you were demanding to know where I'd been, angry as a hornet that I had left you on your own for a couple of hours. Now you want to throw me out. Jill, Jill," he shook his head sadly, "make up your mind, sweetheart. You complain if I sit in your pocket and you complain if I don't. How can a man know how to please you if you're forever so contrariwise?" He laughed at her.

"I certainly *do not* want you to sit in my pocket all the time!" she threw at him over her shoulder, still refusing to meet his laughing eyes.

He sat on the bed with his shirt unbuttoned, revealing some of the makeshift bandage that still covered his shoulder and quite a bit of his darkly matted chest. It was hard for Jillian to ignore so much unfettered masculinity. She felt her temperature, along with her anger, rise to new heights.

"Ah. If I can't sit in your pocket, will you sit on my lap, then?" He patted his lap, inviting her to sit down.

"No, of course not!"

"May I lie in your lap then?"

Jillian allowed a familiar martyred expression to cross her features, then sighed in exasperation, "I suppose you've had many lures cast out to you in your lifetime of raking?"

"Jealous, sweetheart? There's only one hook that has the bait to tempt me."

"You're the one who baits people."

"Sure you don't want to lure me in yourself? If you play your cards right, to mix metaphors, you might just take the trick."

"The *trick* would be to get you to leave right now."

He raised his hands in mock surrender. "Have we been at daggers drawn long enough so that we can now go to sleep, sweeting? A man knows when to thrust and when to parry, and I judge now is the time to put away my, er, sword."

"More of your foolish mischief. You can't expect me to sit here all night long and take your thrusts without parrying them, now can you, Mackinnon."

An expression of unholy glee lighted Jack's face at this sally. "If you're ready to parry my thrusts then there's some other sport I would gladly play with you. Indeed, I've desired little else since I first laid eyes on you in that wretched stagecoach."

He had finally succeeded in goading her past her endurance. She advanced on him again with fists raised and this time she couldn't prevent herself from responding physically to his brazen suggestions. She launched herself upon him, pummeling him about the face and chest, retaining just enough control to avoid his injured shoulder. "You debauched blackguard! Stop insulting me with your lecherous insinuations."

He grabbed her fists, laughing at her puny attempts to plant him a facer, and pulled her more firmly on top of himself on the bed. "Peace, peace, little vixen. No need to give me a leveler. A man knows when to sport his canvas and when to, ah, trim his sails. Threats of violence always cause me to cry craven. I give, I give." She knelt up in his lap, away from his chest. "Ouff! You've proper winded me now, you have, darling." He had to impose an iron control over his desires to prevent himself from pulling her back down again.

"Serves you right, then, to have the wind taken out of your, 'ah, sails.'" She delivered up a most brazen set-down but couldn't prevent herself from blushing fiercely nonetheless as she climbed off the bed.

Jack was bent on yet one more piece of bedevilment as he made as if to unbutton his trousers. At Jillian's very real distress, he desisted.

"I know it's all an amusing game to you, Mackinnon. You take delight in taunting me."

"No, no, love. I can't resist teasing you, you know, but you must know also, my very dearest dear, that I would not harm one hair of your gorgeous golden head," he tried to reassure her. "Come on, love. I promise to behave." He looked at her beguilingly, and though she didn't trust the rascal, she couldn't help responding to his practiced charm. Jack succeeded in calming her, and she agreed to join him again if he would only promise to keep his hands off her body and his trousers on his. Jillian, of course, refused to take off more than her shoes, but she did take her hair down and carefully combed it out before she gingerly lay down beside him once more.

She was just too bone-weary to sleep in an uncomfortable chair, she told herself in excuse. If she were honest, she would admit that she had become amazingly used to his warmth. It was reprehensible of her she knew, but she just seemed to feel more secure when she was lying next to him no matter that he threatened her virtue with almost every breath he took and every move he made.

"May I trouble you for a corner of the sheet,

152

ma'am?" Jack asked sleepily, but with faultless courtesy, some few minutes later. Jillian realized that she was clutching a whole handful of the soft muslin, and she released it as though it were a hot coal. Soon she felt comfortably drowsy and was astonished to remember how tense she had been when he was missing and at how relaxed she was now lying next to the puzzling man. She slept almost immediately.

Unfortunately, sleep evaded Jack for quite some time. He was warm and comfortable, but the sight of Jill's long, lustrous, honey-colored hair had sent his pulses to racing when she had unpinned it earlier and allowed it to cascade down her back. He hadn't realized at the time how difficult it would prove to conquer the temptation to run his fingers through the curtain of its silkiness. Now her soft, little form with its luscious curves, curled so trustingly into his own aroused body, made him grit his teeth with the effort to cool his lust. He longed to touch and be touched, and he had to fight his overwhelming desire to keep from turning her under him and making violent love to her. The strain was killing him, he thought to himself, smiling ruefully at his own folly.

Eventually Jack had cooled down and drifted off into a deep sleep. He was up with the sun, shaved, washed, and dressed, and made ready to leave the inn. Before he departed, he glanced several times at the bed to make sure Jillian still slept while he stealthily picked up her worn gray cloak and deftly made a tiny slit in the inside lining of the hem. He quickly stuffed a much-folded piece of paper into the opening before replacing the garment on the back of the chair where it had lain. Then he tiptoed over to the bed once more and couldn't resist bending over to gaze on Jill's serene countenance.

He noted that all the poor girl's worries had faded from her face as she slept, leaving her features much softened. He took himself severely to task for adding to her troubles and vowed to tease his love less and woo her with more courtesy in future—a vow easier made than kept. With her voice stilled and her flashing eyes invisible, she looked soft and delicate—the veriest schoolgirl rather than the hot-tempered, barb-tongued woman he knew her to be. Jack chuckled to himself. His fingers seemed to rise of their own accord to tenderly stroke her hair where the honey gold curtain spread out on the pillow. He bent to kiss her slightly parted, sleep-softened lips but on second thought pulled back just in time and settled for kissing her hair instead as he ran his fingers through the soft, silken strands. Then he took himself out of the room before Jillian so much as stirred from her comfortable nest among the sheets and coverlets.

Jillian awoke around noon to the sound of insistent knocking on the door of her room. She noted Mackinnon's absence as she sleepily padded to the door in her stockinged feet, neglecting to put her torn shoes on those swollen appendages, to greet the same servant boy who had brought her her food the previous night. He had come on a similar errand and, as before, he informed her he did not know the whereabouts of "Mr. MacCade." She was left to her own devices for the rest of the day and took the opportunity to wash her hair. It proved to be a long morning with nothing to do as she let her hair dry but wait and worry and berate herself for falling victim to the handsome face and practiced charm of her irrepressible companion.

Jack, meantime, was scouting around the old town of Moreton during the busy market day and waiting impatiently for a message to be brought back to him from his colleagues. His impatience finally got the better of him when his young messenger hadn't appeared by noon. He took himself into the largest bank in town and requested to see the manager. It took all the considerable powers of persuasion at his disposal, including revealing his real name and position, to convince the officious provincial bank official to forward his request. He was even reduced to pledging his watch to obtain a small advance there and then, but there was no alternative. No matter how many times he turned his pockets inside out, he suffered the same result—they were always empty. He was "flat busted," as his three young nephews would have said.

Jack wandered back to the White Hart in midafternoon and, seeing the comely barmaid on her way through the hallway with a tray full of drinks, dared to nab one of the glasses of ale and proceeded to engage the flattered girl in a light, bantering flirtation.

Sick of being cooped up all day, Jillian had donned her cloak and pushed her swollen feet into the ruined shoes, deciding to venture down the stairs just at that inauspicious moment. What should meet her eyes but Mackinnon smiling down at what Jillian could only describe as a common trollop. The abandoned girl was pressed

155

up so tightly to Jack's chest that Jillian could see not an inch of space between them—the wanton hussy! And Mackinnon was smiling down at the girl with a most appreciative look on his face—downright lecherous it was, to Jillian's irate gaze.

Jillian put her hands on her hips and cleared her throat. The look on Jack's face was ludicrous in the extreme, she thought, as he turned to see her standing at the top of the stairs. He backed away from the barmaid so fast he very nearly upset the tray of drinks the girl balanced in one hand. He put out his right arm in a supplicating gesture as he came up the stairs toward her.

"So!" she began in ominous accents.

"Now, Jill, I can see that you're displeased," he raised both hands in mock surrender, "but don't start to rip up at me, breathing fire and brimestone."

"Why should I bother to rip up at you, you disgraceful libertine. 'Tis only another example of your unprincipled behavior," she upbraided him. "Oh, yes, I am quite used to your profligate ways by now. I am only surprised that you did not invite the girl to make a third in our bed last night!" She seethed in indignation.

An unholy gleam came into his eyes as he heard her jealous words. "Dear me! How wifely you've become!"

"*Wifely!*" she choked, "I wouldn't marry a hell-bent scoundrel like you if you were one of the most eligible lords in the kingdom!"

Jack tried hard to control his mirth but lost the fight. He sputtered then bent over the stair rail, convulsed with laughter. "Now, Jill," he said when he had recovered somewhat. "If you didn't care, Miss Hot-at-Hand, would you be so jealous?

No, don't eat me, love." He grabbed her hand just as she lashed out, finally goaded beyond all endurance. She wanted to slap the devilish grin off his handsome rogue's face.

My shrew is jealous, is she? Good! Jack smirked to himself.

"There is a fair being held today in the town. I was just on my way up to see if you wanted to go out with me to join in the festivities." He tucked the little hand he still held through his arm. "'Tis market day, you know, and there is all manner of fun and gig going forth. What say you we take in the fair while we wait for—ah, while we wait." He was trying to cozen her, she knew, from the warm, beguiling look in his eyes. The conning rascal was trying to bring her round his thumb again.

Jillian allowed herself to be coaxed out of her ill-tempered mood. It would be amusing to go out and about for a change after the disagreeable last few days she had spent. Jack made it sound the most delicious fun to wander through the crowds of people to see what wares were for sale in the stalls and what the fair booths had to offer by way of games of skill, to look over the livestock brought to market as well as to purchase some of the savory food whose mingled scents, he declared, "made my mouth water as I walked back to the inn."

She agreed to walk out with him but not before letting him know that she was quite angry at being kept cooped up almost all day. He was at his most reasonable as he responded, "But *I* had nothing to do with that. You could have ventured out anytime it suited your fancy."

"A woman venturing out alone in the midst of such a rowdy crowd?" She looked all around at the boisterous horde of townsfolk, visiting merchants, and merrymakers milling about.

"Well . . . mayhap it was better to wait for me," he temporized as they emerged from the cool shadows of the White Hart Inn into the bright, bustling town square.

Every market day in Moretonhampstead was an important event in the lives of the townsfolk, happily disrupting their day-to-day routines and bringing some excitement and variety to their lives and, hopefully, profit to their pockets. The village was thronged with people come to buy and sell, haggle with the peddlers, gossip with their neighbors, or just to enjoy the fun. It made for a noisy, colorful scene. Many of the merchants had traveled from afar to sell their wares at this thriving country market.

The fair itself seemed to have attracted jugglers and fortunetellers, acting troupes and puppet shows, tumblers and acrobats of various kinds, mummery of all sorts as well as games of skill and games of chance. There were pony rides for the young people and donkey carts for them to be driven in. Several children were entertaining themselves by turning somersaults on the green in imitation of the professional tumblers, others were rolling hoops, and a trio of boys stood laughing at a small spotted dog who had a ruffled collar round his neck. The dog stood on his hind legs and danced in a circle while his master held a tidbit before him.

The odd wrestling match attracted much attention and a not-very-discreet bet or two on the side. The obligatory pugilistic contests between professional boxers and local lads anxious to show off their "handy bunch of fives" to their friends attracted a wildly cheering crowd of onlookers.

There were the inevitable beggars, pickpockets, gull catchers, and con artists to keep a sharp eye out for, too. And of course there were all manner of market stands to be visited as well. Peddlers were hawking their wares, calling out from all directions.

As they walked leisurely about, Jack pointed out to Jillian an Elizabethan troubadour cum jester complete with doublet, hose, and a fool's cap who was wandering about strumming a lute and making bawdy comments to all and sundry.

"And what mischievous couplet will he make up for us, do you suppose?"

"Something suitably Shakespearean, I would guess. He's sure to dub you a knave at first glance," Jillian responded with a wide smile, causing Jack to beam down on her with one of his own wicked grins.

She was soon attracted to a booth at the edge of the square where a cobbler was mending and selling shoes. After fierce bargaining, she was able to come to terms with the man and buy the comfortable-looking, but sturdy pair she wanted. Her purchase took the last coins in her reticule. She stepped behind a tree for privacy and slipped them on, discarding her ruined pair behind a bush.

When she emerged, Jack flicked her beaded reticule and asked, "How many coins do you have left now, exactly?"

"'Tis none of your concern, Mackinnon," she answered stiffly.

"Here." He handed her several shillings.

She wouldn't touch them. "No. I can't take money from you."

"Just thought you might want to purchase some meat pies or currant buns or some trifling fairing or other.''

"Where did you get this money? I thought you spent your last penny on our accommodation?'' she asked suspiciously through narrowed eyes. She hoped he hadn't won the money in a game of chance. "I haven't fallen in with another gambler, have I?''

He looked slightly embarrassed. "No, no. I was able to persuade the local banker to advance me a certain sum . . . just to tide us over until my draft comes through.''

"Your draft? What are you talking about?''

"I've sent a message to have some funds put at my disposal. I had expected to hear from Joh—ah, my associate by now.'' After further argument, Jillian knew she really had no choice until she could contact her father-in-law in London. She would have to borrow from Mackinnon though the idea of being in his debt vexed her extremely. Succumbing to necessity, she agreed to accept a loan from him, and she insisted that it should be strictly a loan. Jillian was not satisfied until Jack had written up an IOU which she signed and saw him put away in his pocket.

They wandered through the stalls as the sunny afternoon turned to a mild evening, taking in the sights, sounds, and smells of the fair. They stopped to eat some of the local victuals freshly carried out from a baker's shop. They feasted on mouth-watering sausage rolls and Cornish pasties filled with meat, potatoes, and onions, piping hot and smelling like heaven. Then they went on to stuff themselves on a cream tea. They drank strong, sweet tea to wash down their pasties and wolfed down the freshly made scones covered with strawberry jam and thick, yellow Devon cream as

160

though they were manna from heaven. Afterward, as they licked their lips with great delight, they smiled at one another, each amused to see the other do something so childlike.

Jack suggested they sample the much-vaunted local hard cider. When they had been served and tasted the slightly sweet, alcoholic brew, he poured his out, saying he preferred a tankard of good, strong ale instead.

He spied an archery contest going forth and insisted on trying his skill. "Ah, shall I play Robin Hood for you, sweet Marian?"

"Aye, marry will you, my fine outlaw?" she answered playfully, entering into the spirit of the game.

"Oh, indeed, marry I will, Jill. But I insist it be to you," the fellow smirked in a flippant manner.

"You shall be sorry if I hold you to that promise, Robin."

"No, no. I'm never sorry when you hold me, sweet Marian." Jillian sent him a killing glance, but offered no rebuttal.

Jillian looked at him skeptically as he plunked down his penny and was handed three long arrows and a tall, strong-looking bow. As he knocked the first arrow into the bow, she could see he had had some practice at this sport before. When he let fly the first arrow, she was not surprised to see that it hit the target, though it just touched the outermost ring.

"Damn!" Jack muttered under his breath. "I must be sadly out of practice." His left arm hurt like the devil as he stretched the bow handle out from the string but he decided to ignore the pain. With a look of determination in his eye and a hardening of his jaw, he took careful aim with the

161

second arrow. He let go the shaft with a twang of the bow and hit the edge of the bull's-eye.

By the time Jack loosed the third feathered missile he had definitely got his eye in. The arrow struck smack in the middle of the target. He turned and bowed to appreciative applause from the bystanders and beamed triumphantly when he saw the look of admiration in his companion's eyes.

For a prize he chose a delicate lace Juliet cap for Jill. As he presented it to her, he said, "For my own Marian. May she wear it in honor of her devoted Robin. Shall we hie off to Sherwood Forest, little sweet, and join the denizens there hiding out among the trees?"

"Thank you, but I've had enough of hiding out to last me a lifetime." He laughed as he tucked her arm through his again.

It had grown dark as they joined a large boisterous crowd of happy onlookers who stood watching and applauding a group of costumed merrymakers—young people holding hands, alternating male and female—dancing in a line down the street to the lilting music of strolling musicians, some of whom were playing tambourines, others flutes and pipes. This impromptu band was joined by the jester with his lute.

Jack held Jill's hand as they moved along with the crowd to follow the youngsters to the end of Cross Street where they had passed by the seventeenth-century almshouses on their way into town the day before. Several lanterns had been hung in the branches of a huge and very ancient elm tree that stood opposite these same almshouses. Jill and Jack both were amazed to see that a platform had been fixed in the great elm itself, spanning the width of the tree from one strong limb to another. They watched entranced as the revelers danced not only around the gnarled trunk of the tree beneath its spreading branches, but actually climbed up a wooden ladder to the platform and danced *in* the tree!

It was quite a spectacle to see the gentlefolk of Moreton dancing among the sturdy, leafy branches of the Dancing Tree, for so the giant elm was called, Jack learned after inquiring of one of the local inhabitants. The friendly man told him the platform was always affixed thus on festive occasions in the village.

This unique and quite unexpected sight elevated Jack's already high spirits, and after yet another pint of strong ale, he was eager to join in the lighthearted fun of the revelers.

"You're in high gig, Mackinnon," Jillian commented as she felt his arm sneak around her waist and pull her nearer to him as they watched the young people climb the ladder two by two and dance on the platform while those waiting their turn below danced in a wide circle around the festive tree. Jill did not protest; she felt somewhat more secure in the protection of his arm. The crowd was large and now slightly rowdy and more than slightly inebriated. So relaxed in his company did she feel that he was even able to persuade her to take several large sips of the home-brewed in his pewter tankard.

"It's too bitter for me. I preferred the cider," she smiled sweetly up at him, causing Jack's heart to do a flip-flop in his breast.

Jillian, truth to tell, was feeling decidedly light-headed. It seemed a suitable time to celebrate the end of their ordeal on the moor, and the enchantment of the evening, together with the close

163

proximity of her companion, had cast some sort of spell over her. She was loath to admit it, but she was caught up head over heels in the coils of her madcap rogue. How had the scoundrel wormed his way into her heart? she wondered fuzzily. That organ was beating erratically as he pulled her even closer to his side and whispered in her ear, "Shall we join them, sweetheart?"

"You must be well up in the world if you expect me to climb up there," Jillian offered a token protest as she pointed to the gigantic tree, but the prospect appealed to her sense of excitement the evening had produced.

Before her words had died away, she found herself climbing the ladder with Jack coming up behind her, his hand firm at the small of her back. And then she was whirling around giddily on the platform as Jack clasped her tightly to himself while the tambourines thumped and the flutes piped ever louder and the crowd below cheered lustily. He laughed down into her eyes, and she found herself laughing back up at him—no matter the danger of moving so fast on the elevated platform. She felt nothing could touch them this night. They seemed bound round with magic. With her head spinning and a smile still on her lips, they climbed back down amid much laughter and applause from the other merrymakers. They were still laughing as they stood and clapped as others followed them up.

Jack, in his euphoria at having effected their certain rescue in a matter of hours, allowed his habitual watchfulness in such a fluid situation to lapse. The usually cautious fellow was intent on only one goal as he drew Jillian snugly to himself again and gradually stepped back into the shadows with her until they stood well back from the main body of onlookers. She smiled dreamily up at him in the starlight, reaching up to push back the shock of black hair that had fallen across his brow.

"Jill," he whispered huskily as his hand came up to caress her cheek and his head descended slowly toward hers until their lips met in a kiss so soft and sweet that Jillian felt she was in the middle of a dream. And then his mouth opened over hers, and he demanded and received a response equal to his own hot passion. Her body melted into his, and her arms rose of their own accord to clasp him tightly round the neck. Jack strained her tightly against himself; his body throbbed for her as for no woman ever before.

Jill had never experienced such a hot-blooded kiss, such all-engulfing ardor, and she was lost, surrendering to his hunger.

And then suddenly they were enveloped in darkness as some thick, suffocating material was thrown over their heads. Jack, still hampered by the partially healed wound to his left shoulder, tried to struggle and succeeded in throwing off the portion of the blanket that covered him, but he was quickly overwhelmed by the three unseen attackers. The men took no chances; they immediately pinned Jack to the ground and knocked him out with a blow to the head. Jillian was so stifled that she had not the strength to struggle out from under the covering. She was hit, too, a glancing blow through the blanket that left her but half conscious.

Chapter 11

They had surely been traveling for hours, jolting over what must have been deeply rutted tracks in a muddy road, Jillian thought as she lay dazed in the rough, wooden-floored wagon. Blessedly for her equilibrium the motion of the horses finally stopped, and a minute later Jillian felt herself lifted out of the back of the cart and carried over a man's shoulder into some sort of building. She was dizzy and sore, and as she tried to keep her head from bobbing against her captor's back, she focused all her attention on remaining conscious. At some point her hands had been bound behind her back with lengths of scabrous rope that bit into her wrists most cruelly. She was bruised and shaken in mind, body, and spirit.

Her fear had been so great when she had been thrown into the back of the wagon with the blanket still covering her head that she had fainted. When she came to, she was too numb with shock to do anything other than concentrate on breathing through the heavy, damp, musty-smelling old blanket. The only thing that penetrated her conscious mind was that another body lay beside her and that it was warm. She hoped . . . she prayed . . . that Jack still lived and that it was he who lay trussed beside her.

Jillian was thrown into a chair and the blanket was finally, blessedly, removed—only to be replaced by a foully soiled rag placed in her mouth and tied tightly at the back of her head to gag her. Jack, she could see by the dim light of the one candle in the room, had been flung unconscious to the floor by the ruffians who had carried him into the same small, bare room where she sat. The blanket that covered his head had been removed and thrown across the floor. It now lay at Jillian's feet. Two of the villains bent down and began to search through his clothing, seemingly looking for something in particular as they cast aside the few meager contents of his pockets. The third of their captors kept a guard over Jillian as he watched his cohorts and gave low-voiced guttural orders to the other two to find that "gardamned, bloody paper and be gardamned quick like about it," in a threatening voice.

Abruptly one of the searchers was sent reeling backward by a vicious kick; he fell heavily to the floor. A fist crashed into the face of the other as a flailing Jack surged to his feet, looking wildly about. He took several quick steps toward the door before his eyes alighted on Jillian sitting tied and gagged in the chair. He checked immediately and balled his fists as he charged forward to meet the third man who stood over her. Unfortunately, one of the villains sprawled on the floor recovered quickly, got to his feet again, and charged after Jack. And then it seemed to Jillian as though all hell broke loose.

During the melee Jack was held down and

knocked out once again by the burly individual who seemed to be the leader of the gang. The candle guttered and went out just then, and Jillian was left in suspense while it was relit amid much foul-mouthed cursing from the snarling man.

Tears sprang to Jillian's eyes when she saw that Jack was hurt. Her one consolation was that the man Jack had hit on the chin still lay unconscious where he had fallen.

"Tear off the gentry cove's togs, then, if'n ye can't find it in 'is pockets—search every inch till'n yer bloody well find that bloody paper!" The other man, Daniel, obeyed orders, stripping Jack to his underdrawers and turning his clothes inside out. The snarler shook awake his unconscious accomplice who moaned and sat up holding his head.

"Gardamn it, Jem, ger up! What's a matter witt ye? The flash cove landed ye a flush 'it to yer bone box, did 'e? Knew I shoulda brought Sam instead of ye."

"I fink me jaw's broke," a muffled answer came from the one called Jem.

"Damn me, boy, yer bone box's soft as a girl's if ye can't stand a bit of a wisty caster," the growling bully barked as he scrabbled about on the floor feeling with his dirty fingernails for something. "Where's that bloody catch? Gotcha!" At his exclamation the man opened a concealed door in the boards of the wooden floor that hid some sort of chamber dug out in the ground below.

"Throw the gentry mort down 'ere, lads," the snarler said. No sooner had he spoken than the small man called Jem picked himself up and obeyed his orders. Jem took Jillian, none too gently, under her bound arms, lifted her over the opening, and dropped her down. She tried to hook her feet around the legs of the chair she sat in but only succeeded in hooking them in the folds of the blanket that had fallen nearby. She dragged it with her as she fell several feet to a cold, dirt floor that smelled of onions and cabbages.

Jillian was listening too intently to the sounds coming from above to take much note of her fall. The trapdoor remained open she could see as she squirmed on the dirt floor. She kicked away the blanket twisted round her legs, losing her shoes as she did so, and tried to free her hands. She managed to loosen the gag enough so that it fell to her chin and she could breathe easier. She could hear the snarler say, "Gardamn it to 'ell. Where'd that devil 'ide them papers, then? 'Erbert'll do fer us, else we find 'um.

"Wake 'im up, lads." Jillian heard sounds she took to be the men pulling Jack upright and slapping his face, trying to bring him round.

"''E don't seem to wake up, Badger. Ye think 'e's snuffed it, then?"

"Nah, 'e ain't stuck 'is spoon in the wall yet. Let's leave 'im 'ere; 'e'll be safe enough down below. Jem and me'll search 'is room in Moreton while 'e's trussed up 'ere. Ye get 'Erbert, Dan'l. 'E'll know 'ow to make 'im 'and it over." This last was followed by the sound of a body being dragged across the floor to be followed immediately by Jack's tumbling down on top of Jill through the opening in the floor, unconscious and partially clothed as he was. The trapdoor was slammed shut with a finality that reverberated through Jillian's body—they were doomed. "We'll never leave here alive," she whispered into the darkness.

Jillian was wild with fear. She squirmed out from under Jack's inert form and kicked the blanket over his poor cold, bruised body as best she could, then knelt down beside him: she was never more glad of her heavy cloak in the freezing cellar. With tears running down her face, she began to kiss his unresponsive lips and indeed all of his face, pleading with him incoherently when her mouth was not otherwise occupied, "What have those villains done to you? . . . Oh, my darling, please, please don't be dead. . . . Speak to me, speak to me, my love . . . oh, please! . . . I'll never rip up at you again, I promise, if only you'll speak to me!"

Just as she began to sob uncontrollably, she felt Jack stir beside her and moan. "A rash promise, sweetheart!" the irrepressible rascal murmured. "Think you can keep it for a lifetime?"

"Oh, Jack! You're alive!" Jillian gasped then pleaded, "Hold me! Hold me, Jack. I'm so frightened." She felt an overwhelming need to hold him and be held, and her need was immediately gratified as she felt strong arms move round her and hug her fiercely.

"Are you trying to finish off the job by drowning me, love?" he complained as her tears bathed his face.

"Oh, Jack! I thought they had killed you."

"Hush, sweetheart. We old reprobates are too tough to die—like an old pair of boots, you just have to throw us away. You're freezing, love, and so am I." He felt that her arms were imprisoned behind her back, and he quickly unknotted the ropes and brought her hands round to kiss them tenderly. A wet salty taste assailed his lips, and he realized that her wrists were bleeding. He cursed softly but violently under his breath for several moments.

"Where are we, Jill?" Jack suddenly realized that he was lying on the cold, hard ground in complete darkness. He also realized that he had been stripped of most of his clothing. A rough blanket was wadded up over his waist and legs, and Jill's little body was partially covering his chest. He reached toward the only warmth available and hugged her more tightly to himself.

"In hell, I think," she answered. "Those men who attacked us threw us down in this pit to rot and die."

"It's too cold to be hell, love," he laughed, and she felt the reverberation along the length of her body pressed so tightly to his side.

"We're below the floor in a kind of concealed dungeon. . . . Oh, Jack, darling, we'll never get out of this prison, will we? . . . We've not long to live," she sighed against his neck. She would never, never let him go.

"Such a show of concern, sweetheart!" Jack remarked, investing his voice with mock surprise. "It must be love! Come here, Jill."

"We'll make a paradise of this hell then," Jack murmured as he proceeded to turn her face up to his and kiss her—at first reassuringly, then with the same overwhelming passion that had overtaken them beneath the spreading branches of the Dancing Tree. He reached his hands to burrow underneath her cloak for warmth, and more, as he pulled her fully on top of himself. "We'll reinvent Adam and Eve, shall we, love?" he whispered softly, a slight tremor shaking his voice.

She clung to him and moved her sore arms to hold him tightly round his neck as he whispered against her lips, "'*Vivamus, deliciae meae, atque amemus.*' Then 'let us live, my darling, and let us love,' whilst we still inhabit this mortal coil . . . *'da mi basia mille, deinde centum.'* 'Kiss me a thousand times, then a hundred.' . . . 'If I have but breath enough and time.'" All murmurings of love gave way as his warm breath fanned her face and he found her eager mouth again.

"Oh, Jack we can't," Jill whispered breathlessly as she tore her mouth from his. She was shaking all over and with more than the cold.

"Just when . . . I was finally . . . getting . . . warm!" Jack gasped against her neck as he leaned his face into the crook of her shoulder trying to catch his breath and reorder his senses. He had forgotten who he was, where he was, and everything else except that he loved this woman to distraction.

"You're right, my heart. We can't go on. Not *here.* This is neither the time nor the place. We need somewhere cozier for our 'lovers rites,'" he laughed against her ear.

"We're not to be lovers!" she contradicted automatically.

"Not *yet,*" he corrected.

It was her mad companion, Jack Mackinnon, she had just kissed with complete abandon, Jillian thought as she came back to herself again. She realized that she had surrendered to his passion with nary a thought to the consequences. That she had been carried away by the dangers of their situation, her fears for him and for herself . . . *and* by her attraction to the charming rascal, she could not deny. Why would she, a well-bred woman, used to conducting herself in as upright a manner as she could, behave in such a way? she asked herself. She must *indeed* be in love with the rogue, Jillian realized, startled by the astounding idea.

She tried to look at her companion as he lay with his head against her shoulder, his rapid breathing slowly subsiding. Jack's beautiful face, she saw, was bathed in moonlight. His eyes were closed, the dark lashes fanning his cheek. A wave of tenderness washed over her for this man as her head finally acknowledged what her heart had long known—she loved him. She whispered into the cold, still air " 'and when he shall die I shall take him out and cut him into little stars and he shall make the face of heaven so fine that all the world will be in love with night.' "

As her words penetrated his consciousness, Jack opened his eyes and began to laugh again—the same deep rumble shaking his chest. "You little fraud—ye have the poetry as well as I do, lass," he teased in a broad brogue.

She laughed softly and reached to caress his cheek where the pale moonlight fell on it, then realized something. "My God, Jack! There's *light* on your face! There must be an opening to the outside in this prison. We can get out! We can get out!" she exclaimed excitedly.

"Of course, we can get out, sweetheart. All I have to do is lift you up to stand on my shoulders so that you can push up the cellar door. You'll find it's probably not bolted. Those fools will have pushed something heavy over it but as you push up, whatever it is will slide off, you'll see. I've dealt with a similar situation in the past."

Jillian's mouth formed an 'O of absolutely furious surprise. She was totally speechless while the storm built up within and exploded in a fury about his head. "What!" she raged. "You *knew* we were not trapped! We could have gotten out of here before . . . before you let me make a fool of myself!''

"It's not making a fool of yourself to embrace the man you love, I hope.''

She balled her fists and beat him on the chest, trying vainly to make some impression on him of her displeasure. "Oh, vile worm! *Love* you? Ha! I hate you!''

"I'm desolated that you should think so,'' he said. At times he wanted to hoot with laughter, so fast was his little shrew to come to blows with him. And just after they had exchanged a most passionate embrace, too! Ah, well, he thought philosophically, life with Jill would never be dull.

"Dear me. It's a shame you should regard your future husband with such loathing. 'Twill make our married life a sad trial for you.''

"*Marriage!* To *you?* You must think I'm mad. I detest you, sirrah!'' But in her heart Jill knew that she was weakening. She could no longer deny that the overwhelming attraction she felt for the beguiling rogue was love, but she was cautious. She held back, still afraid after her experience with Reginald. And she was furious with him for not telling her sooner that they could get out of their prison, letting her think instead that they were doomed to die!

She tried to get up, but he held her fast in his arms. She managed to pull her hands up and used them to cover her own face in angry humiliation.

"Nay, sweet, you know that I love you. And you love me—you've just confessed it,'' he soothed her as he pulled her hands away from her face so that he could look at her. "We did tarry here awhile to affirm that which had been growing between us.''

He rolled sideways so that he could cradle her in his arms. "Now that we have reached such perfect accord, we can solve the other dilemmas that lay between us. Don't you see? This was the most important one."

Jillian jerked herself out of his arms and jumped to her feet, grabbing her cloak about herself. She moved as far from him as the narrow confines of the cellar allowed. Jack gritted his teeth against the pain from his recent beating and slowly got to his feet. "How long do you plan to sulk, sweetheart? In case you've not noticed, I'm almost as bare as a newborn babe, and it's damned cold down here. But I am, as in all things, your most obedient servant, so I remain at your beck and call in the matter of when you are ready to effect our rescue."

Jack moved to where she stood and put his arms round her again. "You'll have to help keep me warm, though, else you'll have a deformed spouse whose fingers and toes and other, ah, extremeties were quite frozen off while you fumed, sweetheart."

She tried to pull out of his arms but he still held her gently. "I refuse to listen to you! You're a deceitful rogue, and I won't marry you either!" she sobbed against his shoulder and stamped her naked little foot on the dirt floor.

"Nay, nay, my bonnie lass, a' course ye will. Yer jist a wee bit overwrought," Jack said with a suppressed laugh in his voice as he deliberately lapsed into a burr, rolling his *r*'s over his tongue.

"You're magnificent when you're angry—I can't resist you. Hmm, perhaps I should keep roasting you. Your temper makes you more beautiful than ever—and warmer, too."

"Ha! You can't even *see* me down here!" Jill protested halfheartedly as she leaned against him, wiping her eyes with one hand. Despite her show of temper, she was reassured that her rogue would not take no for an answer. It seemed that he meant to have her, sharp tongue and all.

"Ah, but I can *feel* the anger vibrate all through this tempting little frame of yours. . . . No. I don't think I can resist you at all." So saying, he proceeded to kiss her deeply. Jill fought against responding to him at first, but soon abandoned the struggle and melted into the softness of his kiss for some minutes.

"Before we get carried away again, love, I think we should find a safer—and warmer—place to celebrate our newfound accord. What do you say we abandon this frigid prison, hmm?"

Jack then proceeded to lift a barefooted Jill up onto his bare right shoulder so that she could easily reach the trapdoor. Although it was awkward to balance her thus, he had to insist that she put both of her small feet on his good shoulder while he held her about the knees. He gritted his teeth as he hoisted her up. Even to stretch his left arm to grasp her legs caused him to wince from the pain in his wounded left side.

It was not so easy to open the trapdoor, however. Jillian pushed with all her strength only to be met with unyielding resistance. "It won't move an inch," she said between clenched teeth. "You told me it would be easy!"

"Well, then, if you can't move it, I'll stand on your shoulders, shall I? I know that *I* can move it." His jibe had the desired effect when without more ado, Jillian gritted her teeth and gave a cry of pain as she heaved with all her might. They heard something sliding off the door, undoubtedly the heavy object Jack had predicted would be placed on top to hold it down. She pushed the lid open, braced herself on the side of the floor above, and, with a heave to her backside from Jack, pulled herself up and out.

"Well done, sweetheart! Just give us a hand up, will you?"

"I think I may just leave you down there in hell where devils like you belong. And good riddance, Mackinnon!"

"Come on, sweetheart. I'm freezing!" His teeth were indeed chattering. But even as she taunted him she reached a hand down. When they found she could not reach him, she scouted around in the hut for something to use to pull him up.

"Jill!" he pleaded. "Hurry up!" She smiled to think she held him at her mercy.

"I'm looking, I'm looking! Wrap yourself in the blanket—it's on the floor somewhere down there. And throw my shoes up here while you're about it."

"Damnation, wench, will you hurry! . . . Ah, here it is," Jack exclaimed as he found the blanket.

The shoes came flying out of the cellar while Jillian scanned the almost bare room lighted only by moonlight. There! The chair their captors had tied her to, of course! She handed it down to him, and he was able to stand on it and boost himself up and out.

"Much obliged, ma'am," he laughed as he stood up. The blanket fell from his shoulders where he had loosely knotted it before he maneuvered himself out of the pit. There were no candles now or other manmade illumination in the little cabin, but with a full moon shining in the window,

Jillian could see her bare-chested swain well enough for the first time since they had been thrown down into the cellar. She had not realized that their captors had disrobed him so thoroughly, but there he stood in nothing but his white flannel underdrawers. She averted her eyes immediately.

"So, where are your clothes, Mackinnon? Here on the floor somewhere, I suppose." Jillian began to chatter in an embarrassed fashion as she hunted on the floor for his scattered garments. "I hope they have not been torn to pieces, for it sounded to me as though those villains took not much care when they were ripping them off you. They were determined to search you most thoroughly."

"Ah, yes. We must preserve my modesty at all costs. I can stand it if you can," he teased as he tried to help her find his clothes. He was indeed freezing.

When Jill didn't respond but only kept her head averted, Jack commented, "Such prudery, Mrs. St. Erney!" He located his trousers and picked them up.

When she still didn't rise to his bait, he asked, "What's the matter, sweetheart? I'm not completely bare, you know. And you've seen this hairy chest of mine before, when you so kindly attended to my wound. Surely the sight doesn't offend you now. You must've seen worse than this . . . you've seen a naked man before."

"Well, I haven't, you know."

"What's this?"

When she maintained a stony silence with her back turned to him, he tumbled to it. "Jill," he said softly. "You really haven't seen a man in such a state of undress before, have you, my poor innocent darling?"

"No," she said almost inaudibly.

"How can that be? You were married for four years, you said. Surely Reg . . . ?" Jack began to dress himself in the clothes she handed to him while Jill continued to avoid looking at him.

His attackers had ripped his greatcoat apart at one seam, but his shirt and trousers had not suffered unduly. The incompetent fools hadn't even inspected his boots, he noticed, thinking of the precautions he had taken earlier.

"No. Reg never undressed in front of me."

"What! But surely when you shared a bed. . . ."

"We never did! It was always dark and he always left me quickly after. . . ."

"Oh, my poor love! I've been a sad trial to you with my teasing, haven't I? Well, we shall just have to accustom you to the sight . . . but after we, ah, become more closely related, I can see."

Jill had tried to keep her eyes averted when Jack turned his back to her and donned the clothes that had been torn off him, but she could not quite keep them from straying to his form as she watched the moonlight play over the firm muscles of his back and shoulders as he pulled on his trousers and stretched his arms into his shirt. He grimaced slightly as he extended his left arm but managed to pull on both shirt and jacket without her help. Jillian swallowed uneasily and tried not to think of the heated embrace that had gone forth between them only minutes before.

Chapter 12

They tramped the two miles back toward Moretonhampstead along a dirty, deeply rutted road that had caused Jillian such anguish earlier when she had been bumped and bruised on the floor of the wagon that had transported them to their makeshift prison. The night was soft and mild, and a brilliant full moon lighted the way of the battered pair. Jack kept Jillian's fingers imprisoned in his. Just before they had left, when he had finished dressing himself, he had leaned down beside her saying, "You've caught your cloak here, love. Let me straighten it for you." And thus unbeknownst to the unsuspecting lady he had retrieved his precious paper.

"How can you bear to leave such a snug little love nest?" he had sighed melodramatically as they fled the hut, unerringly turning in the right direction. "This way, love," Jack tugged on her elbow as Jillian tried to walk the opposite way.

"How do you know this course will take us back to Moretonhampstead? You were unconscious when they carried you in."

"Oh, I've a good sense of direction, among other

181

things," he twinkled down at her.

Jack continued to spout his arrant nonsense for quite half an hour without stopping, purposely distracting his companion. He kept a sharp lookout the whole time, in case their erstwhile captors should ride back that way on their return to the cabin. He was ready at a second's notice to shove Jillian into the sheltering trees on either side of the road.

She remained all unaware of the continuing danger. When she could finally get a word in, she took a deep breath and demanded, "I suppose you still have no intention of telling me why those men kidnapped us or what they were searching for in your clothing, do you?"

Jack lifted the little hand he held in his and kissed it. "What I love so much about you, sweetheart, is that you know my mind so well. You are quite correct. I have no intention of gratifying your curiosity. But, alas! I know you well enough to realize that you will never give up. It is what I find so delightful about you. You know that I will not tell you, yet you can't resist asking anyway in your stubborn insistence on coming to cuffs with me at every opportunity."

"You are the most unreasonable, pigheaded man alive," she railed. "I have a right to know. I am not a child or an idiot! My life is in danger as well as yours. How can I protect myself if I do not even know why there are kidnappers and thieves following me, trying to do me an injury as long as I remain in *your* detestable company."

"Ah! You see? You never disappoint me!"

Jillian snapped her lips closed on a sharp retort. She turned her head away as she tugged to free her hand. Of course the fiend would not release it, so she gave up that useless endeavor without further loss of her dignity—she did sometimes know when she had met a will superior to her own—and indulged her irritation with him by refusing to talk, although much needed to be said. Her companion chuckled to himself. He didn't consider himself punished in the least, she could see.

Jack resisted nettling her further. He hadn't any intention of explaining their predicament. It would have been irresponsible of him to place Jill in so much danger. He was confident they would be rescued shortly and proceeded to hum quite merrily for the rest of their walk which was, in fact, not long.

Jillian was surprised that they were such a short distance from the town. Jack had had no notion in his unconscious state how long the ride had seemed earlier. How had he known which way to turn, she wondered. Did he never err? She could not bear it should he *always* prove to have the right of it.

They arrived at the White Hart once more to see a chaise and four standing in the inn yard and could detect signs of life inside the establishment even at such a late hour. As Jack entered the taproom slightly ahead of Jillian, two men who were seated at one of the tables looked up and hailed him with expressions of relief and pleasure.

"Jack! You mad rascal! You've led us on a merry chase, you have, my lad." The two hurriedly got to their feet and made their way to him, each shaking him warmly by the hand as Jillian stood back near the door watching. The men had been cudgeling their brains as to what might have happened to him after he had sent them word to meet him in the White Hart Inn, cautioning them to ask for a man named MacCade.

"By all that's holy! Torrance! Molesworth! Thank God! But where's John?" Jack hailed them with an expression of relief on his face.

"John is awaiting further orders in Plymouth. He has the party there well in sight," David Torrance answered him.

Thank the stars above the head office had sent David Torrance! Jack thought. He was just the man Jack had been hoping to see and the most reliable person to be entrusted with the precious code. It would throw the villains who were evidently after him off the scent if the paper were transferred to another person. Jack was sure Torrance would have no difficulty in making all speed to London while he himself went back to Plymouth, perhaps leading some of his pursuers in a circle, there to join his comrade John and help keep the nest of spies under surveillance while they awaited for developments from London.

After the effusive greeting, Jillian saw that the more reputable looking of the men put his arm round Jack's shoulder and draw him off to one side of the room where they engaged in a lengthy, and seemingly all-absorbing, conversation.

At the back of Jack's mind a plan had begun to form to entrap the traitors. His first priority, however, was to send Jill to safety. He decided to enlist the reliable Molesworth in his efforts to guard her and remove her from danger.

Jillian stood unnoticed near the door, quite forgotten, she assumed. Her temper first simmered as she waited, then began to boil. By the time Jack looked over and noticed her, she was considerably overheated. "How dare he ignore me so, after . . ." Her mind suppressed the thought of what had gone before.

The knave, not knowing himself consigned to perdition, had the audacity to smile broadly and wink at her even as he beckoned to the other man who hovered nearby—the shabbily-dressed, low-life fellow whose sparse gray hair hung down on his collar and who bore a striking resemblance to one of their villainous kidnappers. Mackinnon, Jillian saw—she couldn't help watching avidly—whispered to the fellow and gestured toward her as he took a leather notecase, handed to him by his well-dressed friend, and drew some banknotes out of it. He gave them to the seedy-looking, bow-legged individual who put them in a pocket of his baggy coat.

The man came over, introduced himself as Stanley Molesworth, and without further pre-amble, began giving orders. "Beggin' yer pardon, ma'am, but seein' as 'ow 'is lor—'is 'onor be wishful that ye make yerself ready to leave posthaste, h'it's me job to take ye to yer room to pack up yer gear."

"So 'his honor' is *wishful,* is he?" Jillian answered rebelliously and assumed a haughty air, trying to look down her nose at the man. She failed. The fellow towered her by a good four inches and was in no case ready to take any notice of a female's distempered freaks in the face of his employer's orders. Molesworth took her by the elbow without so much as a by-your-leave and began propelling her out of the room. She was left in no doubt that the so-called "wishes" were in fact imperious commands issued by her overbearing companion. She was led upstairs to her room and given exactly ten minutes by Mackinnon's lackey to refresh herself and gather her meager belongings.

Jillian found that the room had been ransacked—so their kidnappers *had* searched. What had they found and where were they now? She summoned Molesworth who took one look round, then pelted downstairs again—no doubt to inform his boss, she thought. Somehow, after all else that had befallen her in Mackinnon's company, she could muster no surprise at this turn of events.

She collected together her scattered belongings, then looked round one last time at a room that held memories both good and bad. She felt a lurch in her chest as she remembered how scarce an hour ago Jack had held her in a warm embrace, his mouth hotly covering hers, his words of love whispered against her ear—and how she had responded. She blushed even now at the thought. But then her temper began to rise again as she recalled his cavalier treatment. She wished she could ring a peal over his shaggy, black head, she fumed as she made ready to leave.

Molesworth had returned to stand guard outside the door and was ready to escort her downstairs when she emerged some fifteen minutes later. Jillian pointedly glared at him as he took her by the elbow again. Was she to be yet a prisoner?

"Unhand me this instant," she commanded to no avail. "Who does your master think he is that he can force me to go with you? Where are you taking me?" she demanded.

"Never yer bother yer noodle about h'it. 'Is 'onor the capt'n arranged h'it all, ma'am. 'E's sendin' yer to safety."

186

"I want to see your officious 'captain' right now!"

"The capt'n 'as h'urgent business to take care of. 'E'll see yer when 'e's good and ready ter, never ye fear, ma'am."

"Just what is he captain of, anyway? A captain sharp, if I'm any judge!"

"Aye, Capt'n's sharp as a tack," was the only answer from her companion who continued to hold her arm and rush her along.

Just wait until she saw "his honor the captain"! She would give him a blistering reprimand for daring to treat her so. But penniless and friendless as she was, she had little choice but to accompany the little man down the stairs. She was led off to the elegant chaise waiting in the inn yard. She saw no sign of Mackinnon or the neatly dressed gentleman when she glanced in the taproom as she was hurried along the corridor and out the front entrance.

"Where are we going?"

"Lunnon." Molesworth vouchsafed the one word and handed her up into the vehicle at once. Jillian found herself bundled into the carriage without more ado.

She was indignant at such careless treatment, but her protests fell on deaf ears. Molesworth had no sooner handed her inside than he shut the door on her remonstrations and the four strong horses were given their office to start. Jillian was off in the direction of the Exeter Road before she could gather her wits. Her urgent queries to know what was happening and where they were bound now could not be voiced further. Was Mackinnon not coming to join her, then, she wondered in dismay.

Perhaps he would come along after her, she thought, and then she would happily cross swords with him. She tried not to hope . . . fear, she quickly corrected herself, too much that this would be the case. She could not even question her jailer—Molesworth had not elected to join her inside. She knew not if he were left behind or if he sat on the box with the driver.

Jillian slumped back against the velvet squabs of the well-appointed equipage and found to her irrational disappointment that it was a well-sprung and comfortable vehicle. She found, too, that the chaise was moving with considerable speed out of the town; but where Mackinnon was at that moment continued to tease at her mind. He had *talked* about their further acquaintance, twitting her about their being husband and wife one day. He had cast himself as the henpecked husband living under the thumb of a scolding wife, but now, without his large, warm presence to reassure her, Jillian began to think this was just more of his nonsense.

She had failed completely when it came to knowing when he was serious, if he ever was, and when he was roasting her for his own entertainment. Whether she was ever to see him again was something that she didn't care to dwell on. The mere idea that he had disappeared from her life forever caused panic to pull at her insides. She had thought she would be glad to wash her hands of him, hadn't she? Then why was the idea of never seeing his grinning face again and hearing his mocking taunts so devastating?

Jillian was so tired she fell into a deep sleep in

the swaying chaise and awoke with surprise when the carriage pulled into the yard of a busy inn in a sizeable city. This must be Exeter, she assumed with some interest. It was mid-morning and they had made excellent time from Moretonhampstead. She waited in the chaise as she saw Molesworth jump down from the box and go inside an impressive black and white half-timbered building, presumably to make arrangements for her accommodation. The inn proudly bore the name Prince of Wales Arms, Jillian saw as she glanced at the swinging sign hanging above the bustling coaching inn yard where carriages and wagons of all varieties, men and women on horseback, and pedestrians of all stations of life milled about.

Molesworth came to collect her some several minutes later. He led her inside and handed her over to the bombazine-clad proprietress of the establishment who escorted her up a red-carpeted staircase to a quiet room at the back of the luxurious inn.

"Shall you be wantin' a hot bath, dearie?" the landlady inquired, noticing how tired and worn her guest looked.

Jillian perked up immediately. "That would be most welcome, ma'am!"

When the door had closed behind the woman who promised to see to the bath immediately, Jillian walked over to the double windows at the rear of the chamber to see what sort of view she had been afforded. She was pleasantly surprised to see that the room looked onto a wide, gently sloping green surrounding the beautiful cathedral of Exeter beyond. Jillian stood entranced admiring the thirteenth-century early-English Gothic building, gleaming a pale golden in the mid-morning

189

light. The sight somehow soothed her tired and troubled spirits.

The chamber itself was well-appointed with green and white chintz hangings, comfortable-looking chairs, well-polished woodwork, and an elaborately patterned flowered carpet. The sheets, Jillian noted when she inspected the well-sprung bed, were immaculately clean and smelled as though they had been freshly aired.

"Ah, alone at last!" she breathed, feeling free—and sadly deflated. She had been burdened for a week with the company of the most lowdown, outrageous, cunning, devilish, beastly, rum customer it had ever been her misfortune to come across. And now that she was free of his vexatious company she couldn't help missing the teasing creature. Had ever a woman been so unlucky in the menfolk in her life, Jillian sighed—first Reginald St. Erney, now Jack Mackinnon.

A maidservant knocked, bringing hot water to fill the shiny hip bath concealed behind a painted screen in a corner of the room. After several trips up and down the stairs, the bath was filled to the brim with steaming hot water.

"Would you be wantin' anythin' else, ma'am?"

"No, no. Thank you. This is quite heavenly."

Jillian quickly discarded her worn garments, pinned up her hair, and sank into the invitingly warm water. She detected the scent of sweet woodruff in the bath water and sighed with pleasure. "Ah!" She closed her eyes in content as her head fell back against the edge of the tub as the water lapped gently against her soft skin.

But they flashed open again in a moment. Thoughts of her errant knave would obtrude. And they were not thoughts of his rascally behavior. . . .

Indeed not! She blushed rosily as she glanced down at herself in the bath. Her thoughts were of a quite, quite different nature. They were thoughts, in fact, of the several heated embraces they had exchanged in the past few days. Thoughts of warm intimacy, of Jack's lips on hers, of his caress . . . thoughts of his tender words . . . and how she loved him! No! She shook her head violently and sat up—then sank back down with a soft smile on her face. Yes! He had spoken of love and of marriage. Would she entrust herself to a man again? Could she dare to trust him? Her head warned caution, but her warm body and soft heart whispered Yes!

When she had finished her lovely bath, Jillian could not keep her eyes open another second although it was just midday; her sleep in the chaise had been welcome, but she had many days' worth—or nights' rather—yet to make up for. She told herself that she was glad to remove her tattered garments and climb into the inviting bed without having to fight over sleeping arrangements for the first time in a week. Then why, she asked herself some minutes later as she lay still wide awake on the lavender-scented pillow, was she so miserable?

Her evening meal was enjoyed in the same solitary state. She sat eating her dinner in a private parlor, paid for by funds doled out by Molesworth, who seemed to be acting as her nursery maid. On the command of "'is 'onor, the capt'n," she had no doubt. And just why did Molesworth address Mackinnon as "captain" anyway, she wondered again suspiciously. Was he indeed the leader of some nefarious criminal ring as she had begun to think? No! She couldn't bring herself to believe such a thing of him. But why was he called captain then? He had refused to tell her a single thing about himself or about why they had been chased all over Dartmoor. She would have the truth from him, she vowed, the very next time she saw him. How she longed to confront him with her questions.

"If only he were here this minute," she thought, then blushed as she suddenly remembered her thoughts in the bath.

But, alas, there was not a sight or sound of Mackinnon all evening. She had, irrationally it seemed, been expecting him to follow along after her and arrive in plenty of time to harass her again about their being bedfellows for the night. She tried to convince herself that she felt nothing but relief that the jackanapes had ceased to plague her.

Trying to swallow her disappointment, and concealing from herself the soreness of heart Jack's absence had produced, Jillian left the parlor and prepared to make her way upstairs to her bedchamber when Molesworth intercepted her in the hallway. He doffed his well-worn hat to show a balding gray pate with a few hairs straggling down to his collar. He handed her a letter and a parcel wrapped in brown paper. "From the capt'n, ma'am. 'E give me this 'ere letter to present to ye afore ye retired for the h'evenin' . . . and these 'ere h'articles, too."

"What are they?"

"Female fripperies, I call's 'em." Molesworth answered unhelpfully.

With barely concealed impatience Jillian snatched the letter and parcel from his hand. Only with a mighty effort was she able to resist opening the missive then and there in the public passageway.

192

She ran up the stairs, bolted into her room, and slammed the door before ripping open the letter addressed to her in a bold hand. As she did so, several banknotes of a rather high denomination of English currency fell out and fluttered to the floor.

Sweetheart, (she read the scrawled words without stopping to pick up the money) *I hope you will be happy with the arrangements I have made so that you may get to London as quickly and comfortably as possible. My agent will keep the dibs in tune for you. On my instructions he will have purchased a few necessities for you that should see through until you arrive in London.*

Knowing how little you care to accept charity, I recognize that you will not be anxious to arrive on your father-in-law's doorstep being unsure of your welcome. So I have taken matters into my own hands (high-handedly, you will say) and arranged for you to visit Lady Dorothea Gilmore for the space of a few weeks. She is a real love and in need of a companion at present to confide her worries to—among the most pressing of which is how she is to cope with launching her peagoose of a daughter upon the ton. Young Missy is a rare handful and Dolly will be glad of your warm, soothing presence in her household at this stressful time. I know she will come to rely upon your calm good sense, not to mention the evenness of your sweet temper.

Dolly and I will be eternally grateful if Missy can be removed from underfoot with all possible speed. I have taken the further liberty of writing directly to Dolly informing her of your imminent arrival. She has carte blanche to draw on my account for anything you need. I know you will wish to replenish your wardrobe.

Unforeseen complications mean that I must postpone our next sparring match for the time being. I will call upon you at Dolly's when my business is satisfactorily concluded.

I'm devastated to admit that I am already missing our skirmishes and your never failing readiness to do battle, my little shrew. I know you will be as sorry as I not to have the pleasure of sharing our, ah, evenings for some little while. Most particularly, I'm sure you'll agree, as we had just arrived at a most interesting juncture.

> *Love and kisses,*
> *your own Jack*

P.S. Whatever will I do without you to keep me warm at night? The thought occurs that you would fix me with your severe eye and say, "Freeze, as you deserve, Mackinnon."

Jillian flung the hastily written message to the floor, speechless with indignation. She literally wanted to cry with vexation at the high-handed machinations of the lowdown knave. The light of battle flared in her eyes as she paced about the room, uncaringly treading on the banknotes that lay scattered over the carpet in her hurried passage back and forth.

"If only I could get my hands on you this minute, Mackinnon. Oh! I should have left you to freeze in that blasted cellar!"

High-handed arrangements, indeed! Order her about, would he? Force her to be a companion to this Lady Dolly Gilmore, would he? Who was she anyway? Some elderly lady? Or some young and beautiful flirt of his?

Well! she said to herself wrathfully, the over-bearing monster would just have to think again before she would bow to his arbitrary arrange-ments. Just who did he think he was that he had control over her life! She would spite him, that's what she would do! . . . But how?

On such a note of discord, sleep was long in coming. It certainly did not evade her because there was no warm and soothing presence at her side. Not at all! But the morning saw a heavy-eyed Jillian still unresolved on her course of action once she reached the metropolis. She would hit upon something during the journey, she was sure.

Her abominable knight was at that moment engaged in rounding up those who had treated them so roughly the previous evening.

After giving Molesworth a pair of hastily scrawled letters, one to take to London and deliver to a lady there and the other to give to Jill, Jack took two men from the local constabulary—plucked from their quarters where they had been nodding off on the night watch—and a brace of horse pistols, then raced off on borrowed horse-back at a furious clip back to the cabin where he and Jillian had been held. He hoped to intercept the men who would return to look for him. Jack grinned into the darkness as he thought what a surprise his incompetent captors had in store when they did not find him lying battered and bruised in the cold, dark cellar.

It was a deuced shame, he thought as he rode, that he hadn't bid Jill a fond adieu, but on reflection it was just as well. He didn't have the time to get into detailed explanations about his work. He assured himself it was much safer for her not to know, anyway. There was already one woman in his confidence. But he knew he could trust the redoubtable Dolly with his life. Jill was a tiny bit too volatile. If she were angry, she might spill the beans. Besides, he wouldn't risk one hair of her precious honey-colored head over this episode. His protective instincts rose to the fore when he thought of his lovely girl.

When Jack and the now wide-awake constables neared the cabin, they concealed their horses among nearby trees and stealthily made their way to the back of the old stone structure. Jack signaled to the two to cover him as he stepped to the door. The snarling man named Badger was cursing vociferously, "Where in 'ell did that gardamned blighter git to then, if 'e's not bloody well down there?"

Then Jack clearly heard Jem's plaintive voice. "'Im 'ad the devil's 'elp to disappear like 'at."

Jack quietly pushed the door inward, pointing his long silver pistol at the head of Badger, who was bending down looking into the opening to the cellar speaking to Jem. The unfortunate Jem had evidently been sent down to look for the captives.

"Drop your barker, there's a good fellow, and raise your hands over your head. Instantly! Else I shall be forced to discharge this weapon in the region of your belly, you black-hearted knave." Badger complied, a horrible snarl distorting his face. Jack shouted for his men to enter the cabin.

"Jem!" Jack called. "Throw your weapon out of there, put your hands up, and stay where you are. If you don't do so immediately, I shall shut you in." The already frightened Jem gave a low shriek and threw out his gun. One of Jack's men pulled him out of the cellar, then tied his wrists. Badger had already been bound.

"Gardamn it to 'ell! 'Ow'd ye get loose, covey?" the snarler growled.

"Black magic, my fellow, black magic." Jack leered at them, a white grin splitting the black visage of his unshaven face.

"'E's got the devil in 'im, Badger!" Jem's eyes rounded in horror, and he fell back a step or two, only to be poked in the spine by the pistol of one of Jack's men urging him forward again.

"What'll we do now, Badger?" Jem turned to ask the snarler in a shaking voice.

"I'll tell you what you're going to do," Jack answered in a voice of command. "First, you're going to tell me exactly where Daniel and Herbert are at this precise moment. Then, you'll lead me to the person who ordered my kidnapping. After that, I believe you'll be more than happy to share the information about who's behind this operation in Plymouth. I want names, places, dates—what money has changed hands. I'm sure you get the gist of the form your cooperation will take."

Badger spat on the floor in disgust. "We don't know nuffing, goven'r."

Jack stepped up to the bound man and took hold of the loosely knotted kerchief round his neck, giving it a good twist. "You're dealing with the devil now, my fine bully, and I want answers straight and I want them now, or I'll give you a

197

taste of the home-brewed you were so generous in doling out to me earlier. Where are Daniel and Herbert? Following along behind you, are they?" Jack looked over to where the other captive stood, shaking with fear.

At Jem's nod, Jack motioned for the men to hide in the trees outside to try and intercept Herbert and Daniel when they should approach the cabin while he and the captives waited inside. He questioned Jem and Badger closely until he was convinced he had extracted all the information he could from these very minor players in the traitorous spy ring.

It was dawn when one of the men staked out on the road outside finally reported to Jack that there had been no sign of anyone approaching. Jack was convinced that the man they took their orders from, this Herbert fellow, had somehow eluded him for now. He set off back to Moretonhampstead with his captives and the two constables where he took great pleasure in handing Badger and Jem over to the local magistrate before he headed south to Plymouth once more. His two captives had supplied some valuable information and he must put it to good use straightaway.

It seemed the operation was more complicated than he had anticipated and he must contact John and his other associates there and let them know that the gang in Plymouth waited for the arrival of a very important visitor from London. They would have to continue to stake out the ring's headquarters for several days until they were sure of arresting their man. Then the whole operation would undoubtedly move to London and Jack and his men would close the net they had been slowly stitching together round the person or people in the government who had been supplying information to the French.

He dearly wished he could ride to Exeter and join his little spitfire, but this urgent duty called him elsewhere. At least Torrance would be halfway to London by now, Jack thought with relief. He had every confidence the all-important code would be safely delivered by the morrow. And he had every confidence that his trusted Molesworth would see that an equally important, but more personal, duty was done—Jill would be safely ensconced in Dolly's London townhouse before many more days passed.

Chapter 13

After a further two nights on the road to London spent at superior establishments each time, first in Salisbury and then in Guildford, and with her every comfort uncannily anticipated by Mackinnon and seen to with great alacrity by his lackey Molesworth, Jillian was still no closer to resolving her dilemma than she had been three days before. Her inward debate fluctuated this way and that over her equally undesirable choices. Being Jillian Ford St. Erney, she continued to smoulder even as the wheels of the chaise rolled over London Bridge and onto the cobbled streets of London town itself. Each yard she traveled brought her ever closer to the fateful decision.

It was a situation frought with difficulties. Any number of calamities presented themselves to her mind. If she asked to be driven immediately to her father-in-law's establishment, that course would be attended by a certain awkwardness. Old Lord St. Erney was not so much a high stickler in social matters as he was a stiff-rumped old pinch-penny who would not welcome her because she would pose a disturbance to his comfort and make financial demands that would put a dent, however slight, in his pocketbook. In the same way as he had tried to deal with the problem of Reg so that his peace would not be further cut up, he would want her off his hands forthwith—and Jillian would be more than glad to go, as soon as she found another position.

On the other hand, if she gave in to Mackinnon's instructions and directed her disobliging gray-haired postilion to deposit her on Lady Gilmore's doorstep, she would have lost one more battle to the odious wretch and placed herself once again in his firm control.

She decided on what she thought was the lesser humiliation.

"You may take me to the residence of Lord St. Erney in Curzon Street, Mr. Molesworth," she said firmly as she pushed down the glass and addressed Mackinnon's servant in her best prim-and-proper governess voice and manner.

Molesworth returned her look for look, saying, "H'ain't no reason to go 'aring off to Curzon Street, seein' as 'ow I 'as me h'orders from the capt'n to deliver yer to Lady Gilmore's. H'orders is h'orders, ma'am." The impudent servant, equally and odiously as overbearing as his master, would brook no argument. All her agonizing had gone for nought; she was to be given no choice in the matter. Jillian sat back stymied. As devoted as the fellow was to his "capt'n", there was no chance that she could override his precious orders. She was at point-non-plus.

She had not a feather to fly with, nary a sou—not to mention a stitch—to her name other than the ragged clothes she wore and a few necessities that Mackinnon, in his typical high-handed way, had

had his henchman buy for her. The brown paper parcel Molesworth had given her in Exeter had proved to contain a round gown of gray worsted— one size too big, a new pair of shoes—one size too small, they pinched her still swollen feet; some heavy stockings together with a rather prim white nightrail; a hairbrush; even a toothbrush and toothpowder along with a valise to carry them in. She had been embarrassed beyond words to receive such items, but her need for them was too great for her to refuse to accept them as she fervently wished she had been able to do. Doubtless Mackinnon would have laughed at her dilemma!

She was determined not to take any of the "blunt" enclosed in Mackinnon's letter, but when she tried to hand it back to Molesworth, that gritty individual said, "Seein' as 'ow 'is 'onor, the capt'n, gave it to yer, ye'd be best h'advised to take the fripperies and the blunt, ma'am, h'if yer don't want a taste o' 'is temp'r. The capt'n 'as a blisterin' temp'r for all 'is gay graces and devil-me-care ways. 'E's a right thunderin' firecracker for all 'e natters h'along so 'appy-ger-lucky."

A taste of his temper, indeed! Why, she could deal with his temper any day of the week. But accept the money, she could not, would not—for pride's sake, for honor's sake. There was too much the sordid feeling of payment for services rendered, as well as the reminder that the so-called captain had had the ordering of her life for too long a time as it was. Then, too, he may have won the money by playing cards or dicing—just like Reg, she thought in despair—or if he were indeed the captain of some criminal operation, it was tainted money and she would be culpable for having it in her possession. Her anger against her rogue simmered as she counted off his many sins. Then she remembered his intelligence and quick-witted bravery in effecting their rescue from awkward and dangerous situations many times during their adventures and his unfailing good humor even in the face of the painful gunshot wound to his shoulder. She could recall how the ready laughter would spring into his warm brown eyes and how his well-cut lips would form themselves into a mocking grin as he teased her . . . and she remembered how she felt when he held her in his arms, and her attitude softened.

The clip-clop of the horses' hooves on the cobblestone paved street was almost enough to fray Jillian's nerves as the chaise proceeded at a rapid pace to the residence of the unknown Lady Gilmore. Jillian sighed as she tried to swallow her pride. The taste was as bitter as gall in her mouth. She was trapped.

The residence proved to be a modest but tasteful mansion in the very best of residential areas—Mount Street, in fact. As they drew up, Jillian was amazed and impressed despite herself at the neighborhood she suddenly found herself in. Reg had never brought her to London on one of his sprees, for which gross oversight and neglect of family consequence on the part of a son of a peer of the realm she could only be thankful. She had had no desire to see such a sinful metropolis, or so she had convinced herself while her late husband continued to neglect her.

As she stepped down from the chaise, Jillian came out of her near trance to glance sharply up and hear Molesworth address the young footman who opened the door to Number Ten, Mount Street. "Me h'orders is to deliver this 'ere lett'r straightaway to 'er ladyship, me lad, Lady Gilmore that is, and no 'un else. Tell 'er h'it's from the capt'n. H'urgent like." Jillian saw Molesworth conducted inside. She determinedly pressed her lips together at this further reminder of Mackinnon's ordering of her life. What she would give to see the contents of that note!

Molesworth had neglected to help her down from the chaise in his haste to deliver his "h'urgent lett'r." She was bone-tired and disheveled as she lugged her small portmanteau with its few necessities up the imposing steps to Lady Gilmore's Mount Street mansion. Another of the Gilmore servants stood guard at the door as Jillian entered. The young man stared at her, not with suspicion as she might have expected, but rather with an avid, undisguised curiosity. His shock of rather stiff red hair seemed to stand straight out from his head. The poor lad looked as though he had been dragged through a hedge backward. This comical sight caused a brief smile to pull at Jillian's lips. The awkward young man seemed new to his post and belatedly realized that he was standing in her way. He quickly offered to take her small valise and conducted her inside.

She stood in the marbled hallway and looked up to see Molesworth in conversation with a tall, dark-haired woman at the top of the stairs. The woman stood awkwardly leaning on a crutch under her right arm. Jillian distinctly saw Molesworth pass the woman a piece of paper—undoubtedly the note from Mackinnon. As the lady hastily read it, she put her free hand to her heart and gasped. Then a slow smile curved her lips upward and lit her entire face. She glanced to the hallway below, saw Jillian standing there, and gasped again, "Oh, my," as she hastily concealed the paper in her pocket.

The woman came down the stairs as quickly as her infirmity allowed with her unencumbered arm extended in a gesture of welcome when she reached the floor below. Jillian had time to observe her closely as she descended—she was darkly good-looking, with strong, aristocratic features and finely carved lips. Her figure was excellent, regal in fact, Jillian thought, despite her limp. She had an air about her that bespoke a strong-minded woman of sound opinions. She was undoubtedly a mature woman in both manner and age, probably a few years Jack's senior if Jillian were any judge.

"My dear Mrs. St. Erney, I am Dolly Gilmore. Jack tells me you are to bear us company for some little time," Lady Gilmore said, taking Jillian's arm and leading her forward along the marbled hallway toward the ground-floor reception room. Her deftness in this delicate maneuver bespoke a much-practiced use of the crutch. Perhaps the disability was not temporary, as Jillian had first assumed, but of long-standing.

"I'm so sorry to impose on you in this manner, Lady Gilmore . . ." Jillian began, embarrassed.

"Please. Do not feel uncomfortable. If it isn't just like that incorrigible rogue to make arrangements without first consulting the desires of the other parties involved but he's invariably right, you know. Drat him!"

She led Jillian into an elegantly furnished reception room. "I know that Jack can be obnoxiously overbearing at times, but he's a dear really, underneath that bearish temper, and I am truly glad that he has sent you to me. Will you not come in and make yourself comfortable." Jillian was rendered acutely embarrassed by the warmth of her hostess's greeting. She felt all the awkwardness of a stranger imposing herself in the midst of a comfortable household and was only able to murmur a polite rejoinder.

"But then, I am being overhasty in desiring to converse with you when I can see that you are dropping with fatigue." Lady Gilmore was quick on the uptake. "You will want to tidy up and refresh yourself. I shall have Whitby take you up. I'm sure you'll be comfortable in one of our guest chambers," said the lady, already limping forward to pull on the golden tasseled bell rope.

"Thank you, Lady Gilmore. You are very kind," Jillian said earnestly. There was nothing she wanted more than a wash and a rest. In next to no time she found herself in a tidy little bedroom, being cosseted by a tiny, wizened white-haired woman with a Scottish accent.

"Here ye be lass. Just rest yerself awhile. If ye be needing anything, just ring for Rosie and tell her Mrs. Whitby says yer ta have whatever you require."

Jillian's head was in a whirl as the little dynamo of energy swept out of the room, promising to send up a hot cup of tea and some bread and butter "in jig time." Jillian slowly sank down on the soft mattress of the canopied fourposter bed and took stock of her surroundings. The room was small but exceedingly well-appointed. From the well-polished woodwork to the small white stone fireplace to the patterned wallpaper of pink cabbage roses, she could not ask for more comfort. But Jill was very confused. What exactly was her standing in this household? Who was this handsome Lady Gilmore whom Mackinnon had called a "real love" in his letter to her? Was Jillian herself a guest or a hired companion? The room was on the third floor and away from the main bedrooms in the house—surely in the servant's wing? But her hostess had greeted her like an honored guest. It was all very strange.

Meanwhile Dolly once again perused Jack's letter at her leisure over a cup of tea. She pursed her lips as she read, "Keep her with you under any pretext you can think of, my dear love," he wrote. "I doubt not that you can come up with something. I know well your powers of invention— you're a past master at duplicity, my dear." The beast! thought Lady Gilmore humorously. "And for God's sake, don't tell her anything about me or about our relationship! And I mean don't breathe a whisper of our current arrangements. Curb any desire to make her your confidante. Don't let your tongue run away with you as is sometimes its wont. I wonder John's business has not been compromised any time these past twenty years with your propensity for gossip. We must pull the wool over everyone's eyes. It is vital that we keep the *ton* in the dark if we are to meet with the success we hope for in our project. I repose every confidence in you, O my sister in intrigue."

Lady Gilmore bristled up indignantly as she read the words. "I do not gossip! 'Tis you, Jack dear, who have the unruly tongue and well we all know it! As to compromising John—why, 'tis no such thing. I've known well how to bridle my tongue, and indeed my very thoughts, any time these past twenty years. Compromise you, indeed! The very idea is nonsense!"

She considered awhile. "For love of you, Jack dear, I'll do as you ask. It should not tax my 'powers of invention' as you so rudely call a woman's natural turf." She laughed to herself and began to plot in earnest as she absently reached down and tucked the letter into her sewing basket.

"I dare say Jack will call more frequently after Missy's off my hands and we can be comfortable again. She's forever plaguing the life out of him, you know," Lady Gilmore laughingly assured Jillian the morning after her arrival.

Dolly explained that Jack had written that he thought it a good idea for Jillian to go around with young Melissa Gilmore as she made her come-out. "If you are agreeable, my dear, I should be most pleased and grateful. While in general I do not mind going about the *ton*—'doing the pretty,' as Jack would call it—I find the idea of plunging into the *endless* round of social engagements that my daughter has her heart set on a rather tedious prospect just at present. I find myself saddled with extra duties involving the boys as well as Jack's projects.

"I gather that you did not frequent society during your marriage to Reginald St. Erney. If it would give you pleasure to see some of the social whirl, then I hope you will share some of the chaperoning duties for my daughter with me." Lady Gilmore looked expectantly at her guest in bright inquiry.

"I should be delighted," Jillian answered in some surprise. She wanted to please her hostess, whom she liked very much, and, indeed, the idea of seeing a bit of the *ton* that had been forbidden to her as Reg's wife was appealing. What were the "projects" of Jack's that Lady Gilmore referred to?

Jillian was burning to know, but did not feel well-acquainted enough with her hostess to ask.

"I hope you shall still be delighted after a week of Missy's company. Alas! my daughter is a pea-goose, Jillian," Lady Gilmore said humorously. "I hope you don't mind if I call you Jillian." She cocked an eyebrow at her guest, and at Jillian's negative shake of the head and half smile Dolly continued, "I know not how I came to be saddled with such a ninnyhammer for a daughter when my family were ever known for their superior under-standing—even if we have somewhat of a reputa-tion for an odd kick in our gallop, not to mention an unruly tongue or two amongst the present generation. I believe Missy must take after my husband's side of the family. It must be admitted that my mother-in-law was just such a goose, love her though I did."

"Is your husband, Lord Gilmore, in residence?" Jillian inquired politely.

Lady Gilmore colored slightly and answered in some confusion, "Uer, no. Not just at present, that is."

Jillian wondered at the Lady Gilmore's slightly embarrassed stutter. The lady was usually so self-assured.

"What do you think of Jack? Is he not a hand-some rogue?" Lady Gilmore questioned gaily. "One cannot help but be in love with him," she said archly, watching Jillian carefully for her response.

Jillian was pleased to find that she did not blush as she looked her hostess straight in the eye and said, "I find him rather an overbearing tyrant, myself, Lady Gilmore."

Lady Gilmore laughed outright as her warm

brown eyes crinkled with delight. "Yes, my dear, indeed he is that, too. And you must call me Dolly, you know. I shall feel a veritable ancient else," she said with a rather conning smile on her handsome face. Jillian had a vague feeling that she had seen brown eyes crinkled in just such a fashion only recently, but she could not place where.

A shining head appeared round the sitting room door at that moment and a sweet voice inquired diffidently, "You sent for me, Mama?"

"Yes, yes, come in, Melissa, my dear, and be introduced to Mrs. St. Erney."

Jillian felt her jaw drop as she stared in astonishment at the embodiment of an angel. A petite girl-child, who looked no older than twelve but must have been five or six years beyond that if she were being presented to the *ton*, tripped into the room with a hint of rose along her cheekbones adding a blush to her lovely little face. The girl peeped from behind a riot of sunny golden curls with a rather mischievous smile on her rosebud lips lighting up her angelic features. Celestial blue eyes set in a creamy complexion appraised Jillian candidly. The girl was curious as a kitten about her mother's mysterious visitor. Miss Gilmore's morning gown of blue muslin, trimmed with a modicum of lace, was of a color to highlight those eyes that seemed to Jillian to dance with little imps of mischief.

From the top of her shining head to the tips of her dainty satin slipper-clad toes, Jillian could see no obvious imperfection in face or form to mar the girl's beauty. She was petite, yes, but her form was shapely. A man's heart was sure to catch in his throat when he beheld such a little incomparable, and the girl was not even particularly elaborately dressed this morning. Her perfect features set off by the crowning glory of her hair and her trim little figure were enough to turn any man's head.

"Jillian, my dear, this is my daughter Melissa. We always call her Missy in the family, and you will come to see that it suits her precisely."

"Missy, this is Mrs. St. Erney. She is to go about with you this Season, if you make yourself agreeable to her, mind. Oblige me by forbearing to play any of your tricks on her. I doubt not you will enjoy her company, for she's a friend of Jack's."

"How do you do, Missy?" Jillian said in her best governess voice.

Lady Gilmore excused herself, saying that she must consult with Cook about the menus for the day and that she was sure Jillian and Missy would want to become better acquainted. She limped from the room. Jillian looked after her, thinking that she certainly was an expert at handling her crutch and noticing that she wore a special shoe on her right foot, too. Jillian's curiosity must have shown in her face, for Missy piped up, "Mama was born with one leg shorter than the other. Did she not tell you?"

Jillian made a polite rejoinder and concealed her embarrassment at letting her curiosity show.

"Did Jack send you to Mama?" the pert chit questioned brightly. "Mama said you are a friend of his."

Well, she certainly wastes no time in coming to the point, Jillian concluded ruefully as she bowed her head affirmatively. Perhaps the chit was not needle-witted as her mother said, but she was not precisely a featherhead either. Just very young—and inquisitive.

"How did you meet him? Did you have an

adventure? Jack is always involved in such havey-cavey doings. Mama will never tell me what they are—though I'm certain she knows. Jack and Mama are as close as inkle-weavers, you know.''

"Oh?" Jillian raised a delicate brow in inquiry.

"Oh, yes. Though Mama would have forty fits if she heard me calling him Jack. She always says I must call him Uncle Jack—to show proper respect, you know. But it seems to me that I am quite grown up now and he is not *that* much older than I am."

"Indeed," Jillian said, a laugh twitching at the corner of her mouth at the thought of this child parading as a grown-up.

"Besides," Missy added ingenuously, "he is *not* quite respectable, despite what Mama says. You probably know it, anyway." She dimpled up winningly at Jillian, inviting her confidence.

"Your mother has reason to feel uneasy about Mr. Mackinnon, then?" Jillian asked uneasily.

"Oh, well, not precisely . . . with her brother being a marquis and all . . ." Missy looked delightfully confused for a moment. "It's all supposed to be a great secret you know," she confided. "But if he truly is a spy then I think it the greatest joke, for if ever there were a more jolly, fun-loving creature than Jack, I vow I've yet to meet him."

This last was unheard by Jillian as the word *spy* hit her with the force of a hammer blow. So that was it, the reason for all his secrecy. My God! It couldn't be true. He couldn't be a traitor—she would not believe it. Not her brave, resourceful companion. Oh, Jack, Jack, how could you!

Jillian realized that she was sitting like a stock. She recovered from the blow enough to continue

213

the conversation. "Your mother's brother is a marquis, you say?" she asked rather absently, hitting upon one of the tidbits of information Missy had let fall.

"Oh, yes. Lord Letham. Did you not know?" Missy looked at Jillian curiously for a moment, but receiving no reply, launched into further confidences.

"Mama is in quite a pelter to fire me off and get back to that pack of brats of Jack's. They keep them in the country, you know. Not that I mind coming out a year early. It will be the greatest lark, I vow. Now you're here, I'm sure there will be no reason why Mama may not fly down to the country to see to the boys. You will be here to go about with me," Missy prattled on complacently, not noticing the strange look on Jillian's face.

Jillian's head was reeling. First she heard that Mackinnon was a spy. And now Missy was telling her that Jack had a "pack of brats" in the country. What could the girl mean?

Jillian swallowed with difficulty. "Jack—that is, your mother has children in the country?" she asked faintly.

"Oh, yes."

"How . . . how many?" Jillian forced out through suddenly stiff lips.

"I have three brothers. Edward, Marcus, and little Jack."

"Little Jack . . . ?" Jillian knew not why she was torturing herself, but she was in an agony to know.

"Yes. Named after Uncle Jack, you know," Missy replied sunnily.

Jillian could not believe her ears! She felt quite giddy with shock. Jack had some boys in the country and Lady Gilmore had to rush down to see to them, Missy said. They couldn't be *his* children, not his and Lady Gilmore's! That could not possibly be what the girl meant . . . could it?

The pain in her heart was so great that she could hardly keep from moaning aloud.

She had heard of the Devonshire miscellany, but this passed all bounds. And that such outrageous, scandalous goings-on could exist and be spoken of quite freely by a young girl of presumably gentle birth was beyond her understanding. Why, Missy openly acknowledged her three illegitimate half-brothers! What a ménage Mackinnon had sent her to! That shameless, depraved blackguard! The gall of the despicable scoundrel to send her here to his mistress, the mother of his three illegitimate sons! She would kill him, she surely would if he ever came within a mile of her again.

Jillian quickly rose to her feet, made some excuse to Missy, and beat a hasty retreat to her room there to dwell on all the wrongs she had suffered at the hands of that contemptible, infuriating man, Jack Mackinnon—a spy and a rake. Yes, and she had allowed herself to fall in love with him, too! She had tried and tried to convince herself that he loved her. He had said so, hadn't he? and declared quite insistently that he intended to marry her. And just when she had come round to the thought that she might try marriage again, even though he was an overbearing, infuriating monster . . . *this!* It was too much to bear.

Chapter 14

Jillian determined to visit Curzon Street the very next day to call on her former father-in-law and throw herself on his mercy. She didn't see how she could continue to reside in Mount Street after what she had learned. What was that rat Mackinnon about, anyway? she wondered. Did the foolish man expect her to wait for him at Lady Gilmore's and submit to being part of some sort of Anglicized harem? She was outraged at the very thought. Missy's information that he was a spy slipped from the forefront of her mind as the more painful knowledge of his dissolute behavior occupied all her thoughts.

Alas for her hopes to remove from Mount Street, her call was fruitless. Lord St. Erney was from home and not expected for two weeks. And she had had to abandon her best intentions to the contrary and dip into the money Mackinnon had given her in order to pay for the hackney carriage that had driven her to Curzon Street. If she had known beforehand that the journey was not above a mile, she would have walked. In any case, she saved half the fare by walking back, indulging herself in a fit of the blue devils as she did so.

'Twas plain that while she was forced to continue her residence in Mount Street, she could not decline to participate in Missy Gilmore's come-out. To have refused to help after all the gracious hospitality she had received while she had been with the Gilmores—why, Dolly had not begrudged her food, shelter, clothing, and friendship—would have branded her an ill-natured, ungrateful guest and rendered her acutely uncomfortable to boot.

Established in the Gilmore household as she was for the time being, Jillian found herself helplessly slipping into a new way of life, caught up in the social whirl as soon as an appropriate wardrobe was assembled for her. She protested against the expense, but to no avail. Dolly was very discreet, not to say devious, in persuading Jillian to have a few modestly elegant gowns made up by her own modiste.

After first being confused as to what her role was to be—chaperon to Missy or companion to Lady Gilmore—Jillian began to appreciate the friendship openly offered to her by her hostess and, as the days went by and she grew to know Dolly very well indeed, she found it difficult to credit Missy's talk of "a pack of brats" in the country. Dolly was just Jack's friend, that was all, Jillian assured herself. She tried to convince herself that she had misunderstood what Missy was saying. It *must* be a mistake to think that the regal Dorothea Gilmore was the mistress of a vagabond like Jack Mackinnon and that they had three illegitimate children!

And try as she might, she could not banish the man from her every waking thought. Jack had hinted over and over again that he wished to marry *her* and in her heart she wanted to believe him, however much she was angry with him for his continued absence and worried about his possible involvement with spies. There must be some good explanation for that, too, she thought in her calmer moments.

Dolly Gilmore had a wicked sense of the ridiculous and was ever ready to share her humor with Jillian. And underneath her polished social exterior, the lady was fiercely intelligent and exceedingly kind. She seemed to have a genuine interest in promoting Jillian's place in society. Whenever Dolly was entertaining visitors, Jillian was encouraged to sit with her and thus was she made acquainted with some of the social lionesses of the *ton* who would be entertaining young Missy and herself during the season. Why, Jillian thought with astonishment, she treats me almost as a sister! She wondered at the open, friendly warmth of the lady.

She noticed also that Dolly frequently tried to draw her out about the time she had spent with Mackinnon and her feelings for the man. Despite the lady's humorous quizzing and the smile in her eyes on these occasions, Jillian for the most part refused to be drawn, remarking only that it was an ordeal the sooner forgotten the better. She preferred not to reveal what was in her heart.

"I shall be driving down to the country tomorrow for a few days, Jillian, my dear," Dolly said one morning a sennight after Jillian had been with her. "I hope that you will agree to accompany

219

my daughter without my support for the next five days or so, if you don't find it too arduous a chore. I shall return in time to oversee the preparations for Missy's ball. Never fear that I shall land you with *that* daunting task, as well," Dolly laughed.

"Why, I shall be pleased to accompany your daughter if you so wish, my lady."

"Please . . . I thought we had agreed that you were to call me Dolly." Lady Gilmore smiled at Jillian. Her wide, engaging grin revealed the dimple usually invisible in her chin. "And I do wish. But is it what *you* wish to do? I would not ask you to do something you find irksome. Missy can be a sad romp, I well know."

Jillian assured her hostess that it would indeed be her pleasure to go about with Missy and then asked curiously, "Does something particular take you away?"

"Why, yes. Did you not know? My boys are at home and I am sadly missing them as I would wager they are not me! The are perfectly ready to go on with Perkins—their nurse, you know—and not give a thought to their mere mother. I must admit, she is a jolly soul and manages them well. I should not envy her their affection. Jack, of all people, put her in my way."

"Missy said something about Mackinnon's 'pack of brats,'" Jillian said on a catch of breath.

"Ah, she told you about them, did she?" asked Lady Gilmore warily. "Do you like boys, Jillian? If not, I hope you won't object too violently. Jack would be distressed if you were to find his 'boys' disagreeable. I daresay he wanted to tell you about them himself. I must see that they are being properly looked after as well."

Jillian sat numb, her heart breaking in her

breast. Dolly's speech brought all her suspicions to the fore once more. She had tried not to believe it. It had seemed so impossible that the well-bred Lady Gilmore could be the mother of Mackinnon's three by-blows. Yet Dolly's very words seemed to confirm Jillian's worst fears.

Dolly was such a dear. Undoubtedly she had been sadly taken in by Mackinnon's devilish charm at some point in her life and now was tied to him so strongly by their children that she could not break the connection, Jillian rationalized. Somehow she could not help but like her hostess — just as she continued to feel an unwilling and irrational affection for her unprincipled, detestable monster of deception.

It seemed apparent that by sending her to Mount Street Mackinnon expected her to accept the situation and not condemn them for it! But he was in love with *her,* she knew he was. Did he intend for her to continue to reside with his mistress and be willing to receive him when he finally did see fit to call on her? The very idea was so audacious that Jillian could well believe it of him.

As much as Jillian worried that her hostess was her rival for Jack's affections, she missed Dolly's sensible but stimulating conversation and found Missy's giddy company a bit wearing to her spirits, sunk in the doldrums as she was. Especially when Missy chattered on and on in the praise of one Jack Mackinnon. To the admiring seventeen-year-old, he was a Corinthian of the highest order, outshining all others in every manner of sport. He could do no wrong and every facet of his person was perfection.

It was quite trying to listen to Missy's comments about how Jack was "at home to a peg in every situation" and how his various horses, carriages, clothing, manners, indeed the very way he had of lifting his quizzing glass and saying "Dear me!" were "all the crack." Jillian had a hard time imagining the vagabond she knew even *owning* a quizzing glass, anyway, much less knowing how to use one to such effect.

"Jack told me I was slap up to the mark, Mrs. St. Erney. He winked at Mama and said she would have to beat off the suitors with a stick once I was brought out. He thinks the *ton* will consider me a toast once they clap eyes on me, you know," said the little minx, twinkling up at Jillian, "and he is always so top-of-the-trees himself that I vow he is in the right of it."

"Do you not consider that it would be more gratifying to your vanity if the *ton* were to make that judgment for themselves?"

Missy stared at her out of round blue eyes. "Whatever do you mean?"

"A girl should exhibit some modesty about her appearance, some humility, even if she is rag-mannered enough not to feel any, do you not agree? And not boast openly about her own attractions. Then the gentlemen may admire her without being forced to do so and will see how well brought up she is."

"Oh, but they know *that*. Papa is quite well to grass, and my dowry is quite respectable, you know."

"Then you must watch out for fortune hunters who praise your beauty just to turn your head, must you not?"

"Papa and Jack will protect me," Missy answered with great unconcern.

"*Both* of them?" Jillian asked in consternation. "Do you mean that they *know* one another and would act in concert?"

"Of course they know one another. How could they not when Jack is Mama's . . ." Missy was round-eyed again. She felt that this chaperon who had been foisted on her was a trifle touched in the upper works. "Oh, but perhaps you mean—" the widgeon clapped a hand to her mouth. "I am not supposed to even know about that, much less speak of it. Mama would *kill* me if she found out!"

"How can a young girl like you be exposed to such things?" Jillian was once more taken aback that Missy seemed perfectly aware of the clandestine nature of her parent's dealings with the treacherous Mackinnon and that she was even willing to cover up for them.

"Well, silly," she giggled, "they don't *know* that I know, of course. But it's perfectly obvious to anyone who has a brain in her head," the girl said cavalierly. "All their secret carrying on and passing notes written in secret code almost right under my nose. Why, Mama keeps them in her desk. I know where she keeps the key and I could easily read them if I wanted, but I give not a fig for their secrets," she said snapping her fingers, seeming to dismiss this dangerous, perfidious activity as a dull and boring adult game.

Yet again Missy's thoughtless, indiscreet chatter had stunned her chaperon. Notes from Mackinnon to Lady Gilmore were in her mother's desk, the girl had said. Jillian felt a burning curiosity to know if they were love notes. Everywhere she turned there seemed to be more and more evidence that Dolly and Mackinnon had enjoyed, and continued to enjoy, an illicit liaison.

But then why would Dolly welcome her so warmly if she were indeed Mackinnon's mistress. Perhaps Dolly knew she had nothing to fear from Jack's chance-met acquaintances. Or was Dolly bowing out of the picture so that Jillian could take her place—not that Jillian had any intention of being her successor. Certainly not! But what could be Dolly's motive in conducting a clandestine correspondence with Jack? Continued contact—though perhaps no longer amorous—with the father of her three sons? Jillian was at a loss to puzzle it out. Her endless speculation was fruitless and painful. She knew not what to think. . . . And where was the author of the devilish situation she found herself in anyway?

It was a sorely troubled, blue-deviled chaperon who accompanied the scatterbrained Missy on a round of social activities after Lady Gilmore had departed for Kent to see to the "pack of boys." At one such engagement Missy and Jillian met for tea at the home of Missy's particular friend, the Honorable Miss Eliza Wentworth. The gaggle of giggling girls was enough to distract Jillian from her woes for an hour or so. She was all ears even before the first pot of tea was ordered and poured out into the delicate Sèvres cups. No sooner did they sit down than the other girls began to question Missy about two gentlemen: Lord Letham, a mysterious gentleman wholly unknown to Jillian, and the other only too familiar—Mr. Jack Mackinnon.

Miss Mary Delderfield, the thin brunette, accepted her cup of the rich India blend and wondered casually, "When will your relative, the divine Lord Letham, deign to return among us, Missy? I declare, it seems an age since anyone has laid eyes on him."

"Soon, I should think," the chit said coyly, sliding her eyes to her chaperon as she stirred two lumps of sugar into her cup. "He's away on business. And, I declare, his particular business always takes such a monstrous amount of time. It's a wonder we ever have a chance to see him. I hope he will take me up in his high-perch phaeton when he returns, for everyone knows no one is a better whip than he."

Jillian wondered who this marquis was and what connection he bore to the Gilmores. She recalled that there was some mention that Lady Gilmore's brother was a nobleman, perhaps it was he Miss Delderfield spoke of.

"Ah, yes, the elusive marquis," breathed Eliza, holding her cup most daintily in her lap. "Such a distinguished man. So tall. . . ."

"So dark," gushed Miss Amanda Falquhar of the flaming red tresses.

"So dangerous, deadly, and devastating, I declare," interjected Mary.

"So *lethal!*" tittered Amanda.

"The fatal marquis—complete to a shade." Mary sipped her tea and lifted her thin brow insinuatingly.

"'Pon rep, he puts all others in the shade," Amanda laughed.

"Yes, quite casts them into oblivion," Mary topped Amanda's sally.

"Oh, 'tis a riddle!" Eliza said as she poured a

second cup of tea for Violet Richardson who was too busy eating to participate in the conversation as yet. "You mean a play on Letham's name, I suppose. . . . How naughty," she chided them even as she emitted a silvery laugh and turned to pass the biscuits to her red-haired friend.

Amanda refused the biscuits but accepted a thin slice of bread and butter before demanding agreement from the others: "Is Letham not the most accomplished Corinthian you have ever seen! I vow, he outshines all others!"

Jillian marveled that the girls' chatter should be so bold and full of gossip for ladies so young. And the way they treated one of their number was a bit catty.

"Actually, 'tith well-known that I shall retheive an offer from Jack Mackinnon when he returnth," Violet Richardson interjected as she reached for another biscuit. She was a girl with a charming lisp and a dumpy figure.

Jillian's teacup rattled in its saucer. What! I can't have heard aright, she thought to herself as she goggled at the girl. This surely was a preposterous bag of moonshine. Jillian couldn't imagine Mackinnon proposing to a schoolroom miss, at least not *this* schoolroom miss, she amended to herself as she looked round at the lovely Eliza, Missy, and Amanda. Miss Richardson was a young lady of stolid conformation—the girl had not lost one ounce of her childhood puppy fat and her unfortunate die-away airs and graces were not suited to her face or figure. They were more suited to a girl of tall, wispy bearing like the Honorable Miss Wentworth.

"'Twill be quite a feather in my cap when I bring your Uncle Jack up to thratch, Mithy,"

Violet said complacently, biting into her biscuit.

"Good heavens!" Jillian, shocked into unthinking speech, exclaimed aloud. "You mean the relationship is known?" Did all these seemingly innocent young ladies know of the arrangement between Jack and Dolly? Why else would Violet refer to him as Missy's "Uncle Jack"? Jillian was horrified.

"Of course the relationship is known. What would be the point in denying it?" Missy giggled. "It's not as if Uncle Jack were anyone to be ashamed of."

"*Au contraire,*" piped up Amanda. "If I had such an *uncle,*" she emphasized the word unnecessarily, "I should shout it from the house tops."

"But Violet," Missy protested. "How can you say you are betrothed to Jack? Mama thinks he is—" She stopped with a conscious look on her face and glanced at Jillian. "Ah, that he has other interests."

"Well, I didn't thay *betrothed* prethithly. But 'tith of a thertainty an offer ith forthcoming. Hith other intereth will thop when he marrieth me, you may be thure!" Violet stopped and pulled an intricately worked gold chain from beneath the bodice of her gown. "Look! If you muth know, he gave me thith on my lath birthday. He'th forever coming to our houth for dinner." She showed her necklace to each lady in turn. And each bent forward eagerly to see the golden medallion that hung from the chain. It was embossed with a coat of arms unrecognized by Jillian. Violet dropped the chain down inside her gown again, patting her bosom in satisfaction as she did so.

"But there is some connection through your father, is there not? I believe Jack's your godfather or some such thing, is he not, Violet?" Missy, persisted pugnaciously. "I make no doubt you plagued him for it most insistently."

"And he spends his time closeted with your papa when he visits, if I mistake not, not making up to *you*," Mary chimed in, taking spiteful satisfaction in scoring a hit. "They have political interests in common, I believe, and often consult together."

Violet chose not to respond to this last shaft, turning up her chin and looking toward Jillian as she reached for yet another biscuit. "I proteth, Mithith Thaint Erney, theth girlth are jutht jealouth, would you not agree?"

Jillian was saved from a reply as Eliza Wentworth addressed her, "More tea, Mrs. St. Erney?"

"I daresay your mama would know the truth of this preposterous claim, Missy," Mary cut in. "I believe Lady Gilmore is his nearest and dearest."

Jillian choked on her tea at such plain speaking. Why, these girls had just emerged from the schoolroom. Yet they were so worldly!

"Yes," Missy answered on a giggle, "Mama knows *all* Jack's business. I believe she would tell you he has other, er, game in mind. Violet is just air dreaming."

Much offended, Violet sniffed affectedly and had recourse to her vinaigrette. "Well! You will all thee, and then you'll be thorry for mocking me!" she promised darkly with a shake of her fair sausage curls. Clutching her lace handkerchief in her pudgy hand, she consoled herself by finishing off the plate of biscuits.

The evening after the tea party Jillian accompanied Missy to a ball at the home of one of the *ton*'s most fashionable society hostesses. There was a certain glitter to the occasion that Jillian enjoyed and, although she felt guilty, she loved wearing the new blue silk ball gown Dolly's modiste had made for her. Her low spirits lifted somewhat as she looked forward to the occasion.

But she got no respite for her sins. Young Missy attracted her fair share of attention and it was Jillian's lot to shepherd the girl about. She had her hands full preventing Missy from falling into mischief—it had proved to be a full-time job whenever they were out together. She could no longer wonder at Lady Gilmore's wishing to share the chaperoning duties with someone else. She realized that Dolly's infirmity often left her tired, and in some pain, with too much racketing about and felt a sisterly sympathy for her absent hostess as she tried to keep her eye on Missy.

Halfway through the evening she felt obliged to caution her charge. "Whatever are you about, Missy, flirting so outrageously with Mr. Blake? I overheard Lady Jersey, no less, remarking in a loud voice to her companion that the man is a gazetted fortune hunter. You must hint him away before your name becomes linked with his."

"Well, you needn't scold. I have already taken care of that. I told him *you* were a rich widow with a sizeable dot. He'll look to you now and you can give him a piece of your mind," the impertinent chit giggled behind her fingers.

Jillian gasped in surprise but before she could draw breath to express her indignation to the mischievous child, Missy floated away on the arm of her hostess's son, a most eligible young man. And soon she found the bandy-legged, sandy-haired

Blake in hot pursuit of herself.

"I am quite destitute, sir, despite what you may have heard," she informed him in no uncertain terms when he had cornered her in an alcove of the ballroom.

The dastard looked at her out of considering eyes. "If what you say is true, Mrs. St. Erney, then perhaps you would be amenable to accepting my protection for a period."

Why, the audacity of the man! Jillian thought outraged. He wasn't even hinting, he was actually offering her a carte blanche now that he had realized how she was circumstanced. "For I find your person highly desirable," Blake had the gall to inform her boldly. "I'm sure we could be everything and all to one another for a certain period."

With a mighty effort, Jillian restrained herself from slapping his blotched, calculating face. Who would have thought such a little man could be such a great rake? she thought angrily.

"Take yourself and your repugnant offer to the devil, you underbred mawworm," she ground out.

"Ah, I see how it is. You're after bigger game. Undoubtedly that spiteful cat Sally Jersey is spreading it about that my pockets are to let. Well, they are not so threadbare that I could not keep a creature such as yourself." He bowed supercili-ously and took himself off just in time to prevent Jillian from punching him in the nose and creating a shocking scene. Her temper was in tatters from the encounter when she came upon her charge.

"I saw Mr. Blake look sharp about and go haring off after you at supper," the saucy baggage said laughingly.

"How could you set that ill-bred rake onto me, Missy! I shall refuse to accompany you to Lady Carlisle's drum tomorrow."

This statement had the effect of wiping the smile from Missy's face and set her to offering a coaxing apology. "Oh, Mrs. St. Erney, I am ever so sorry to have caused you upset. He had been pestering me so. I thought it a great joke. . . . Do say that we may go to Lucy Carlisle's drum," the minx wheedled as she took hold of Jillian's arm and gazed soulfully into her face. "Please, please, beautiful, *kind*, Mrs. St. Erney."

Jillian weakened as she looked into that lovely, innocent face, but despite the wheedling, she stood firm. Perhaps the girl would learn not to play off her tricks quite so readily in future. Besides, Jillian had an errand of her own to perform next day. It was time and enough for Lord St. Erney to have returned from the country. Tomorrow she would seek him out and request his assistance. She felt that she was obliged to stay on in Mount Street until Lady Gilmore returned, but when Dolly was in residence once more, Jillian would depart.

She needed to start putting Jack Mackinnon and all those associated with him as far from her thoughts and her person as she possibly could. She needed to start healing her broken heart.

Jillian found when she returned to Mount Street that she could not get to sleep after the agitation of the evening. She went down to Lord Gilmore's library to choose a book that she hoped would have the desired soporific effect. As she scanned the shelves, she accidently brushed against a workbasket left near the comfortable leather chair Dolly liked to sit in to do her embroidery. A sheet of letterpaper fell out, and Jillian reached down to replace it.

Light from the candle she carried fell on the paper. The words "your own dear boy, Jack" stood out damningly on the stark white sheet. Jillian had no thought of stopping once she started to read—to have done so would have taken an almost impossibly Herculean effort, certainly one beyond her command. The letter was exceedingly revealing, for the most part, with its several phrases providing compelling evidence that the scoundrel Mackinnon was in league with Dolly Gilmore in a scandalous liaison. With ever-mounting hurt Jillian dwelt on the words referring to Dolly as his "dear love," and "for God sake, don't tell her anything about me or about our relationship! And I mean don't breathe a whisper of our current arrangements . . . it is vital that we keep the *ton* in the dark." So the relationship hadn't ended as Jillian had so fervently hoped.

She castigated the absent fellow with every damning phrase that she could think of, desperately trying to keep the pain at bay. But when she read that Mackinnon requested Dolly's assistance in some sort of plot against herself she found the wording rather puzzling. There seemed to be no possible explanation for this request.

And who was the "John" Mackinnon referred to? It must be Dolly's husband, Lord Gilmore. What mysterious and clandestine business was Lord Gilmore engaged in that Dolly was admonished to "hold her tongue." Were the Gilmores, then, in link with Mackinnon in this dreadful spy network that she suspected him of leading? Had Dolly gone into the country on clandestine business then? Jillian's heart positively fluttered as she considered the danger they all stood in should they be discovered.

She looked once more at the note and frowned. Mackinnon had had the unmitigated gall to sign the missive "your own dear boy, Jack"! Why, he sounded like a baby and Lady Gilmore his mother, and the *post scriptum* asking Dolly to look in on his boys for him when she visited her own three in Kent was the outside of enough to Jillian's already severely wounded sensibilities.

"Why, oh why, did I give in to temptation and read this damnable letter!" she groaned to herself. Her conjectures and suppositions had been bad enough, but to have incontrovertible proof in her hands was almost too painful to bear. It was said eavesdroppers heard no good of themselves, and she would add that those who snooped into private letters were similarly fated. What Mackinnon and Dolly had done was scandalous, but she was culpable for trespassing into their private correspondence.

But she wouldn't place any of the blame for the affair on Dolly. No, she shared a sisterly feeling for Lady Gilmore. Jillian was generous in making allowances for her friend—Dolly had undoubtedly fallen victim to the deceitful charm of the captivating rogue as she had herself. . . . Perhaps he had transferred his affection to herself, Jillian sighed, remembering his loverlike words, and actions, of their last night together, then caught herself up short. What had she been hoping, wishing? It was a mistake of the worst kind to trust the fellow an inch! First he had made love to her, then he had abandoned her. Surely her experiences with Reg had taught her that men were vile creatures, always ready to take advantage of women.

There was a great aching void in her midsection, but she would not give in to tears. They would do no good whatsoever. Well, she would cut him out of her heart if it took all her strength to do it, Jillian vowed as she pounded one tightly fisted hand into the palm of the other. She was quite glad she'd found out about his affair with Dolly and his "pack of brats" in time. It had certainly opened her eyes to what kind of reprobate he *really* was. It was just as she had always feared . . . he was not all that different from Reg. Except that Reg had never touched her heart.

Whether Jack intended to set her up in Dolly's place—as Jillian feared he meant to do—or not, it was even more imperative to leave Mount Street before the rascal returned. She must convince Lord St. Erney to provide her with some assistance until she secured another post.

As Jillian donned her hat and gloves next morning for her visit to her former father-in-law, Missy descended the stairs with a determined tilt to her little chin. This was their first encounter since their uncomfortable carriage ride home the previous evening, the young girl sulking in uncharacteristic silence all the way.

"Still in the boughs, Missy? I hope you will mind your manners next time and *think* before you tell such an outrageous faradiddle."

Missy ignored the lecture and tossed her golden head, setting the curls to bouncing. "I've received a letter from Mama this morning. But I shan't show it to you. She is still in Sussex and she says that Jack is with her and that he will accompany her back to town in a few days. But you're being so strict I shan't tell you any more about Jack!''

Despite her discovery of the previous evening, this news struck Jillian like a thunderclap. Jack! She would see Jack in a few days. He would be returning here—with his mistress! They were even now with their children. Cruel! Oh, how could he be so cruel! After letting her think that he was in love with her, saying that he wanted to marry her, refusing to take no for an answer! She had been a fool of the worse kind even to have believed him for a minute. Having had one rotter in her life should have been more than enough.

Yet, despite the overwhelming evidence that Dolly had been his mistress, Jillian had convinced herself that the affair between them was now over. And, worse yet, she had come to believe that somehow Dolly knew about and approved of Jack's interest in her, Jillian, and was doing her best to promote it. Perhaps Dolly suffered from a guilty conscience at having deceived Lord Gilmore all these years, Jillian speculated. She had seen John Gilmore's portrait hanging over the mantelpiece in the drawing room. Missy must have inherited her looks from her father, for he was a fair man with golden blond hair and bright blue eyes set in a kind, comely face. Lord John Gilmore was a very handsome man—quite a bit better looking, in Jillian's estimation, than the dark, harsh-featured Mackinnon. Why would Dolly want an outlaw like Jack when she had a nobleman such as Lord Gilmore for a husband? she had asked herself. It was too much of a conundrum for a woman of her limited experience of the world to solve.

Missy's news, intended to change Jillian's decision not to take her out to the Carlisle drum, with

235

the implicit threat that she would inform her mother otherwise, had the opposite effect. It hardened Jillian's determination to leave the girl to her own devices for a morning and made her own errand to see Lord St. Erney all the more urgent. She knew, too, that Missy was withholding information of vital interest to her, but she would not bargain with the little baggage. Jillian controlled her features and willed down the tightening in her throat that always signaled tears, and was able to address the incorrigible Missy with tolerable composure. "I shall be going out this morning. I trust that you will spend your time on improving your manners if you wish me to accompany you to the theatre this evening."

So saying, Jillian left the sulking girl standing on the stairs, staring down at her with rebellion in her eyes. But Jillian hadn't the time to placate Missy. She had to make other arrangements for accommodation with all possible speed—before Jack returned and all her anger at the scoundrel and good resolutions to tear him from her bruised heart evaporated at one lift of his mobile black brow.

She was followed on her walk to Lord St. Erney's house by the red-haired footman called Ewan who had been given the task to attend her whenever she ventured out otherwise unaccompanied. Lady Gilmore had insisted that the young footman was just the one to go out with Jillian "for he's another one of Jack's projects. Jack found him beaten and half-starved in a Glasgow slum, you know, and he would want Ewan to attend you. Ewan, of course, is devoted to Jack."

"Does Mackinnon make a habit of befriending such boys?" Jillian had asked, full of wonder at this new aspect of the baffling man. She would never have thought of him as a rescuer of destitute children. She did not think he had a soft enough heart.

"Why, of course! I thought you knew," Dolly had replied in some surprise with the characteristic arch of her dark eyebrow.

Chapter 15

Jillian strode along rather hurriedly in the bright spring sunshine, too preoccupied to take note of the trees and flowers just coming into bloom in the pleasant residential section she passed through. She remained oblivious to the sights and sounds of the busy streets of Mayfair as she passed peddlers and sweeping boys, ladies' maids out on errands for their mistresses and gentlemen out for a stroll who raised their hats to her. The gangly Ewan walked two paces behind her, not calling attention to himself but ready to spring to her aid, should the need arise. When she reached Lord St. Erney's house on Curzon Street, Jillian felt a momentary dismay at calling on her former father-in-law. Her marriage with Reg had not been happy, and the old man had not troubled himself about her after Reg's death. With a determined lift of her chin, Jillian bravely mounted the steps and knocked at the door.

The footman who answered was the same lad she had encountered on her previous visit. He invited her to step in while he took her request for an interview to Lord St. Erney. Jillian had never been inside this boyhood home of Reg's and stared around in wonder. The place was built on a grand scale, but the uncarpeted pink marbled hallway was bare. There were no tables, bureaus, paintings, or other furniture or accoutrements of any kind visible—just bare plastered walls and a curving grand staircase of unvarnished wood. Only the great sparkling chandelier, its candles unlit, of course, at this hour of the day, that hung above her head in the vaulted hallway gave any indication of wealth or indeed habitation.

To her relief, the footman reappeared quickly and relayed the information that Jillian was invited to step upstairs to take tea with Lord St. Erney. Ewan, who had not even a chair to sit upon while he awaited her, was left standing in the cold, austere entrance hall.

As Jillian stepped into the upstairs sitting room indicated by the footman, she was aware not only of a stooping, white-haired man rising to greet her with an impatient look on his face but of a young girl, clad all in pink tulle and white lace sitting in a chair at his side. The room had a minimum of furnishings, Jillian could see at a glance, but there was a roaring fire in the fireplace to add warmth at least, if not comfort, to the grand chamber.

"So, Jillian, you've called to see me, have you?" said Lord St. Erney, giving her hand a perfunctory shake. "This is Lady St. Erney, m'wife, you know." A satyr's grin spread over his wizened countenance. "Hee, hee. Given you a shock, ain't I." The old man chortled gleefully.

Jillian indeed was taken aback to know that the young girl sitting next to the man old enough to be her grandfather was in fact his new wife. Why, the new Lady St. Erney looked almost the spitting image of Missy Gilmore! Jillian gaped at her. The two were alike as two peas in a pod except that Lady St. Erney had red-gold hair instead of golden blond and green eyes instead of blue.

"I had no idea. Er, congratulations, my lady, my lord."

"Won't you be seated, Mrs. St. Erney. Oswald has told me that you are his son's widow," the girl said in a sweet, low-pitched voice. "Shall I ring for tea, dearest?" This was to her husband.

"Ain't she got pretty manners. No one would tumble to where I found her." The old reprobate winked at Jillian as he rubbed his hands together. "Birmingham, by gad! Who would have thought it? Chanced to look in at the assembly rooms there. Can thank my lucky stars I did. For there she was, pretty as a picture, the little minx, all decked out in her pink finery. Gave me quite a leveler, I can tell you. The little baggage led me quite a merry dance before she shackled me up tight in Parson's mousetrap," he chortled in glee at the memory. "You go ahead and ring for the tea, Millie, my love."

Jillian gazed at the bride in disbelief. Millie St. Erney didn't look as though she had the spirit to lead anyone a merry dance much less an elderly nobleman of Lord St. Erney's stamp.

"Now, Jillian, what brings you here? Pockets to let, m'girl? Ain't been outrunning the bailiff, have you? My annuity should keep you in fine fettle. Learn to economize, girl, economize." The clutch-fisted old skint put a finger beside his nose as he regarded her out of small, birdlike eyes.

Jillian was mortified. She knew not how to proceed. All the urgency to secure the means necessary to leave the Gilmore household fled. She

241

would not beg. "As it happens, Lord St. Erney, I am staying with friends in town—Lady Gilmore in Mount Street—and I thought I should pay you a call. I was here some days before—"

"Aye. So I've been informed. This is just a social call, then? Don't want any of my blunt, do you? Good thing. All tied up in Mildred here. And what if she presents me with another heir, heh?" He looked lecherously at the girl who colored up fiercely and dropped her eyes to her lap. "You never gave me a grandchild—failed in your duty there, m'girl. Had to look about me."

"But Randolph, your older son, should be the one to provide you with heirs," Jillian spoke up, unwisely flying to the defense of the young Millie.

"He don't care to remarry since his first wife died—the heiress, you know," the old man looked at Jillian with a nod and a wink. "Spends his time with a rackety crowd on the Continent. And Billy's in orders—'holy orders,' he calls 'em. Follows the popish precepts and refuses to marry."

Jillian did not care to pursue the conversation, nor did she care to pursue her mission. Her request was doomed to failure, she could well see, and only an ingrained sense of social decorum kept her in her seat to politely endure the brief tea-drinking ceremony. No doubt she would contrive on her own in some other way. She couldn't help feeling sorry for the new Lady St. Erney, though she knew it was none of her affair. But upon reflection, Jillian decided that the girl knew well what she was about when she had chosen to marry the elderly nobleman. No doubt Mildred would outlive her ancient spouse by many years and be a rich widow with a chance to please herself in a second marriage.

Jillian took her leave after the most perfunctory of social inanities were exchanged. Lord St. Erney let her know that he was off again to the country as soon as Lady St. Erney had replenished her wardrobe. He was anxious to get a start on his second family, he said gleefully, not sparing the blushes of either lady.

"Can give you the direction of a fine lady's modiste in Cheapside before you go," he said to his former daughter-in-law, "who don't charge the earth for all these silly female fripperies." He grasped the lace edging his wife's sleeve and chuckled in a lecherous manner. Jillian politely refused his offer and took her leave.

Blast it, she thought crossly. I'm well and truly trapped now. I have nowhere to go. . . . I shall just have to use some of Mackinnon's no doubt ill-gotten money to advertise for a position. But I'll pay him back, she vowed. With the characteristic determined tilt to her chin, she descended the steps of the St. Erney mansion with Ewan at her heels.

"I beg your pardon, ma'am," a bored voice interrupted the flow of her thoughts as she bumped into someone just as she reached the pavement. The stranger appeared to be on the point of ascending the steps to her father-in-law's townhouse. A fine gentleman, decked out in the latest fashion, stood raking her with cold eyes that then narrowed as he looked more closely, trying to recognize her.

"Ah, pardon me, ma'am. Have we not met somewhere before?"

Jillian barely glanced at him before she began, "Oh, no, I think not. . . ." She felt, rather than saw, Ewan bristle to attention behind her.

"Mrs. St. Erney, is it not? I can't believe my luck!" The well-dressed gentleman lifted his curly-brimmed beaver hat, revealing pale blond locks, and smiled at Jillian in anticipation of a greeting.

"I really don't think . . ." Jillian was puzzled, then enlightenment hit her. "But wait! Why, you're the gentleman from the stagecoach in Yelverton!" she exclaimed in astonishment. "However did you get away from the highwaymen?" The man bowed in acknowledgement, a wide smile lighting his handsome face. He did not choose to answer her second question for the moment.

"However did you come to be calling on my father-in-law, ah, my former father-in-law?"

"Why, to seek you out, dear lady. Why else? I learned your name from the roster of passengers carried by the coach company and could not rest until I found you."

"But why?" Jillian was mystified and vastly flattered.

"Oh, I had a hunch that you had not been killed after all that you were left for dead by those shockingly violent rapscallions."

"No, I was only battered and bruised. It was the most unpleasant experience of my life, I can assure you," Jillian said, knowing even as the words left her mouth that somehow it was not quite true. In fact it was a howling bouncer. She had never had a more exciting adventure in her life!

"And that rascal who was left with you . . ." Here several passersby jostled them on the pavement and the gentleman extended his arm. "Allow me to escort you. Are you on your way to Bond

Street to visit the shops, perhaps?"

"No. Oh, no," Jillian said, embarrassed. "I'm afraid you mistake, sir. I do not *live* with Lord St. Erney. I have been paying him a visit merely. I reside in Mount Street. I am on my way back there now."

"Ah, how fortuitous for me! You will allow me to accompany you, will you not?" he inquired with such an appealing smile spread across his fair countenance that Jillian found it impossible to refuse him. Though she did glance back to be certain that Ewan was still with them as she set off on the stranger's arm.

"Thank you, Mr. . . . ?"

"Did I not introduce myself in the coach? How remiss of me." And careless, he thought to himself. "Peters, Warren Peters at your service, my dear Mrs. St. Erney. After our mutual misadventure I feel that we are quite old friends. Indeed, I feel a kinship for *everyone* who shared that unpleasant experience with us."

Jillian began to feel uncomfortable at his familiarity, and little prickles of alarm ran down her spine. She glanced once more at Ewan trailing behind them.

"Tell me, ma'am," Peters continued with some urgency, "how have you come to be here? Were you rescued soon after the holdup? Did you see what happened to the other passenger—that ill-mannered and drunken Scot who was thrown out of the coach? He was shot, I believe. The highwaymen were convinced they had killed him. I, er, overheard them boasting of it before they released me. You are in a position to know. Was he in fact shot dead?"

Jillian, caught off guard, did not perceive the

impropriety of this inquisition by a stranger and could only address the last of his barrage of questions.

"Oh, he was most certainly shot," she answered with a sorrowful look on her face as all her grievances against Mackinnon were brought freshly to mind. She missed Peters's small, satisfied smile.

"What became of his body? Was it ever recovered?"

"I don't know what became of him," she answered truthfully.

"Crow's bait then, we must assume."

"Oh, yes, the scoundrel undoubtedly deserved to be left for crow's bait," she muttered angrily under her breath. Peters took her low-voiced mumble for agreement with his assessment.

"You were rescued . . . ?" Peters asked leadingly.

"Yes, er, I was picked up by a farmer who was driving to market the next day."

"You spent the night on Dartmoor, then?"

"Yes." Jillian shivered. "It was cold, wet, and altogether frightful. I know not how I survived the dreadful experience. But what of you, Mr. Peters? You haven't told me how you got away from the highwaymen. They kidnapped you, did they not?"

"Indeed they did. Evidently I was not the man they were looking for and they decided to let me go." Jillian looked an inquiry at this statement. Had it indeed been that easy to make his escape, she wondered incredulously.

"When they unknowingly shot the rogue who was their rightful quarry, they lost his body when they dumped him on Dartmoor. So careless of them. A pity for the rest of us, though," he commented.

"Pity?" Jillian wondered in some confusion at this unnatural statement. Had he no sympathy for a fellow passenger, then?

"Pity they did not realize that at the time. It would have saved the rest of us a most unpleasant experience."

"And you sought me out to assure yourself of my safety?"

Peters bowed, "That, too," he had the audacity to say with a flirtatious look on his face.

"Well, here we are, Mr. Peters." Jillian had increased her pace with every sentence the man uttered and found herself back in Mount Street in short order. She began to think him a decidedly shady character. "Thank you for your company." She pulled away from his arm and extended a gloved hand to him. "I am glad that you survived the holdup and suffered no unpleasant consequences as a result of your kidnapping."

He tipped his hat to her as he said, "May I call to take you walking in the park tomorrow?"

"I am sorry, Mr. Peters, you are laboring under a misapprehension. My time is not my own." Jillian fobbed him off as best she could and turned to go inside before he could make further awkward inquiries. Jillian didn't notice, but after seeing her enter the house, Ewan kept Peters under narrow observation before taking himself round to the mews at the back of the Gilmore residence. The alert footman was not surprised to see Peters cast a speculative glance after Jillian's retreating form— then Ewan saw an unpleasant smile cross the man's face. He took out a notecase and seemed to be scrawling something down on a piece of paper as he glanced up once more to note the number of the house. Ewan, being a lad used to living on the

247

streets by his wits, duly stored up his interesting observations and decided to bring them to the attention of his employer at the earliest opportunity.

And Ewan was not the only one observing the meeting of Jillian and her unknown escort. Missy, on the lookout for her chaperon's return, had been peeping through the curtains of the drawing-room window and saw her approaching with the stranger. As soon as Jillian gained the hall, she was greeted by her charge and the question, "Who was that man?"

Jillian, startled, dropped her bonnet onto the floor. Not knowing how much her mother had told Missy about the unfortunate circumstances leading to her presence among them, Jillian answered cautiously, "A chance-met acquaintance merely."

"What would Jack say to your casting out lures?"

Jillian's lips tightened. "I beg your pardon? How dare you insinuate such a nonsensical thing, young lady! Jack Mackinnon has nothing to say to the matter." She shook her finger at Missy. "Your manners appear to show no improvement since I left you this morning. I fear we shall have to cancel our engagement to the theatre this evening."

Missy was immediately contrite and prettily begged pardon, excusing herself on the grounds that she had only been joking, for "as you say, what would *Jack* have to say about anything you do or anyone you see, anyway?" As this impertinent question was unanswerable, Jillian let it go, merely reminding Missy to try and mind her manners and comport herself with more decorum in future.

The evening brought a light mist, but the two ladies who mounted into the Gilmore town carriage for the trip to Drury Lane thought nothing of it. Each was pleased to be going out: Missy because she was a giddy young thing and any evening spent at home during her Season she would characterize as sadly slow; Jillian because she rather thought she would enjoy the theatre, and besides, she didn't want to be left alone with her troubling thoughts. They always revolved endlessly around her absent, black-haired tormentor who had affected her to such an extent that she didn't know whether she loved him or hated him.

She didn't understand the man. When she had been with him, half the time he had been tender and loving and the other half maddeningly teasing and odiously offensive. He was a rogue and a spy, but apparently his vagabond appearance was only a disguise, for he seemed to have some standing in the *ton*. If one believed half the nonsense spouted by Missy and her friends, he was quite a paragon . . . quite a catch, even.

He was involved with another woman for pity's sake! Jillian had to keep reminding herself. . . . And wouldn't he just smile that heart-stopping smile of his to know how disturbed she was! He would cock an eyebrow and say, "Thinking of me, sweetheart? How flattering." Oh! she could kick him in the shins if she could conjure him up before her at that moment.

Jillian succeeded in banishing the wretch from the forefront of her mind during a spirited performance of *The Taming of the Shrew* at Drury

Lane. She had read the play, of course, but never seen it performed. The ending was not exactly to her taste—Kate had become very poor-spirited, in her opinion, to allow Petruchio to browbeat her into submission. Well, it was just like a man to write such a thing.

Missy had behaved with a mixture of pleasant high spirits and demureness whenever she felt Jillian's eyes upon her, and the two were in charity with one another as they left the theatre. It had come on to rain somewhat more heavily as their carriage was called and they waited in the foyer. Ewan came with an umbrella, and Jillian motioned for him to shelter Missy under it first as he led the girl to the carriage; she would follow. Ewan handed Missy up and had just turned around to see that Jillian hadn't waited for him to bring the umbrella to cover her and was stepping toward the carriage. Suddenly she was grabbed from behind by a man in a flowing black domino. The man clamped a hand over her mouth, giving her no chance to scream as she was dragged away into the shadows. Ewan dropped the umbrella and rushed to her rescue only to be felled from behind by an unseen blow to his bright red noggin.

Chapter 16

Jillian came to with a splitting headache some hours later. Kidnapped again, she thought wrathfully. And where was she this time, she wondered. She could only remember that she had been grabbed suddenly outside the theatre, then she had known no more as a heavy object came down on her head, rendering her quite insensible.

She looked about the dark room where she now sat bound hand and foot, feeling sick. Every movement seemed to set off a wave of dizziness behind her eyeballs. Tied and gagged but not blindfolded, she was seated on the floor in a small, high-ceilinged room with dirty rags littering the entire area. The room had the musty, salt-tinged smell of a wharfside warehouse—disused, she guessed. A stub of a candle sat precariously on a broken crate, its flame guttering in the melting wax. The amount of light it provided was minimal, but it did serve to cast flickering shadows on the walls that set Jillian's heart to hammering against her ribs. Why had she been abducted? Think, Jillian, think! she commanded herself. It must have something to do with that scoundrel

Jack Mackinnon. He was a blasted spy, wasn't he? And now someone had associated her with him. . . . And where was he, anyway? her mind screamed silently.

She heard a sound at the splintered door directly across from where she sat pinioned. Her heart caught in her throat as the handle slowly twisted. The door creaked open and a masked man, caped, booted, and spurred, stepped into the room. He swaggered forward, swung his cape over one shoulder, and dropped to one knee in front of her.

"So, my dear Mrs. St. Erney, we meet again. And what have you to tell me this time? No more of your evasions, I think."

She knew that voice. Why, it was Warren Peters! What was he talking about? And why had he kidnapped her?

He leaned forward and with black-gloved hands removed the gag from around her head. Her mouth felt dry and unpleasant as her breath rasped in her throat. She couldn't make her tongue move to give him the rating he so richly deserved.

"Now, Mrs. St. Erney. Where is the man who calls himself Jack Mackinnon? We know he isn't dead. The area was thoroughly searched after you and he left. You were traced to Moretonhampstead, then to a small cabin outside that town. He escaped by means unknown and took two of our men. But where is he now and what is he up to?"

"I . . . I don't know what you're talking about," Jillian croaked. Her mouth and lips felt as though they were cracked and bleeding from the rough treatment they had received. She couldn't take in Peters's words, her head was in such a whirl.

"Oh, come, come, Jillian, my dear! We know that you were sharing Mackinnon's bed when you were together. You must know his business as well. We are convinced, you know, that you are in league with him. My superiors will take it ill—very ill indeed, Mrs. St. Erney—if you refuse to cooperate. You have information that is very valuable to me." He ran his gloved hand caressingly down her cheek. Jillian thought she had never felt such a thrill of terror. "You can—and *will*—tell me where Mackinnon is and what he has discovered about us."

"I don't know! I don't know anything about the beastly man," Jillian cried breathlessly. "He didn't tell me what he was about. I haven't seen him in weeks. I know nothing—you must believe me!"

"How can you say so, when we know that you're staying in Mount Street with his—" They were interrupted by a knock on the half-opened door followed by the entrance of an unsavory individual whom Jillian, with horrifying clarity, recognized as Sam, the highwayman who had made his amorous intentions concerning her person unmistakably clear during the holdup.

"Ye wanted Sam 'ere to 'elp ye wit the gentry mort, surr?"

"No, not yet, you fool! Leave us be—get out!"

"*You!* You were involved in the holdup! You told me yesterday that you were a victim along with the rest of us. I . . . I don't understand what's going on here. Sam, Daniel—you are in league with those men?" she asked Peters.

"Idiots! Fools! But they will prove their usefulness now, Jillian, my dear, if you will not cooperate any other way," Peters said threateningly.

"I don't know anything. You must believe me! Don't send that man back in here! Please!" Jillian begged, terrified that Sam would be called back.

"Hmm. I don't believe you, you know. I shall give you half an hour to reconsider. Then," he paused and smiled sinisterly, "we'll just have to let Sam see if he can succeed in convincing you to tell us what you most certainly know."

Peters began gagging her again, saying, "Think carefully, now. I'm sure you will remember many things that Mackinnon let drop . . . even in his sleep, perhaps, hmm? if you just put your mind to it."

Jillian was left shaking in terror—and fury. That damn Mackinnon! she thought, infuriated. He had caused her more heart-burnings, more emotional upset, and more fear in less than one month than Reg had done in four miserable years of marriage!

The minutes passed second by agonizing second for Jillian. Beads of perspiration formed on her brow as she thought feverishly of some bogus information, some false trail—call it lying, my girl, she said to herself—that sounded plausible enough to feed to the men and have them believe it.

No more than fifteen minutes could have passed by Jillian's calculations when the door opened again and the hated Sam came into the room with a leering grin on his gap-toothed, walleyed face. A scream formed in her throat as the foul creature bent down beside her and pressed a loathsome kiss on her cheek. His breath reeked of gin, nauseating Jillian behind her gag as his hands went to the bodice of her cloak. He began to unfasten it with rough, impatient hands. Jillian felt she would faint.

Just as her eyes began to roll back in her head, she heard the sound of a loud crash outside the door and the retort of a pistol split the air. Sam jumped to his feet but not in time to avoid the creature who hurled himself out of the darkness beyond and plowed into him. The two fell to the floor grappling with one another in a great tangle of twisted arms and legs. The sound of flesh hitting bone came unmistakably to her ears as one of the combatants pounded the other with his fist. Jillian, watching the melee wide-eyed, could not tell who had the upper hand. Who was the second man? Not Peters, she was sure. This man was taller and built on sturdier lines than her kidnapper. She could not be sure that he intended to rescue her, either. Perhaps it was merely a falling out among thieves and she was the prize.

There was a sickening sound as the larger man once more sent his fist crashing into Sam's face and at the same moment the candle flame flickered and went out. Then all was quiet for a moment before Jillian heard the movement of the larger man as he disentangled himself and stood up.

Once more Jillian tensed as she felt someone touch her. A man's hands ran over her body—her pulses raced. The man's breath was coming in gasps from his recent exertions as he tried to loosen the bonds biting into her wrists, Jillian realized. Her pulses slowed somewhat—then the unseen man paused, brought his head near to hers, and kissed her gently on the same cheek that had been befouled by the villain Sam moments before. Jillian pulled back and twisted away from this new assailant, though she knew her struggles against his superior power were hopeless in her bound state.

"Don't struggle so, sweetheart. It's only me." Jillian made inarticulate sounds behind the gag as the man fought to remove it. As the rag was pulled free, the shameless creature bent to take her lips in a hot and fierce kiss. She would have none of it.

"Mackinnon!" she spat out when she had succeeded in freeing her mouth from his. "I might have known . . . !"

"Yes, so you might, my heart." She saw the flash of his white teeth as he grinned down at her in the dark.

"Unconscionable blackguard, you debauched libertine! Rake! Traitor! Devil's spawn!" Jillian was so astonished—and grateful—to see him again that she felt herself in danger of losing all control and bursting into tears of relief on his shoulder. She hurled insults at him instead. "Shameless, wicked, heartless deceiver! Ohhh! I cannot think of names black enough to call you!"

Jack was busy loosening the bonds tying her wrists even as she continued to rip up at him. He put her failure to greet him as her savior down to overwrought nerves and laughed softly under his breath.

"Well, you seem to have come up with every name in the book, sweetheart," he laughed down at her. Jillian could see the familiar flash of his white grin even in the gloom that enveloped the room as he bent to kiss her again, more tenderly this time. She allowed him to press his lips to hers for a moment, but when she felt his tongue seeking entrance to her mouth, she damped down her treacherous response and pulled back. The ropes binding her wrists fell off, and he pulled her hands forward and began to chafe them. "Pluck to the backbone, as always. I expected you to be having the vapors by now. . . . Did those villains harm you much?"

"Oh, no! Not at all! How could you think they did me any harm? Why, they treated me as though I were a priceless piece of chinoiserie that they were conveying to Prinny!" she replied sarcastically.

He laughed. "Did you receive my letter?"

"What letter?" she asked suspiciously.

"I sent you a *very* private message while Dolly and I were in Kent. I made sure she enclosed it with her letter to Missy. Did the chit not give it to you?"

"So *that's* what the minx meant . . ." Jillian recalled Missy's cryptic words of the morning, then she also recalled that Jack had just admitted he had been with Dolly in Kent and flashed hotly. "I trust the missive contained abject apologies for your unconscionable behavior toward me and your solemn promise to reform your black character in future!"

"Ah, my shrew, how I've missed you!"

"Missed me! The *deuce* you have!"

"Indulge me for once, love. Do you suppose we could skip the preliminaries and kiss and make up without the fight first?"

She ignored his wistful request. "How can you have the cheek to say such a hoaxing thing to me after all your broken promises, you weasel!" As Jillian spoke, Jack reached over and found the still warm candle and relit it with his flint. He turned back to see his Jill fiercely scowling.

"What broken promises?" Jack looked blank. Then as he continued to rub and caress her wrists and fingers, he gazed into her eyes with a conning look on his face. The moment she saw the ready laughter spring to life in his warm, dark orbs,

257

Jillian's temper soared accordingly.

"All of them," she said comprehensively. "And your mistress—have you missed her, too?"

"Ah, you are my only mistress, sweetheart—the mistress of my heart! And of course I've missed you. I've just said so, haven't I?"

"Humph! A likely story! And what about your children? Have you missed them . . . and their mother?" Jillian shook her hands free of his grasp and pushed him farther away even as she continued her diatribe. Jack judged it wisest to let her harangue him to her heart's content. He had plenty of time to kiss her into submission later.

"Heh? What children would those be?"

"The ones Lady Gilmore was so anxious about and rushed off to see were being properly looked after."

"Oh, ho! So you've found out about my boys, have you? I hope you don't object."

He seemed to be teasing her, but Jillian found herself gasping for breath, so irate was she at his joking about the matter. "Not object . . . ?" Her mouth opened and closed in rapid succession, like that of a fish out of water. She was too outraged, and exhausted, to upbraid him further. Was Mackinnon so depraved that he could openly admit to fathering Lady Gilmore's sons and then laugh about his own by-blows? *And* expect that she would have no objections! The man was crazed, as mad as a hatter, so far gone in the arts of seduction that he could not see what those with moral standards of decency could object to in his unconscionable behavior!

"Is *everything* a joke to you?" she asked ironically.

"I know you will find it difficult to credit—but I

am known for the seriousness of my disposition in some quarters."

"Balderdash! Who told you that I had been kidnapped? How did you know where to find me? Devil take it, Mackinnon, I thought you were in Kent. How did you get here so quickly?"

He laughed. "It was Ewan, love. Did you not know? The clever lad has been keeping an eye on you for me. His assistance has been invaluable; I shall reward him accordingly. I was afraid the villains would try anything to get their hands on . . . well, something that is of vital importance to His Majesty's government." Jillian shivered. "The information is in the proper hands now—and you are safe, love. No more abductions, I promise. My men have rounded up our kidnappers in Plymouth and here in London—Peters, the highwaymen—the lot. There's just Samuel here to be carted away."

"Is it true? Are you a spy?" she asked disbelievingly.

"Well . . . I'm a government agent, sweetheart. You might call it being a 'spy,' but I prefer to think of myself as a 'minister of information.'" He was laughing at her again, Jillian knew. All this time he had been working for the government and his country, and she had thought him a desperate criminal! Well!

She glared at him ferociously. He had refused to tell her anything about the business all along—she was not judged worthy of his trust, was she? It was her country, too, she wanted to shout. But then in the dim light of the candle lighting the room, she finally noticed the ugly-looking gash across his cheek that was dripping blood all over the both of them.

"Oh, Jack, you're hurt!" Jillian cried in distress as he untied the bonds at her feet. As soon as he had finished with the last of the ropes binding her, she tried to reach up to wipe the blood away only to find that her hands would not obey her. She couldn't seem to get them to work; they were still numb from the tightness of the bonds. Jillian turned her face aside to hide tears that arose unbidden to her eyes; the effects of her ordeal, seeing Jack again, and to see him hurt suddenly overwhelmed her.

"It's just a scratch, Jill sweetheart," Jack said as he reached to take her hands in his again to chafe them back to warmth. He leaned forward to try to kiss her cheek again and then to whisper, "I meant to get back to you much sooner, sweeting, but I was prevented."

"Just leave me alone, Mackinnon," she said fiercely in a low voice that shook with anger and nervous reaction.

He reached out a finger to run it along her averted cheek. "My dear love, I have no time to explain things to you now. I'll see you soon. We'll enjoy another of our comfortable cozes, and you can pile on the insults I'm sure you've been storing up."

He briefly kissed her lips then stood up and turned to his men who had congregated outside the door waiting for further instructions. Inevitably, Jillian thought, his first order was to his faithful lackey. "Take Mrs. St. Erney back home to Mount Street, will you, Molesworth. You may tell Lady Gilmore that John's information was correct; he should be with her soon now. All else is satisfactorily in hand."

"I do not need your interference, Mackinnon. I

can take care of myself, you know," Jillian shouted at his departing back, but he was soon out of earshot and there was no further opportunity to come to cuffs. She submitted to the inevitable with as much grace as she could muster and allowed Mr. Stanley Molesworth to take her "home."

Jillian returned to Mount Street exhausted, her emotions in the usual turmoil after her sparring match with Jack Mackinnon. She didn't dare admit that she had been so exhilarated to see him, so exultant when he called her his "love" that she had almost fallen on his neck in gratitude. Molesworth had seen her properly to the Gilmores' door this time, with every attention to her comfort.

Dolly, who had returned from the country with Jack when Jillian and Missy were at the theatre, was waiting with Mrs. Whitby to fuss over her when she arrived. They had exclaimed over her as they bound up her wrists with a soothing salve and fed her on hot tea laced with a little brandy. Their solicitous attention made her feel treacherously close to tears. They were so kind whilst she had been wishing the whole Gilmore household at the devil. And despite everything she had learned about Dolly, even if she had been Mackinnon's mistress, Jillian couldn't help but like her a great deal. It was strange, she mused, but Dolly seemed to share some of the same characteristics that drew her to Jack, with her roguish sense of humor and strong character. Why, they even looked alike with their black hair and warm brown eyes.

It was typical of the man to make mock of them both by arranging for them to shelter beneath the same roof. Such an idea would occur only to such a mad monster of teasing provocation. He would think it a great joke, the scheming wretch!

It was long past noon the next day when Jillian arose. After her prolonged and restful sleep, she found herself fully recovered physically, if not emotionally, from her ordeal. Dolly took her aside when she finally came downstairs to explain in some measure why Jack thought she had been kidnapped.

"Jack has said that I may enlighten you about last night's events."

"Oh? Mackinnon has given his lordly permission for me at least to learn why I was hit over the head, kidnapped by a gang of thugs, tied up, gagged, threatened, imprisoned, and terrified out of my wits, has he? How magnanimous of him!" Jillian seethed sarcastically.

Dolly repressed her smile at Jillian's show of temper, thinking Jack had met his match at last. He would have to take care or he would find himself living under the cat's paw.

"Jack and John—my husband, you know— were entrusted by the government with a most sensitive and secretive job." Jillian, all attention now, raised her brows at Dolly's revelation. "They were given the dangerous job of rooting out a nest of spies who were passing information to French agents somewhere in the vicinity of Plymouth. They managed to intercept the coded messages the spies were using, and Jack was on his way to London with this crucial information the night you met him on the stagecoach. John remained behind in Plymouth to keep the suspects under surveillance while Jack was to deliver the code to

262

the cryptographers in London who were to decipher it.

"Unfortunately, the traitors discovered that Jack had stolen the code and the highwaymen who set upon you were in the employ of these dangerous men. I take it they mistook their man when the stage was held up—Jack being in disguise at the time no doubt accounted for their mistake. Peters was some little fish—a thief, who, when they had mistaken him for a government agent, fell in with them and agreed to act as their cover man to help find Jack. When you and Jack were kidnapped in Moretonhampstead, the spies were attempting to recover the code, but Jack had hidden it well—in the lining of your cloak, he tells me." Dolly looked at a fuming Jill, and a humorous grin tugged at the corners of her mouth. "He is resourceful, this mad Jack of ours, you must admit."

"Indeed!" Jillian exploded. "It seems he was a more deceitful knave than even *I* gave him credit for!"

Dolly laughed. "Jack passed the information on to his colleague David Torrance whom I take it you met in Moretonhampstead after you had been kidnapped the first time. Jack dealt with your kidnappers, then joined John. First they waited in Plymouth for the next informant to show up, then they rounded up the traitors there and jailed them after thorough questioning about their contacts and activities here in London. John was instructed to oversee the port in Plymouth to make sure that no further messages were smuggled in or out there.

"Jack was ordered to lie low until he received further orders. He rode to Kent to join me, bringing the latest news, while he awaited his orders. He was on tenterhooks to be off to London, and I think it was more than getting this business settled that kept him in a high state of impatience the entire time," Dolly said laughingly with an arch look at Jill.

"David Torrance, meanwhile, was able to deliver the cryptic message safely to the government ministry. Once the code was deciphered and the Plymouth gang had been forced to supply certain information about their 'friends' here in London, Jack and his cohorts were able to move in on those in the government who were supplying the information. Fortunately for the prime minister, one of the members of his cabinet was not involved, as had been much feared. It was a secretary in the War Office who had access to all manner of sensitive information who proved to be the brains behind the operation. The lot of them were rounded up last night, and you may rest easy, my dear: they are all now securely imprisoned in Newgate," Dolly concluded.

"And Mackinnon . . . ?" Jillian despised herself for asking.

Her hostess answered with twinkling eyes. "Was here earlier to see that all was well. Gone to his lodgings now, I'm afraid. He has orders to—" Dolly caught herself up short. Momentarily forgetting Jack's instructions to keep Jillian in the dark for her own safety, she had almost revealed that he had gone to Plymouth once more with a party of government agents to join John and bring the men under arrest there back to London. "But I mustn't let my tongue run away with me. Rest you easy, my dear, he will return in good time for Missy's ball on Saturday."

"And Lord Gilmore . . . ?" Jillian questioned.

"Is well and will soon return home, also." Dolly evidently intended to tell her no more.

As it was Tuesday already, this meant that it would be only four days until she saw Jack again. "But what am I thinking of!" Jillian castigated herself roundly. Never mind that Mackinnon had been working on behalf of his country—he had proved a veritable hero, in fact, and not a foreign spy after all. That didn't change things as far as his behavior to herself and Dolly was concerned. A man could evidently be a hero and a scoundrel at one and the same time, she huffed. Jillian vowed she must be gone by the time he returned and never look on his black countenance again, else she would forget all her good intentions and cast herself on his chest in an ecstasy of delight to see him once more.

Her hostess, seeming to read her mind, tried to forestall her. "There will be time enough to have a ball dress commissioned for you. I thank my lucky stars that Missy's is completed already, else we should have no end of pets and tantrums."

"Oh, Lady Gilmore, I don't think I should attend Missy's ball. 'Twould be inappropriate for me to appear at such an important family occasion."

Dolly raised her eyebrows at Jillian's attempt to avoid the ball. "You weren't planning to run away before Missy's ball, were you? And I thought it was agreed that you were to call me Dolly. I shall fear I am in disgrace else," the good lady teased as her eyes laughed at Jillian's predicament. "Think of me as a sister," she added with a meaningful lift of her shapely black brow. "For we quite think of you as part of our family already. And you must give my husband a chance to meet you, you know. If all goes well, we shall expect to see him by Friday at the latest."

The four days before the great event passed in a whirl for Jillian. She did prepare a notice for the newspapers, advertising her availability to serve as companion to some elderly lady. Hoping it would bring her luck, she used the same wording that had secured her her former happy position with Mrs. Bakewell: "Gentlewoman seeks post as companion to genteel lady of mature years." As she had not the means to leave the Gilmore residence until she secured such a post, she steeled herself to see Mackinnon one last time. She stored up a thousand things to say to him. He deserved one last good tongue-lashing before he disappeared from her life forever, she vowed.

Missy's friends gathered at the Gilmore residence on the Thursday before the eagerly awaited ball. Dolly asked Jillian to sit in for her as hostess since she had a million and one things to do before the festivities on Saturday. The group of girls were in the habit of meeting frequently, Jillian already knew, ostensibly to take tea, but in fact to exchange tidbits about the newest fashions, tear up the reputations of their absent friends, exchange the latest *on-dits*, boast about their most recent conquests, and generally try to outdo one another in every area dear to the hearts of young debs fresh on the *ton*. The unfortunate Violet Richardson came in for the most ragging when Jack Mackinnon's name was mentioned.

"Have you heard from your *betrothed* lately, Violet?" Mary Delderfield questioned archly.

"That ith a private matter, Mary." Violet puckered up, trying to stand on her nonexistent dignity but unwittingly giving Mary and Amanda Falquhar scope for their needle-witted remarks instead. The Honorable Miss Wentworth remained composed and aloof throughout.

"Which means that you haven't. Just as we all thought. I assumed Jack would have returned to town by now, Missy," Mary probed.

"Oh, yes, he was here earlier in the week. He promised Mama that he would be sure to attend my ball," Missy said blithely.

"Oh, good! I should love to have a dance with him." Amanda clapped her hands. "La, I shall have to look to my wardrobe for my most alluring gown—not that my mama will let me wear anything daring, of course," she pouted as she remembered her mother's strictures. "Just wait until next year when I'm no longer a deb. Then she will no longer be able to forbid me the styles I favor." Amanda shook her bright locks at them, knowing that even if red hair was unfashionable, hers was the best figure among the lot of them.

"What will you wear, Eliza?" Missy asked her sophisticated friend. All the girls rather admired the cool, statuesque beauty.

"Oh, something demure in lace, I suppose," Elizabeth said languidly as she gracefully lifted her teacup to her lips. She had more suitors than the other girls but was in no hurry to choose among them this year.

"You are so elegant nothing looks *demure* on you!" Missy gushed.

"And what shall you wear to captivate your beau, Violet dear?" Mary turned her feline attention on Violet once more.

"Mama thayth my pink thatin lookth pothitively perfect on me," Violet replied complacently.

"Oh, Violet, no!" Amanda giggled. "Jack Mackinnon won't be allured by a dress like that! Why, that gown positively makes you look like one of Gunter's iced confections—a pink one." The girls all laughed while Jillian regarded their cutting remarks disapprovingly, feeling sorry for the silly, buffleheaded Violet.

"He is a gentleman who prefers something much more sophisticated and . . . and *dramatic*, would you not agree, Mrs. St. Erney?" Amanda turned to Jillian.

"Oh, I would say there's no accounting for what Mr. Jack Mackinnon will prefer or what he will do next. The gentleman has odd tastes, not to mention a most peculiar sense of humor, to say the least." Jillian couldn't resist venting some of her pent-up feelings although she knew that it was dangerous to discuss him with these girls. She felt it was not her place to warn them away from the scoundrel, no matter how much she was tempted to do so.

"Do you *know* him, then, Mrs. St. Erney?" the watchful Mary exclaimed, quite curious about the extent of the acquaintance between the two.

"Of course she does," Missy interjected as Jillian nodded briefly. "She was Uncle Jack's friend before he sent her to Mama."

Mary's eyes lit with avid interest. "He is a most charming rogue, would you not agree?" She watched Jillian carefully. "How did you become acquainted with him?"

Before Jillian could answer these leading questions, Violet piped up earnestly, "I am perthuaded you think him an honorable gentleman, Mithith Thaint Erney."

"Why, I think him top-of-the-trees, of course. Doesn't everyone?" She tried to laugh off the question in hopes that the subject would be dropped. "I try not to think of him at all," was what she wanted to say.

But Mary was tenacious when she was on the scent of an *on-dit*. "Do you plan to attend Missy's ball, Mrs. St. Erney? You must be anxious to see your *friend* again."

Jillian decided it was time to deflect this line of questioning and turn the subject. She put her hand on the teapot remarking, "The tea has gone quite cold. I shall order another pot." She rose and went to the bell-pull to summon a servant, effectively putting an end to Mary's impertinent inquisitiveness for the moment.

By the time Jillian had instructed the butler to have more tea and macaroons sent up, the girls had turned their attention to another subject. Jillian busied herself with the teapot and contributed nothing more to the chitchat beyond polite inquiries as to who wished for more refreshments. Violet was not behindhand in passing her cup and plate forward.

The phantom Lord Letham's name also surfaced once or twice in the girls' conversation. Jillian paid not much attention, but if the man lived up even halfway to the flattering and exaggerated paeans of praise the young ladies heaped on his head, he must be the ninth wonder of the world!

"Lethal Letham," the girls called him. "Able to

slay female hearts at a hundred paces," Amanda had sighed. It was strange that this lord had not called on the Gilmores, if he were indeed related to the family. Jillian could distinctly recall that Missy had said he was her uncle—Dolly's brother, in fact. Yet not only had he not called, but to her knowledge they had not encountered him at any of the social engagements she had accompanied Missy to, either. Apparently he also was from town. She wondered if his lordship and Mackinnon were acquainted. They seemed to be two people from entirely different social worlds from all she could gather.

Chapter 17

When Jillian met Lord John Gilmore on Friday next, that gentleman proved to be every bit as elegantly handsome as he had been represented in his portrait. Why Dolly preferred that black dog of a Mackinnon to such a gentle, good-looking, perfectly *civil* man left Jillian quite mystified.

And Dorothea Gilmore seemed to dote on her husband, too. Even as she limped along at his side when he escorted her into dinner that evening, she leaned heavily upon his arm and gazed lovingly up into his face. Jillian saw him lift his wife's hand briefly and bring it to his lips. They seemed a couple very much in love. The whole situation was extremely confusing.

When Lord Gilmore had arrived earlier that day, Jillian had been sitting with Dolly and Missy in the library. When he came in, Dolly had dropped the book she was reading and stood up hastily, forgetting to use her crutch, a most uncharacteristic action for the usually composed Lady Gilmore. Her husband had come straight to her, caught her up against his chest and kissed her before lifting his head, whispering something to her then extending his arm for Missy who ran to him and hugged him tightly.

"Papa!"

"Missy!" he responded with a gentle, teasing glint in his eye. "And how is my best girl?"

"John," said Dolly somewhat breathlessly as she emerged from his embrace and picked up her crutch, "you must allow me to make you known to our guest, Mrs. St. Erney. Jack sent her to us, you know. Jillian, my dear, this is my husband, John."

The tall, laughing man with his quiet aura of authority had turned to greet his wife's guest. He had been everything that was polite and correct in making her welcome, taking Jillian's hand and saying he hoped she would make his home hers for as long as she cared to.

"Thank you, Lord Gilmore. You are very good." Jillian had been flustered. Such a kind man and so handsome. He dominated the room with his presence, quiet and gentle though it was. And his wife was deceiving him with that snake of a Mackinnon! And then she remembered that Mackinnon was Lord Gilmore's colleague. No doubt Jack had met Dolly in the course of his business with her husband. What a coil!

After a few pleasantries were exchanged, Dolly Gilmore could no longer restrain her impatient desire to have her husband to herself for some little time and bore him off to her boudoir.

Jillian was embarrassed by Missy's comment as they left the room. "Oh," she giggled, "Mama and Papa won't come out of her bedroom for hours. You may as well agree to drive in the park with me, you know."

*   *   *

The charming Dolly had had to use all her considerable powers of persuasion to convince Jillian to have an elaborate gown made up for the ensuing ball. "You have saved me considerable effort, you know, in bravely agreeing to serve as Missy's chaperon for these last several weeks. It would have been difficult for me to go to Kent if not for your kind offices, my dear."

Jillian tried her best to resist this expensive gift of clothing, but Dolly skillfully played on her guest's fear of offending her hostess. Lady Gilmore had made Jillian feel positively inconsiderate to refuse the Gilmores' gift of expensive clothing and gear to outfit her in the first stare of fashion so that she might accompany Missy to *ton* events. Jillian remembered Mackinnon's letter to her saying that Dolly would outfit her at *his* expense and wondered exactly who was paying the bills. She tried valiantly to dig in her heels. Her efforts were in vain.

Dolly would not hear of Jillian's protests over the issue of a gown for Missy's ball. "You must allow me to overbear your scruples in this matter at least, my dear Jillian. You have been of immense help in squiring Missy about for me. For all we love her, my little ninny leads us all a merry dance, I well know. I should feel I have taken monstrous advantage of your good nature if you will not allow us to repay you in some way. And what better way than to help replenish your wardrobe somewhat? 'Twill give me great pleasure to outfit you for the occasion, you know."

"Have I been such a thoughtless guest? You make me feel positively ashamed of myself for not wanting to put you to the expense of outfitting a perfect stranger," Jillian smiled at her hostess.

"'Tis your duty to be a compliant guest," Dolly twitted, wagging a finger at Jillian.

"Well, then, I will accept your kind offer, ma'am. Just this once more. You have been much too good to me already." Jillian had laughed as Dolly overbore her reluctance and literally forced upon her a gorgeous silk dress, more costly than any she had ever owned, for the forthcoming festivity. The misty green of the silk gown brought out lights in her eyes Jillian was not aware they possessed. The soft material clung to her every curve, and the unbroken span of color made her feel gracefully slender and positively two inches taller. Jillian was pleased. An impatient excitement began to seep into her blood that grew hourly as Saturday approached.

The evening of the ball was at hand. The Gilmore household had had an air of expectant anticipation all day, and as dusk fell, the various occupants retired to their rooms to dress. Dolly came to Jillian's room and professed herself gratified beyond her dearest hopes when she saw her protégé attired in the green silk.

"Ah! How lovely you look, my dear. I see you have allowed my dresser to style your hair. Quite glamorous with the curls held up by that gold band and allowed to cascade down the back of your neck. I must say, she has outdone herself—but then she had so much more to work with than when she tackles this shaggy mane of mine. You do have beautiful hair, Jillian. This style sets off the gown to perfection, I think." Dolly tried to press her own pearls on Jillian but was met with an adamant refusal this time.

"But, my dear, do you not wish for some jewelry at your neck?" she had persisted.

Jillian picked up a golden satin band on her dressing table. "I shall tie this round my neck. It matches the ribbon in my hair. You see," she said, fitting action to words, "it complements the gown wonderfully well. But thank you for the offer." Jillian impulsively reached over and kissed Dolly's cheek.

"Are you looking forward to seeing Jack this evening?" Dolly questioned archly. "He will be captivated when he sees you looking as you do tonight. I must confess, I am burning with curiosity to see the meeting between you two."

Jillian tried to look unconcerned. "I daresay he and I will contrive to exchange a few words," she said offhandedly.

Dolly grinned. "Fie on you, my dear. Do not think to flummery me! I cut my eyeteeth long since. You may choose to be nonchalant, but *I* choose to believe you feel quite otherwise," the lady said laughingly before tucking her crutch under her arm and limping off to her daughter's room.

She could not but wonder at Dolly's words—would a cast-off mistress speak so? Jillian fully intended to give Mackinnon a piece of her mind for blighting the Gilmore's marriage, indeed Dolly's very life, and to assure the scoundrel in no uncertain terms that he had no chance of upsetting her own life in similar fashion!

She was unable to eat a bite at dinner, her emotions were in such turmoil. Her senses positively reeled—with anger, she told herself—when she thought of the forthcoming meeting with Jack. The meal concluded with a toast to Missy's health and the success of her party. Jillian dutifully smiled and lifted her glass, but she did so in a fog.

And then Lord and Lady Gilmore stood at the top of the stairs greeting their guests, with their daughter Melissa, demure in debutante white, between them. Jillian wandered aimlessly about the ballroom, trying to calm her disordered nerves. When would he come?

The room began to fill up rather rapidly. Just as she had convinced herself that he would not dare come (the rogue would not have the audacity to show his face in Lady Gilmore's ballroom, would he?), there he was! The fiend! He had an arm around Dolly's waist and bent to kiss her cheek even as Lord Gilmore clapped him on the shoulder in a friendly masculine gesture of affection. Jillian's mouth dropped open. She stood stock still as she observed the tableau, a look of pure amazement on her face.

The dirty, tattered, unshaven rogue of their many adventures was gone. She could not recognize any trace of her erstwhile companion in the elegant gentleman garbed in correct evening gear who stood not thirty feet away from her. A severely tailored black velvet jacket stretched across his wide shoulders covering a pristine white shirt. A full two inches of delicate white lace showed at the cuffs. Why, the formerly careless vagabond was even wearing a starched cravat! Black knee-breeches above white silk stockings encased his muscular legs, and shining black evening pumps on his feet completed his flawless ensemble. Even his barbering was of the first stare of fashion. His hair—his beautiful, thick, curly hair—had been cropped quite short and styled conservatively. Could this sartorially splendid gentleman she was gazing at indeed be the Jack Mackinnon of her memories? Jillian asked herself incredulously.

The laughing devil was swinging Missy up now, lifting the girl quite off her feet and twirling her around as though she were a child. What was the madman about? Before Jillian could think what to do, he had spotted her. He set Missy on her feet, gave the laughing girl a quick peck on the cheek, and was striding across the room straight toward her, his flashing, white-toothed smile decorating his tanned face.

Jack laughed at the wide-eyed expression of disbelief on Jillian's face as she took in the full magnificence of his evening garb. By God, she looks beautiful, though, he thought to himself as he bore down on her.

"Here comes Lord Letham!" exclaimed a young lady to Jillian's left. "Ohhh, isn't he the most handsome man you've ever seen!" she giggled.

"Well," temporized her companion, "if you like them looking devilish, then yes."

"Oh, but wouldn't it be a feather in one's cap to capture the interest of such a one! I should love to tame a rake," the first young lady simpered in die-away airs.

"I don't think I could stand the excitement," her friend answered drily.

Jillian belatedly came out of her trance as Jack was two steps from her, and turned on her heel to flee. She felt a hand snake out and take her elbow in a tight grip. "Whoa, there, sweetheart."

He linked his hand through her arm in a reversal of the usual male-female configuration. Jillian, bent on escape, batted at his hand on her arm and said "Shhh" at his teasing endearment as she continued to move toward the ballroom door at a rapid pace.

"Where do you think you're going in such a hurry when I've come all this way to see you?" He did not loosen his grip. Many heads turned curiously in their direction as they transected the ballroom. "Ah, I can see what it is. You don't recognize me in this unfamiliar regalia."

Jillian kept on walking, dragging him along with her.

"On second thought, since you're so bent on leaving the ballroom, I think I shall accompany you. What a good idea! Shall we adjourn to John's study?" he inquired innocently, matching his pace to hers.

Jillian stopped dead in her tracks and turned toward him. She could see at such short range that he had shaved so closely there was no trace of the black beard that made him look so devilishly villainous. Why, his skin must be almost scraped off, she scoffed, uncommonly agitated by how well he looked. She tried to tamp down the treacherous thought that she would like to run her fingers along his smooth cheek. "Unhand me, you brute," she said in a low, fierce voice. "Who do you think you are, coming here like this."

Jack smiled winningly down at her, "Why, I thought I was your beau. You know, the man you love to chastise with your sharp tongue, your confederate in crime, your companion in a haystack, the Jack Jill tumbled down a hill with, the prince of a fellow you plan to live with happily ever after. . . . Dare I say, the man of your dreams?"

"My nightmares, you mean."

"Ah," he sighed satisfied, "there's my shrew.

278

Always ready to come to blows. Let us suspend our verbal fisticuffs for the nonce.'' The musicians had just struck up the lovely strains of a waltz, and several couples had already taken the floor. ''Shall we dance?'' Jack propelled her onto the floor before she could give voice to her protest.

The young lady who had been standing beside Jillian minutes earlier glided by on the arm of a rather spindly looking young man. ''Good evening, my lord,'' she turned her head and said in carrying tones to Mackinnon.

On an intake of breath Jillian exclaimed, ''My lord?''

His warm brown eyes twinkled down at her. ''Just so.''

''And what are you a lord of, besides mischief and scandalous behavior?''

''I'm afraid you've caught me out this time, sweetheart,'' he said as he twirled her about. ''I don't like to admit it, but since you force me. . . . I'm afraid that my father had the misfortune to be a peer of the realm. As Papa departed for celestial spheres some ten years since, you must see I had no choice.'' The atrocious creature actually had the nerve to look abashed as he made this statement, gazing down at her with a crooked half smile on his chiseled lips.

''So,'' she said, looking at him through dangerously narrowed eyes, ''it has pleased you to make a fool of me, Mackinnon, or my Lord Rogue, or whoever you are.'' Jillian succeeded in bringing them to a stop at the edge of the floor and pushed herself out of his arms as she stepped backward into a darkened semicircular alcove.

He laughed down at her. ''No, no, sweetheart. You were never interested in my genealogy. As I recall, you never inquired about my social connections." He put his hand to his chin in a mock thinking posture. "I'm quite sure I should have presented you with my visiting card had you done so. Dear me! I quite thought it was my untitled, unadorned—dare I say bare—self you had a hankering after."

"So! You are a member of the peerage. I might have known from the way you carry on that you would belong to that class of persons." She intended him to take this disparagement as an insult.

Naturally her tormentor pretended to understand it otherwise. "If I'd known a handle to my name would have carried any weight with you, I should have produced it immediately!"

Jillian looked for a way to even the score after this mocking speech. She glanced at his evening clothes and took in the splendor of his regalia at close range. Jack stood playing with the ribbon of his quizzing glass. "Like what you see, do you, sweetheart?"

"You look like an affected, dandified fop in those clothes," she said to pay him back for his baiting.

"But sweetheart," his countenance took on a pained expression, "you were always complaining about how dirty, smelly, and untidy I was. I thought if I took particular pains tonight, I could not fail to meet with your approval. Why, I even bathed—though I was without benefit of Mrs. Manaton's hip bath," he said outrageously.

"You look silly!" was all she could think of to say as the memories he deliberately conjured up of their time in Widecombe did not fail to bring a blush to her cheek.

"You don't like my attempt to rig myself out as a gentleman! That's a facer for me. *I* quite thought this a rather elegant rig-out myself. Dear me! There's no accounting for the vagaries of a woman's taste." He clucked his tongue at her. "I've been assured it's all the crack. Now you tell me you prefer me in rags, smelling of sweat."

"I certainly said no such thing!" she flared through clenched teeth as she gestured vaguely at his legs. His shoulders were shaking suspiciously, she saw.

Jack looked down at himself. "Ah, it's my breeches you don't like. Well, we can remedy that. I should like to oblige you by removing them here and now, but I hesitate to do so in the middle of the ballroom. 'Twould not be thought quite proper, you know, love," he leaned down and whispered in her ear confidentially.

She batted at him with her fists as the musicians continued to play and laughing couples danced by them while they stood brangling, unobserved in the shadows of the alcove. He caught up her hands against his chest and said, "Much as I enjoy this cross and jostle work with you, my love, we are missing our waltz. I particularly wanted our first dance together to be a waltz, too. There's something so irresistibly wicked about embracing in a roomful of people."

She tried to free her fists, but he held them easily. "Dear me! Has it actually come to blows between us? I fear you'll catch cold at this game, love. I'm *much* the stronger, you know." He laughed down at her with his eyes.

A couple dancing near them smiled knowingly in their direction, and Jillian saw that they were observed. She ceased her physical struggles. "Your presumption exceeds all bounds, Mackinnon," she addressed him through gritted teeth.

"Jack," he corrected with a conning smile tilting up one corner of his mouth.

"Let me go, you unprincipled, lecherous brute!"

"And then, too," he continued, ignoring her scolding, "the gentleman can imprison his lady's hands when the need arises, like so." He put his arms round her. "Let us not waste the remainder of our dance." So saying, he swept her into the waltz once more. Jillian did not resist. She thought he was indeed a fiend to enchant her senses so. The room about them was filled with couples whirling past in time to the irresistible strains of the deliciously sensual dance. Jillian gave herself up to the music and the intoxicating magic of Jack's presence. Being once again in his arms was where she had longed to be—where she belonged.

Jack tightened his hold and bent his head closer to hers. "I thought we might discuss marriage." The odious wretch had the audacity to hold her eyes with his own while he delivered up this decidedly intriguing statement as though it were a bland subject suitable for polite ballroom conversation. Jillian jumped to the conclusion 'twas a prime bit of mischief, guaranteed to provoke her.

"Marriage! I'm surprised you're even acquainted with the subject, Mackinnon!" she scoffed. Jack laughed appreciatively. "Just whose marriage do you plan to discuss? Or is it an abstract examination of the subject you have in mind?"

"Oh, yes, long and learned. I plan to spend a lifetime investigating every aspect of the, ah, subject." He smiled down at her with a decided glint in his eye. Jill didn't trust that look an inch. He tightened his hold on her and bent closer.

"I thought we might announce our betrothal

tonight," he whispered against her ear, tickling it with his breath and sending a shiver coursing down her spine.

"Of all the contemptible things to say!" Jillian ignored the quickening of her heartbeat at his words. She pounded him on his still-tender left shoulder, causing him to wince. "Sorry," she said, abashed as she realized that she had hurt him.

Jack grimaced from the pain but managed to grin at her nevertheless. "Contemptible?" He feigned surprise at her outraged reaction. "What, sweetheart! You think me incapable of knowing my duty . . . which is my pleasure as well. After all, with us the cart has truly preceded the horse."

She looked an angry question at him, and he murmured for her ears alone, "We've already slept together more than most couples do in a year of marriage."

Jillian colored fiercely and tore herself out of his arms despite his muscular grip on her hand and waist. She almost flew from the ballroom, blown along by a storm of angry emotion. She fled down the stairs into a vacant room, slamming the door shut behind her.

Jack followed her leisurely, letting her have her lead until he saw that she had indeed gone into John's study. He grinned broadly as he turned the handle of the door and entered the dark room lighted only by a fire blazing in the grate.

"Now, Jill sweetheart, let us have this out with gloves off. We must discuss *our* marriage—yours and mine—to each other," he laughed.

She turned on him and spat, "How dare you, you deceiver! How dare you come here to the house of your mistress and make up to me! Have you no shame?"

"Eh?" He looked completely dumbfounded for

once. "What's all this about a mistress?"

"Dolly . . . Lady Gilmore—the wife of your friend. She . . . she is the mother of your three sons, is she not?"

"Three sons? What on earth can you mean? Dolly is my elder sister. Surely . . . surely you knew that." He exploded with a great guffaw of laughter. "Why else would I send you here, if not to my most beloved relative," he said, wiping the tears of laughter from his eyes.

"You . . . your sister?" Jillian whispered, ready to die from the humiliation of it. Could she have made a more ghastly mistake! Her appalling jealousy had blinded her to what was staring her in the face from the moment she had arrived in Mount Street. Why, Mackinnon was the mysterious Lord Letham—Dolly's brother!

"But the three boys, Edward, Marcus, and . . . and little Jack—Missy said he was named for you."

"My nephews." The devil had the temerity to laugh at her again. "How could you believe such a ridiculous thing? And little Jack is named for his father, John. It is one of the usual nicknames, you know. Although I stand little Jack's godfather, he is not named for me. My name is actually Jasper," he admitted somewhat shamefacedly, "but I've always been called Jack. I hope you don't mind?"

"But Dolly—Lady Gilmore—said that she was going into Kent because you wanted her to see to your boys. You've admitted you have boys in the country."

"Oh, yes, *those* boys!" The gleam in his eyes reflecting the bright firelight was almost past bearing, Jillian thought as she peered at him in the darkened room. Only her burning need to know the truth of the matter kept her glued to the spot.

"I know you will find it hard to believe, sweetheart, knowing as you do what a black-hearted scoundrel I am and having certain proof of my depravity, but the fact is that I *do*—just occasionally, mind—allow myself to succumb to my better feelings.

"I *do* have some boys in the country—in a house on my brother-in-law's estate where Dolly and John's three sons live in the manor house. However, the boys I speak of are not my *sons*. No, indeed. I have no children—yet." He wagged his brows at her suggestively. Jillian just stared at him wide-eyed, his shaft going wide of the mark for the nonce.

"You . . . you take in homeless children?" She swallowed with difficulty.

Jack nodded.

"I . . . I do recall Dolly mentioning that you had rescued her footman from the slums of Glasgow. He had been dreadfully mistreated, she said."

"Yes, Ewan is one of my boys." He took Jill's hand in his and caressed it warmly as he continued his explanation, serious for once. "I have, on more occasions than I care to remember, come across young lads living on the streets, trying to keep food in their bellies and the strap from their backs. Sometimes they beg, more often they steal, pick-pockets, and grub for a living any way they can. I've found that our society makes little provision for these unfortunates. It is not an isolated problem; they are to be found all over the country but particularly in the larger cities, London and Glasgow especially. Sadly, I've been able to rescue only a very few. I've taken these poor, homeless urchins and housed and fed them, given them a chance to gain a little education and a little training so that they may have a chance for a better future."

Jillian felt her spirits sink lower and lower with every word he uttered. She was mortified beyond words. How could she have been so lacking in judgment, in sense? Why had she not trusted Dolly and Jack, the two people she liked above all others? She drew her hand from his and turned her burning face away from the man who stood regarding her with a mixture of tenderness and merriment. She was glad they stood in the dark; the gloom provided at least some concealment for her burning cheeks. There were no words adequate enough to frame her apology. She wished she could sink into the floor.

Jack turned her gently by the shoulders so that she faced him. "Oh, Jack! I've been such a fool!" she admitted, disgusted with herself, keeping her face averted from him. "How could I have mistrusted you? I could not understand how even *you* could be depraved enough to send me to your mistress . . ."

"Now, now, sweets. You somehow got the wrong end of the stick. 'Twas a hilarious muddle— quite a comedy of errors—you fell into. But don't be taking yourself to task. I liked it much better when you were upbraiding *me!*" He lifted her chin with one finger so that she looked into his warm eyes gleaming in the firelight. "Now that you know what a pillar of society I am, will you agree to marry me, my shrew?" And before she could speak, he bent his head and kissed her lightly. It was all too brief a touch for Jillian.

She reached her arms up round his neck and brought his mouth down to hers once more. Jack nibbled at her lips playfully, then stopped to say, "By the way, ma'am, did I neglect to mention that I love you beyond endurance. It's been all holiday with me since I first laid eyes on you. I tumbled head over heels even before I fell down that blasted hill."

"What a perverse person you are to profess to love someone you are constantly provoking and humiliating, someone you call a shrew and a termagant. I should think my 'ill temper,' as you call it, would have given you a disgust of me by now. I can't promise to *temper* my tongue in the future, Mackinnon."

"What! No more sparring matches? I absolutely forbid it. Why, I should positively think you had grown bored with me and found me a feeble old stick if you ceased to rip up at me—only on occasion, mind, for I've other plans to keep your mouth occupied." He ran a finger lightly over her lips. "For all I've grown accustomed to the sting in your tongue, my little spitfire," he said as he ran his hand over her derrière "and to your curvaceous tail, all play and no brangling would make this Jack a dull boy."

"Who could live with your incessant blather?"

Jack continued to kiss her lightly along the edge of her sensitive ear, over her closed eyelids, along the outline of her lips, saying between kisses, "You'll find after we're married that I'm a man of few words and bold action."

Jillian wanted still more reassurance. "Can you really love me, Jack? You behave as though you don't like me in the least when you are forever teasing me at every turn, disapproving of my every action, my every word—"

"*I!* Now when did I ever say I didn't like you or approve of what you were saying or how you were acting? I distinctly remember enjoying some of your 'actions' enormously," he quizzed her warmly.

"Oh, you're always laughing at me!" she protested.

"But, sweetheart, I love to laugh!"

"You see, you admit it, you monster! I'm just an amusement to you."

"Yes, you amuse me, tickle me, entertain me, and fill me with joy. I want to spend a lifetime laughing with you. . . . You also frustrate me enormously—always arguing when I'd rather be doing this." So saying, he tightened his arms about her until her curvaceous little body was fitted fully against him and opened his mouth over hers to kiss her hungrily. Jillian, whose heart had long ago been given to the rascal, surrendered her body to his fierce possession as she arched into his heated embrace. Passion flowed between them for a considerable time before Jack came up for breath, lifting his head to whisper huskily, "You will wed me, you little termagant, whether you will or no."

Jill surrendered, saying breathlessly, "Only to preserve propriety, you understand, Mackinnon."

"To be sure, we wouldn't want to offend the gods of propriety, especially when we both know what a timid and thoroughly proper little person you are," Jack teased before he once more bent his head and took her lips in a deep, sensuous kiss that had her clinging to him again and both of them throbbing with passion.

Jill molded herself to him as his hands stroked boldly over her tingling body. What would have happened if someone hadn't peeped into the room at that precise moment neither could say. They just knew that the next time they were alone in a room together, Jack would have to be considerably quicker and a lot more nimble in vaulting across the room to lock the door!